The Ocean Raiders

A Nicholas Foxe Adventure

Jackson Coppley

Contour Press

The Ocean Raiders
A Nicholas Foxe Adventure
Second Edition

ISBN: 9798644343713

Published by

Contour Press

Chevy Chase, Maryland

www.ContourPress.com / / (301) 587-4343

To Ellen

The Ocean Raiders

A Nicholas Foxe Adventure

Chapter 1

NICHOLAS FOXE waited by the canal while the Venetian police fished the corpse out of the water. The large body was laid in a peaceful repose as though asleep. The smashed rear of his skull remained hidden from view.

Nick sat on a crate borrowed from the nearby fish market. Separating him from a crowd of onlookers, the police strung yellow tape marking this as a crime scene. Nick pondered a question the dead man could no longer answer.

Why did you try to kill me?

The flight into Marco Polo airport was uneventful. Nick's private jet made great time in clear skies. He would not have accepted the offer from billionaire Nevin Dowd to come to Venice were it not for Christine Blake's involvement. It had been years since he'd last seen Christine and had fond memories of their time in Paris. He was pleased to hear from her, but surprised she now worked for Dowd. Nick had seen an interview of Nevin Dowd. The man displayed a remarkable public persona, yet there was something unsettling about him. Nick expected Christine would build a career in a blue-chip company. She had perfect business decorum. Nick smiled, remembering the personal side he discovered in Paris.

Christine offered to have a car pick him up, but for Nick, there was only one way to enter the city of water. He contacted Guido Bartoli who ran a water taxi service from the airport. Guido, a tall Italian with a streak of gray emphasizing his dark hair and cinema-star looks, was Nick's go-to guy for getting around Venice. In a place where a street number has little meaning, he needed a man like Guido who knew the city well. Guido stood front and center among the limo drivers holding a sign reading 'Foxe.' Nick was surprised seeing Guido himself and not one of his people. It spoke to the value he placed on their friendship.

Nick walked over to him and exchanged a firm handshake.

"Guido! So, the boss is picking me up. Where's the boat driver?"

"I will be your driver for the day."

"Well…" started Nick.

"I would not have it any other way, my old friend. Let me have your luggage tickets."

Nick fished the stubs from the side pocket of his khaki travel vest and handed them to Guido, who handed them to the short, young man beside him.

At least he brought someone to do the heavy lifting.

"Let's walk this way," Guido said as he motioned to the right. "My man will see to it your bags reach your hotel."

The walk from the baggage area to the Darsena piers would take ten minutes through a covered promenade using moving walkways. Nick was particularly interested in the last flood and of course, the virus outbreak. Venice has its *acqua alta* several times a year when the tide washes over the banks of canals. Tourists wearing boots navigate through iconic Saint Mark's Square on elevated platforms. But this was no simple high tide. It was a devastating flood.

"I haven't been here since the last flood."

"You mean the big one?"

"Yes. Has Venice recovered?"

Guido smiled. "We have always recovered. But this one was big. You'll see signs of it still."

"And what about the virus?" Nick asked. "I saw photos in the news that made the city look deserted."

"You must remember, this city made it through the plague. We are resilient. Speaking of the news, I've seen reports about you lately." Guido smiled. "Seems you like caves."

"Great places to visit," responded Nick, "if you like people making attempts on your life."

"I saw the news of the big find. Is it as dramatic as they say?"

"It was nothing to brag about."

Guido stopped and faced Nick as other passengers hurried by them.

"You are coy, are you not?"

Nick grinned, but said nothing.

"I know, I know," said Guido, tossing his hands in the air. "You cannot say. It is my business to keep out of my client's affairs." Then he winked. "But maybe as friends?"

Nick just smiled.

Guido resumed their walk and changed the subject. "So, it is Signor Dowd you have business with, is it not?"

"That's right." Nick had told Guido why he was coming and the reason for it. "You know the man?"

"Only from the news. He's made a hit here. Wants to save the city from the rising sea level."

"You must feel the effects of that more than me, being a man of the water."

"How can anyone live in Venice and not be a man of the water?" responded Guido. "But yes, we appreciate his efforts. When I started as a young gondolier many years ago, water taxis like the ones I now own could move anywhere. Now, when the tide is high, most bridges are too low. It is the gondoliers who can squeeze beneath, but my taxis cannot. It means lost business."

"The government is doing something about it, isn't it?"

Nick's question drew dramatic gesticulations from Guido, ones best delivered by an Italian, the culture that perfected them.

"The government!" Guido exclaimed. "You mean the project Mose? Gates to halt the rising tides? Behind schedule and over budget. Why am I not surprised?"

Stopping to look Nick in the eye, Guido said, "This Dowd person is involved in that project. Is that why you are here?"

"No," responded Nick. "Dowd is dredging up artifacts he wanted me to examine."

"Is that so?" Guido asked, unconvinced.

"And it's a chance to reacquaint myself with an old friend."

Guido lifted an eyebrow. "A woman friend?"

"Well, yes."

Guido laughed. "Ah, Nicholas, my old friend. I knew it had to be a woman. Who is it? Is she someone I know?"

"Christine Blake. I don't think you would know her."

As they reached the pier where water taxis shuttled people to and from the airport, Guido turned to Nick, looking as though he was about to tell his friend something offensive.

"I am so sorry my friend, I must take other passengers with us. We are swamped with customers today. I hope you do not mind."

"Of course not."

Nick's simple response made Guido's pleasant demeanor return as though the weight of the world had been lifted from his shoulders.

Water taxis filled all the slips at the pier, each a sleek, low-slung thirty-foot wooden vessel similar to those in Guido's fleet. Most riders of any height at all had to duck to enter the boat's enclosure where couch seating lined both sides. Tourists preferred to head to the rear of the boat where they could stand in the open. It was a clear, warm day and most passengers stood.

Guido walked Nick to his boat where they saw other passengers waiting. A couple of retirement age were clearly tourists from the camera around the man's neck to the map in the woman's hands. They were engaged in an excited discussion, pointing to sites on the map. Off to one side stood a large man dressed in a black suit with a white open shirt. If water taxis had bouncers, this man would be one. Nick hoped this wasn't the other passenger. He oozed malevolence.

The couple looked up expectantly as Guido approached them.

"*Scusate.* You are the Wagner couple, no?" Guido asked.

"Oh, yes, we are!" chirped the little woman.

The man shook hands with Guido. His wife provided enough enthusiasm for the two of them.

"We're so excited to be here!" she exclaimed.

"I understand you will be staying on Murano. Is that where I am taking you today?"

"That's right," said the wife. "We were here before and visited the glass factories. I told my husband we had to come back and spend plenty of time to pick out a piece or two."

Nick observed this conversation thinking looks are deceiving. Since the couple said they had been to Murano before, they must have realize the price of the least expensive hand-crafted piece was thousands of dollars. They didn't look the part of customers with that much money to burn.

The man asked, "What do we do with our luggage?"

Guido snapped his fingers, getting the attention of one of the porters standing nearby who responded by loading the bags on the boat. Guido directed the couple with a simple "please," and motioned them to climb aboard. The Wagners followed the porter, who helped them board the taxi. The porter left while Mr. Wagner caught up with his wife. His wife had darted to the open rear of the vessel and was looking around like a puppy dog in a car window.

Guido then addressed the dark-suited stranger. "Signor Smith?"

"Yeah, that's me."

Nick couldn't place the man's accent.

"Where is it you are going today?" Guido asked the man.

"Drop me off at the Rialto Bridge."

"As you wish. Please board and make yourself comfortable."

The large man climbed into the water taxi. He appeared unaccustomed to a boat and the rocking caused by his appreciable weight.

Nick whispered to Guido, expressing doubt about the man's responses. "Smith? Rialto Bridge?"

"Yes," replied Guido. "They were, how you say, generic answers."

"Let's keep an eye on this one," said Nick, watching the man who, by then, sat on the port-side couch near Guido.

"Why not join him and keep him company?"

Nick winked at Guido and got on board, moving past the man with a simple "excuse me," he took a seat further back on the starboard couch near the Wagners.

Guido removed the ropes from the pier, took a seat behind the wheel, and backed out like a man who had done the maneuver a thousand times. He was well in tune with his boat. Heading forward, the water taxi soon sped across the lagoon toward Murano.

Nick entertained himself by talking to the Wagners, all the while keeping the large man in his peripheral vision. The Wagners introduced themselves and Nick responded, "Pleased to meet you. My name is Nickolas Foxe."

Mr. Wagner replied, "Hey, aren't you the guy who found that tablet in a cave?" and turning to his wife, "You know, honey. It was all over the news."

Nick nodded, noticing the large guy glanced toward him with a vague look of recognition. Now that Nick had revealed who he was, the large man knew he was tailing the right person. It was a moment defining the hunter and his intended prey.

Guido slowed the taxi to avoid creating a wake and slid dockside at Murano. A young man on the pier tied up the boat and assisted the Wagners off. Once the luggage was placed on shore, Guido backed out with his two remaining passengers and headed to Venice. The large man stared dead-eyed at Nick. Guido slipped into the canal that would take them from the North side of Venice to the Grand Canal. As the engine quieted, the man spoke for the first time.

"So, you're Nicholas Foxe," he said, looking at Nick from his seat in front.

"That's right."

Through a sneer, the man said, "That's good. I've been waiting for you. I'm taking you to a meeting."

"A meeting? With whom? Do I know you?"

"With whom?" the man repeated, mocking Nick's proper use of basic English. "The whom is someone who wants to see you in, let us say, 'the worst way.' That person has a proposition for you."

Nick understood 'the worst way' not to be in his best interest. Guido shot a glance at Nick over the man's shoulder. Guido's expression indicated he knew the danger of the situation but didn't look worried. He had a plan.

Nick pondered as though he was thumbing through a mental calendar. He replied, "I'm sorry, I don't have room in my schedule for unplanned meetings."

They passed under the bridge at Strada Nova. Nick looked up at the brick arch only a few feet away. He knew by the limited clearance they must be at high tide. Guido knew it as well.

The man pulled a 9mm Glock pistol from beneath his coat and pointed it at Nick.

"Perhaps this will help you make room in your calendar."

When he saw the pistol, Guido took action. He gunned the boat into the Grand Canal. The man lost his balance and dropped the gun. The acceleration threw both the gun and the man past Nick to the open rear of the craft. Nick leaped from his seat toward the gun, but the man reached for it at the same time. Now on a wide waterway, Guido jerked the boat back and forth, throwing the man away from the gun.

The Grand Canal became a raceway with Guido making erratic turns, much too fast, dodging a variety of watercraft.

The boat's wake slammed against a vaporetto causing the water bus to rock violently, startling tourists waiting to board.

Out of a side canal, a police boat gave chase, its siren blaring. Guido was well aware of the police behind him, but Nick and the large man were now wrestling on the floor of the boat. Guido decided his wild piloting was his best contribution to keeping Nick alive.

The man got to his feet. He tried to pull Nick up. But Nick, at six-foot four and two-hundred-ten pounds, was no small package to lift.

Approaching the Accademia Bridge, Guido swung into a wide arching curve from one side of the canal to the other. The boat leaned to one side, toppling the man to the seat beside Nick. Nick swung his body to straddle the man. He braced his knees against the seat, in order to deliver a series of punches to the man's face. Nick pounded the man's jaw to the right and to the left, but the man seemed unfazed.

Nick's fists ached.

What is this guy made of?

In a canal-side café near the Accademia, a pair of young American newlyweds were enjoying a late breakfast. They had a destination wedding in the city the day before. Taking advantage of Daddy's wealth and her own pretension, she wouldn't have had it any other way. Her new husband, equally pretentious, was dressed in a Gucci jacket and black tee. She wore a blue silk garden dress complemented with matching hat to shade her from the morning sun.

They only had eyes for each other and were unaware of the theatrics taking place until another tourist yelled, "Look out!"

Guido was finishing his turn too close to the café. He turned the wheel of the boat sharply to the left only a few feet away. The couple saw what was happening only a second before the wave hit. Water rushed over them as though they had stepped into a wave pool. Drenched, her hat drooping to one side, this delicate flower of a bride erupted in a string of obscenities that would make a longshoreman blush.

The Fondaco dei Tedeschi is a palace turned into a shopping mall providing a rooftop view of the Grand Canal. The few morning sightseers there had an unmatched view of the entire event. Though no one had met before, the chaos below generated boisterous conversation among strangers trying to make sense of what they were witnessing.

One figure stood apart, silent, watching events unfold.

As Guido straightened the boat, the man being pummeled shoved Nick away. The gun slid toward them. As each man reached for it, Guido gunned the boat. The gun slid to the back of the boat with the men tumbling behind it.

Nick grabbed the Glock and stood. But before he could get a good grip on the gun, the man delivered a hard, backhand blow to Nick, knocking him to the couch at the rear of the boat. Nick lay on the couch, dazed. He thought he still held the gun until he saw it pointed at him. The man steadied himself against Guido's maneuvers by bracing himself against the corner of the boat's roof.

"Sorry, Foxe. I have orders. You might say this is a dead-or-alive situation. Looks like you made your choice."

Guido steered the boat straight across the canal toward the Rialto Market. He rocked the boat as the man tried to hold a steady bead on Nick. The man had his back turned and did not see what was coming. He should have.

Several small boats were tied up to slips on one side of the market. Between the market and these boats was a small canal. A water taxi could handle the canal bridge only at low tide, and then just barely. It was not low tide.

Guido's aim was perfect. The speeding water taxi entered the canal and passed under the ancient bridge. It all took a split second. The underside of the bridge scraped the top of the boat a moment before it struck the man in the back of the head. The impact's momentum lifted the man over Nick and into the water where he floated face down, unmoving.

Guido pulled back on the throttle and put it in reverse to stop the forward motion. He killed the engine and joined Nick at the rear of the boat. They looked back under the bridge where the body floated.

The police boat, that entered the chase on the Grand Canal, arrived. The policeman who first approached the scene recognized Guido, who began his explanation of events.

On top of the Fondaco dei Tedeschi the conversation among strangers continued.

"What was that all about?"

"I think I saw a gun?"

"A gun? No way!"

"I think they must have been filming a movie."

The figure who stood apart from the others knew exactly what happened.

The fool. How clumsy. I trusted Bosch when he recommended this man. I'm glad I had a backup plan. Bosch better get that one right. I tried to play nice. No more.

Chapter 2

ALTHOUGH IT HAD BEEN YEARS SINCE PARIS where Nick last saw Christine, he felt he was right back there picking up where they had left off.

She walked up to Nick with a forced and tentative smile one might expect at a high school reunion.

"Nick, you old scoundrel!" she said as she kissed him on the cheek and gave him a short hug.

Scoundrel? Says a lot about what she thinks of me, I guess.

"Christy!" Nick exclaimed with a broad smile. He stepped back to take her in. "You haven't changed one bit."

Nicholas Foxe was the only person to call her Christy, except for her father. That connection had always bothered her. She never told him that, thinking it would cast a pall on the relationship.

The other problem, beside using the nickname, was the way he inspected her. Sure, she was shapely and attractive. Her stature at five-foot-ten put her in the range of modeling possibilities, and her face was beauty-shot photogenic. However, an agent once told her she was too shapely for modeling. Perhaps, she was told, if she dyed her hair blonde. That wasn't going to happen. She was pleased with her brunette locks and she thought blonde would never go with her brown eyes.

Besides, she had a good head on her shoulders. One does not get into advanced studies at the Sorbonne on looks. She was a people person, too. That combination served her well in the high-tech business world. She could sell ice to Eskimos, although for men, she first had to raise their sight to make eye contact, something she never sensed with Nick until this moment of physical appraisal. She remembered him as the one to first make eye contact and focus on each syllable she uttered. Nicholas Foxe had been easy to love.

In her work life, she wore sensible business clothes. This morning, she wasn't sure what to wear. What was this reunion with Nick all about? She sensed Nick was here because of her, even though the invitation came from her boss, Nevin Dowd. She pinned her choice on the weather; it was a bright, sunny day. The direct sunlight was toasty, and they were meeting on the patio by the canal. So, she chose a light, flowery sundress that showed a modest amount of cleavage. Not business-like at all. She knew of the trauma of the day before. Everyone in Venice knew about the attempted murder of Nicholas Foxe. Perhaps her dress would lighten Nick's mood and make him forget about that event. At least, that's what she told herself. She denied trying to rekindle an old flame.

Nick arrived at the Pensione Accademia by water taxi, driven by a man Nick seemed to know well. This was Christine's favorite place to stay while in Venice. If you arrived at the pensione by street, you entered a nondescript walkway under a small sign identifying the place. But the true front faced the Grand Canal, where a large patio and garden separated the water entrance from the hotel.

Nick wore a pair of navy linen pants, white sneakers, and a beige cotton sweater that looked dashing on his tall frame.

Had he been spending time in the sun, or did the clothes accentuate his olive skin?

After they embraced, she had to comment on it.

"Nick, you look so tan," she said. "From what I've been reading, you've spent most of your time underground."

"Ah, yes." He grinned. "Caves and castles. That's me. No, I've been cruising. Needed some air and the smell of the sea."

"Oh, Nick. I heard about what happened yesterday. That must have been awful."

"It was not the best of welcomes to Venice."

"Let's sit and talk about it. I want to catch up on everything."

"It has been some time, hasn't it?"

They took a table in the hotel garden. A waiter came by and they each ordered coffee.

"Why was somebody trying to kill you? Did it have anything to do with your discovery?"

"You know about the discovery?"

Christine looked askance at Nick.

"Who doesn't?"

"So, tell me what you've heard," said Nick.

Christine knew Nick had heard many versions of his search for The Tablet but was flattered that he wanted to hear the one she knew.

"OK. You found an ancient tablet in a cave in New Mexico. It led you to a castle in southern Italy where you found a document that decoded The Tablet and pointed you to a device in a grotto. The device contains a lot of advanced knowledge that now safely resides with a supercomputer in Germany. What is the device called? The Omni Scientia?"

"That's right." Nick omitted that, although the Omni communicated with the supercomputer in Germany, the Omni itself was in a hidden place in Basel, Switzerland.

"So, what happened to the man trying to kill you?"

"He succumbed to a massive headache."

The newspapers didn't give details, but she could imagine a variety of ways in which the bad guy came to an end.

Nick closed the conversation by saying, "The police are looking into it and I'm sure we'll know more later. But I want to hear about your boss. What's he up to and what are you doing for him?"

"Oh, yes. The reason you are here."

Nick corrected her. "Dowd invited me. You're the reason I'm here."

Did I just blush? she thought.

"Thanks, Nick. But what Nevin is doing is important. That's why I'm here."

"Nevin? On a first name basis, are we?"

"Everyone's on a first-name basis with Nevin. You'll see when you meet him. He's very personable."

"Oh, I'm sure I'll be charmed," Nick said with a hint of sarcasm.

Christine made a face.

Was this one rich guy's alpha-male remark about another rich guy?

"Nick, Nevin is doing important work here in Venice."

"So, I understand."

Nick knew about the work Nevin Dowd was doing. Dowd was a billionaire who invested in a wide range of ventures, each unlike the other. He introduced a solar cell that was ten times more efficient than those previously available. His company made tons of them in China for export. No satellite was launched into space without them. He began buying internet streaming services from fading cable companies and united them into a powerhouse entertainment company. Dowd always showed up at the Oscars with the hottest starlet on his arm. Did Nick harbor some envy? Probably.

But it was Dowd's work in water management that brought him to Venice. The Dutch, experts in keeping the sea from overtaking them, now used flood controls manufactured by one of Dowd's companies. The Italians had been working for years on a project where sea walls could be quickly moved into place to abate the flooding of the ancient city. Dowd arrived on the scene to save the project, or at least, that was the hype. The leaders of the project might quibble with the word 'save.' His participation was widely publicized, in part due to Dowd's network where a made-for-TV series followed the project.

Nick remained silent as he considered Nevin Dowd and whether he wanted to work with him. But he had not yet met the man. Better wait and withhold judgment.

Christine watched Nick as though she could read his thoughts. Nick returned Christine's gaze. They each knew they were not talking about the elephant in the room, or on the patio, as it were.

Nick was first to open that conversation.

"What happened, Christy?"

"What do you mean?" she responded knowing full well what he meant.

"It seemed we had something in Paris, you and me."

"It was good, wasn't it?" She smiled, remembering.

"I had to get back to New York. Dad died and I was executor. It was a big deal."

Christine knew that's why Nick left, but she didn't admit to how much she had craved his return. Anyway, that was a long time ago and she didn't want to go there. She let him off the hook by admitting how she had been busy as well.

"And we were going public with our company. It was crazy."

They paused, considering that point in time.

Christine broke the silence. "I guess life got in the way."

Nick considered this and agreed. "I guess it did."

Christine wondered if they could rekindle those flames. Nick said he was here because of her.

Was that just a favor? Did he think he owed her something?

Just seeing him again sparked something she thought no longer existed.

Nick snapped her out of her dream and back into the here-and-now.

"What about Vanessa? What's she doing?"

Christine noted that Nick never used a nickname for Vanessa. He used those little creations for people he liked. He never liked Vanessa.

Christine and Vanessa Fabre had met at the Sorbonne where both were in postgraduate studies working in robotics at Le Institut des Systèmes Intelligents et de Robotique. Together, they started a company to build and distribute robots used in surgery. A leading French neurosurgeon was on their board of directors. Christine was the sales leader and Vanessa the brains behind the operation.

They seemed an unlikely pair. Even their appearance was in contrast. When side by side, one saw two women the same height and proportions, Christine was the olive-skinned woman with dark hair and brown eyes. Vanessa was the pale, platinum blonde, blue-eyed version.

Unfortunately, the partnership was doomed. Vanessa held a patent on an amazing advancement in robotics. Investors were throwing money at the company to have a stake in the next great thing. As time went by, Christine suspected Vanessa had overpromised in her patent and the final device might never live up to its potential.

Nick was an investor in the company. When suspicions arose about the validity of the device, he came to investigate. Christine was in charge of entertaining this major investor, but it led to an affair between the two of them. Vanessa was under pressure. Her partner enjoying an affair with Nicholas Foxe didn't help her mood.

The company soon dissolved, as did the friendship between Christine and Vanessa. Nick and Christine's affair was short. Years passed. Now, Nick was back. Soon, Vanessa would be, too.

"In fact, Vanessa is coming to visit."

"Do tell," Nick responded, his disdain unhidden. "It's going to be old-school week."

"Nick, I know you never liked Vanessa. Why?"

"Forgive me if I seem politically incorrect…"

"You, Nick? Never!"

Nick let the remark about his bluntness pass.

"She seemed to me to be an icy bitch."

"Gee, Nick, what do you really think?"

Nick snickered. "Well, really. She harbored no great feelings toward me, and it showed."

"Wow! The great Nicholas Foxe met a woman that did not worship at his feet. That would hurt, wouldn't it?"

"Come on, Christy. I don't see how you two hit it off. You're so different."

"Not that different, Nick. When we worked together, we shared the same passion for what we were doing."

"Then what happened?"

Christine paused. She wasn't sure herself.

"It was a tough time. You know it yourself."

"Yes, I do," agreed Nick. "The company made promises it could never keep. I hold her totally responsible."

"Nick..." Christine began, trying to calm him down.

"No, really. I thought she should be in jail."

Christine came to the defense of her friend. "That's ridiculous. Vanessa poured her heart and soul into her work. She meant no harm. She was fooling herself as much as anyone."

Nick calmed, slowly. Christine changed the subject to a fonder memory.

"Nick," she said, laying her hand on his arm. "Remember the cooking class we took that evening in Paris?"

Nick smiled. "How did you get me into a cooking class? Of all things!"

"I don't know, but I remember you convincing the proprietor to let us stay behind after closing up for the night."

"Ah, yes, I told him we wanted to try doing that tart again. Just didn't have it right." Nick winked.

"The flour was everywhere!"

"I thought you looked delicious wearing nothing but white."

They paused for a moment, taking in the memory.

Nick smiled. "I wonder where cooking classes are held in Venice?"

Chapter 3

NICK AND CHRISTINE TALKED FOR HOURS. From their spot at the Pensione Accademia under a garden awning near the dock, they watched as water vessels passed along the canal. But mostly, they were attuned to each other. They talked about what each had been doing over the years and, of course, about Paris.

Nick summed it up. "It seems trite, doesn't it?"

"What?"

"I feel like Humphrey Bogart in Casablanca."

Christine smiled and understood immediately what Nick meant. "We'll always have Paris," she said.

"Guess so."

"Nick, I have something for you." She reached into the bag she had placed beside the table and drew out a slender gift box about a foot long. "Here."

Nick opened the box and recognized its contents.

"Christy. I appreciate it, but I'm embarrassed."

"You should be. I gave this to you in Paris and you left it behind. Why?"

Nick pulled a letter opener from the box, a fancy model with a pearl handle.

"You don't remember?" Nick asked.

"Remember what?

"This thing is sharp. I put my finger on the blade and nearly cut it off."

Christine grimaced. "I remember it drawing blood, but not much. Anyhow, I came across it recently and thought I'd give it another try."

Nick returned it to the box and held the box to his chest. "I'll cherish it forever."

There was a pause as they considered this summation of their connection.

"I have tickets to the opera tonight. Want to join me?" she asked.

"Sure."

"Nevin will be there and I'm expected to be available when he ventures out in public. But, I'm in another box across from him."

She had to prepare. Her sundress was hardly suitable for evening wear. Nick had not yet checked in to the Gritti Palace, where he was staying. So, they parted until that evening.

Nick returned that night to the Pensione Accademia in a gondola.

Christine walked across the patio to meet him. She smiled at the craft, usually occupied by tourists.

"Why, Nick, how romantic."

Nick explained as he helped Christine into the gondola.

"Guido tells me that the tide makes it impossible for a water taxi to get under the bridges we need to get under. Isn't it so, Guido?"

Guido, now dressed in full gondolier regalia, replied, "*Si, Signorina*. It is so."

Christine took Guido's hand and sat down beside Nick. "You seem to know Mr. Foxe," she observed.

"That I do," Guido said as he pushed away from the pier and began to pole the gondola.

"Let me introduce you," Nick said. "Guido Bartoli, this is Christy. I mean, Christine Blake."

Guido tipped his straw boater to Christine with a smile.

"It is our honor to have Guido as our gondolier tonight," explained Nick. "He is *il capo* of his own fleet of gondolas and water taxis. He picked me up at the airport."

Christine's somber expression told both men she knew how that trip almost cost Nick his life. "You mean the trip…"

"Yes, Christy, that trip. In fact, I owe my life to Guido. He maneuvered the boat to keep the killer off center, and he…" Nick paused, reluctant to say the rest.

Guido stepped in, "I did the deed. It was a fitting end." His expression revealed his disdain for the assassin. Were a lady not on board, he would have spit on the man's grave.

"Let's just say I took advantage of the unfortunate rising tides."

"Oh, I know about the tides," said Christine. "That's why I'm here."

"Is that so?" said Guido. Of course, he knew. Venice has the day-to-day population of a small ocean town at around 60,000 souls and like a small ocean town, the visitor population swells far beyond that. However, little escapes the citizens who live there year-round. But Guido graciously let Christine tell the tale. She seemed to take pleasure in doing so.

"Nevin Dowd came to help the Mose project."

Guido looked as if she stated the obvious. Everyone knew the project had been delayed for years by multiple concerns and government bureaucracy.

Christine smiled even more broadly. "Nevin worked on the latest technology in Holland. He's bringing the ideas they developed there to Venice."

"You speak highly of his efforts."

Nick sat back to enjoy the exchange and to witness how passionately she spoke about her job. It reminded him of her days with the company in Paris. And that reminded Nick of how that passion translated to an intimate level.

Snapping out of his little daydream, Nick said, "And you can now see why she is Dowd's spokeswoman."

"Indeed, I can."

The sun was setting, casting long shadows on the Grand Canal as lights began to flicker on here and there.

"I need to shut up and enjoy where I am," Christine said as she settled back in her seat and Nick put his arm around her. "Nick, I've been here for four months and you know what?"

"What?"

"This is the first time I've been in a gondola."

"Ever? Like, within your lifetime?"

"Yes, I'm embarrassed to say." She looked skeptically at Nick. "Are you sure this was the only way over?"

"I think you will soon see for yourself, but remember, once upon a time, this was the only way anyone ever got anywhere in this town."

"Yeah, but horse-drawn carriages were the only way anyone once got around in New York. Now they're strictly for romantic drives through Central Park."

Nick smiled. "So, you think this is romantic?"

Christine wouldn't give him that. With as serious a demeanor as she could muster, she said, "Not what I meant."

Guido came to Nick's defense.

"*Signorina,* I can remember a time when there would be no problem getting you to the opera by motorboat at any time of day. Now, perhaps when the tide is at its lowest, but not most of the time."

The man looked wistfully away. One could feel his mourning the slow-motion loss of his beloved city year-by-year and inch-by-inch.

Guido soon had an example. "Here is what I mean," he said. "We come to our first bridge."

It was a short trip directly across the expanse of the Grand Canal to the opening where they entered a maze of smaller canals to reach the Teatro di Fenice. Knowing the location of each bridge, Guido ducked at the exact moment needed to get under. It was second nature to him. As they passed under the second bridge, Nick could nearly touch the underside. Christine marveled at the tight passage. Nick observed that, for all the passion for her work, she understood the rising-sea dilemma from data and not from living it. Guido lived it.

They silently made their way to the piazza near the theater. Guido pulled over to the stone edge of the canal and held the gondola steady. Nick stepped up to the street first and extended his hand to Christine who was soon beside him.

"We may walk back," he told Guido.

"If you need me, just call."

Christine held her hand out to Guido. "Thank you. It was a pleasure to meet you."

Guido turned Christine's hand over and kissed it in a flourish of old-world charm. "The pleasure was all mine."

As Nick and Christine walked toward the front of the theater, Christine turned to Nick.

"Guido is quite the charmer."

"Yes, that he is."

"How do you know him?"

"Guido played an important role in a find I made in Venice long ago."

"What kind of find?" she asked.

"Long story, but let's just say that there were people who weren't pleased I had something, and Guido protected me."

"Sounds like Guido is making a habit of saving your life."

Nick smiled. "Something of a guardian angel, don't you think?"

"A very handsome and charming one."

He studied Christine's wistful expression. "Should I be jealous?"

Christine looked amused. "Why. Nick, is there something to be jealous of?"

Nick avoided the question as they arrived at the front of the building. "Ah, here we are."

The entrance to the Teatro di Fenice was tucked into a small piazza and hid the large theater attached to it. It appeared more like a classic style bank building with four tall columns announcing the entrance.

"You know, as a kid, my parents brought me to the previous version of this theater."

"The previous version?" asked Christine.

"Before it burned down, or rather the last time it burned down."

"The last time?"

"Yes. The theater seems to have a history of burning down from time to time."

"Guess that's why the name," Christine offered.

"Teatro di Fenice? Theater of the Phoenix," Nick said. "Yep, the name fits."

"Nevin will be waiting inside."

"Shall we?" Nick asked, offering Christine his arm.

The lobby to the theater was a broad expanse of beige marble and red carpets lit by crystal chandeliers. At either end of the lobby were dual staircases standing between marble columns leading to the first level of box seats.

Opera fans and those who dressed to be seen crowded the lobby.

"That's Nevin over there," Christine said, pointing to a small group of people surrounding a tall man with straight, jet-black hair. Dowd was the center of attention, regaling the crowd with something that appeared to amuse him. A short man, a ringer for old-time movie actor Peter Lorre, had just come up to Dowd to tell him something. Dowd made his apologies and took Peter Lorre aside. It seemed Dowd didn't like what the man told him and produced a series of stern instructions complete with ample finger jabbing. The man left quickly. All that was missing was a snappy salute given by the minion.

"Who was that?" asked Nick.

"You mean the little guy?"

"Yeah."

"That's Preston Smith."

Christine reported the name as though it was something dirty.

"You don't seem to be a Preston Smith fan," Nick said, reacting to her obvious disdain.

"The man acts as Nevin's majordomo. But, for the life of me, I don't know why he has him around. The guy gives me the creeps."

As Dowd walked back to his admirers, he spotted Christine across the room, broke out in a big smile and waved her over to join him.

"So, let's meet the boss," she suggested.

As they approached, the crowd parted to allow the new people in. Dowd embraced Christine as though they hadn't seen each other for ages and kissed her on each cheek.

"Christine, so good to see you. It's been what... forty-eight hours?" He laughed.

"Nevin, I would like you to meet Nicholas Foxe."

Dowd turned to Nick as though he had just appeared and took his hand in a hearty shake.

"Mr. Foxe, it's good to meet you. Christine has praised you so much. And now your adventures have made you famous."

"Well, fame is fleeting," replied Nick.

"Not if you have a corporate publicist like mine."

Dowd had a hearty laugh, which he used frequently.

Nick liked this man right away. He had one of those personalities that drew you in. Dowd stood just a few inches shorter than Nick. His dark eyes and round face portrayed his Asian heritage. His gentleman manners revealed his British roots.

"Nicholas," he said. "I'm glad you're here. I want to talk to you about a discovery we've made. Can't make hide nor hair of it. We need your expertise."

"I'm intrigued," Nick said.

Dowd grinned. "I thought you would be."

Dowd turned to Christine. "See what looks good on my calendar and set something up. OK?

"Sure thing," Christine responded.

The lights began pulsating, signaling the opera was about to begin.

"Looks like we need to find our seats," Dowd said taking Nick's hand once again for a hearty handshake. "So good to meet you. I look forward to our talking again."

"Me, too."

With that, Dowd and his entourage left to one side of the theater.

Christine looked at the tickets she had.

"We're on the other side."

Christine and Nick made their way to their box seats on the right side of the theater. An usher walked them to one door among many matching ones curving around the theater. He took an old-fashioned key, unlocked the door, and held it open. As they took their seats, Nick noticed Dowd sitting in a box on the other side of the theater with the couple he had been talking to in the lobby. They were all in an animated exchange, laughing and enjoying themselves. But, when the orchestra began the overture, Dowd hushed his company and focused completely on the stage.

"I love Madama Butterfly," Christine admitted to Nick.

Nick nodded toward Dowd. "It appears someone else does, too."

"He's an opera buff. It's not by accident we're here tonight at the opening."

"Do tell."

Nick glanced over at Dowd from time to time, noting his reactions to the opera.

Nick had seen Madama Butterfly enough to know the opera well. He thought it interesting Puccini wrote an opera about an American naval officer. Perhaps, that's why the play used the English name 'butterfly' rather than the Italian *farfalle.* The opera was set in the nineteenth century when the American great white fleet gained prominence, but the story line was timeless.

Local Woman Falls in Love with Sailor. They marry. Sailor leaves. She has baby, faithfully waits for baby's father to return. He does not. And, this being opera, she kills herself.

Nick noticed that Dowd was spellbound during the final scene.

Interesting. The man has a reputation for being ruthless in business. But he appears to have a romantic streak.

At the end of the opera, Dowd exploded with more than his share of bravos and bravas.

Nick commented on Dowd's reaction. "Dowd seemed to be rapt by the opera."

Christine noticed as well. "I think he sees the resemblance to his own life."

"How so?"

"Nevin was born in China. He's adopted. Madama Butterfly may be the mother he never knew."

"Interesting."

Nick and Christine returned to the lobby. Among the crowd appeared an unexpected beauty, Vanessa Fabre. She stood out wearing a silver gown that blended with her pale complexion and platinum hair. She looked like the ice queen Nick remembered. The large man in a tux beside her seemed to be a bodyguard more than a boyfriend.

"Vanessa!" Christine called out. "I didn't expect you until tomorrow. What a surprise!"

Vanessa was less charmed. Her smile was slight and obligatory.

"Hello, Christine," she said as she and Christine exchanged kisses on both cheeks. "Nevin told me you would be here. He had extra tickets. So, I thought I would surprise you."

"You're always full of surprises, aren't you?" quipped Nick.

Vanessa returned an icy stare. "Hello, Nick. Long time."

Christine intervened before unpleasant sparks could spoil the evening. She scolded like a mother separating fighting siblings.

"OK, you two. Stop it!"

Vanessa snickered. "All right. That's all water under the bridge."

"Great place for that metaphor," quipped Nick. "What brings you to Venice?"

Vanessa glanced at Christine. "Didn't Christine tell you?" Then back to Nick with a sneer. "I'm working for Nevin. I'm providing diving robots for his work here."

"Still in robotics? Even after..." Nick began before Christine shot Nick a look that meant 'Don't go there.' He was about to complete the sentence with 'your catastrophic failure in your business in Paris,' but stood down.

Vanessa knew where Nick was going.

"Yes, Nick. There appears to be life after death after all."

"All right, you two," Christine said. She put her arm through Vanessa's. "We've got to catch up."

"I'd like that," Vanessa responded. "I have to get back."

She gave Christine a hug.

"Nick," she acknowledged with a perfunctory nod before she walked away.

Nick's gaze followed her across the room. He saw squirrelly Preston Smith talking to her. He had no idea what Preston told her, but it made Vanessa smile.

A smile that made Nick uncomfortable.

Basel, Switzerland, is a town filled with old world charm. It was an unlikely place for a team of men dressed like ninjas. Each was selected for his special skills by an unseen leader, known to them only as Frost. Frost spoke in a disguised voice like the AI utterances from a virtual assistant. Each of the mercenaries thought it odd, but the money was real, evidenced by rich deposits in their bank accounts.

They didn't know each other's real identities. Frost had assigned them operative names using the Dutch masters. They figured Frost must be an art fan, but the aliases had little to do with each painter, save for one. Rembrandt was first recruited for his skill with locks of all types, especially sophisticated electronic ones. Vermeer was the weapons expert. Steen knew computers. But the team leader was most aptly named Bosch. He was a menacing force who seemed to come from the hideous nightmare world of Hieronymus Bosch. All the men were first-time contractors for Frost save for Bosch. He had worked for Frost before, but the others didn't know that, nor did they need to.

Frost had secured a warehouse in a forgotten part of town where the 'Dutch Masters' would practice a raid. A reasonable reproduction of their designated target was assembled in the warehouse. That target occupied a large room hidden underground in another part of town. Since they couldn't dig a pit into the floor of the warehouse, they erected a platform to represent the upper floor where the men would enter via steps down to the main floor. Tables were in place at the bottom of the stairs for the computer console work area. Partitions created spaces where their ultimate objective would be housed. The arrangement did not have to look like the real thing, but layout and distances were paramount. Timing was key.

Over and over, Bosch put the men through their paces. They timed entry. They practiced neutralizing guards. Steen would handle the computer. Rembrandt would unlock the cage. Vermeer would seize the target.

In two days, they would deploy.

Chapter 4

NICK FELT ODD SWITCHING TO A TUX. After all, Christine and he had just been to the opera, where he wore a simple turtleneck and jacket. But this was a star-studded evening, or as much of one the celebration of an engineering project could be.

He dressed in his suite at the Gritti Palace. The room was elaborate, decorated in period Italianate style. He looked across the room to Christine's letter opener on the desk. No longer in the box, he was sure to keep it now. He thought of last night at the Pensione Accademia with her. It was as though the years had disappeared.

The water taxi took Nick to the dock of the Pensione Accademia, where a bellman helped him onto the small pier.

Nick walked across the patio to the hotel, passing several covered tables where guests were enjoying their evening Spritz. Mostly foreigners, they had already adopted the Spritz as an evening drink. Nick was one of them. A decent martini was a rare find in this country.

Nick traversed the small lobby. The desk clerk smiled and welcomed him with a *buona sera, Signor* Foxe.

"Buona sera, Michael." When someone called Nick by name, he was almost always able to respond in kind.

It was only a dozen steps from the front of the small hotel to the door opening to the garden where Christine's suite was located, but Nick did Michael the courtesy of letting him know what he was about.

"I'm picking up Miss Blake."

"Very good."

The garden contained another couple of tables and a brick walkway. It was bordered by a grass lawn, a rare amenity in Venice. The garden was enclosed on all four sides; two sides were hotel rooms. To the right, a tall brick wall provided privacy. The back wall was a building containing two suites, the right one was Christine's. Peculiar to Venice is that individual floors of a building may have different owners. The hotel owned the ground floor of the building containing the suites. The upper floors had a different owner. Those floors faced the street on the other side.

Nick strolled along the brick walk, ending under an arched trellis of vines with a fountain mounted on the wall. To the right was a private patio, table and chairs for the suite. Written on a name plate beside the door were the words, Fountain Suite.

Likely name, considering.

The heavy oak door to the suite was the type common in Italy. There was no doorknob, but rather a large brass pull in the center. The door was unlatched by placing a plastic room card on a sensor to the left. Nick needed no card since the door was ajar.

He knocked and announced, "Christy. I'm here."

"Come on in."

As Nick entered, he could hear Christine's voice from behind the bathroom door.

"I'll be out in just a minute."

The room had a small sitting area with a couch, a table, a TV and little else. Nick thought it odd that the bathroom was off this room and not connected to the bedroom. It made sense if someone was sleeping on a pull-out, which the couch must have been. The suite was cozy and plain. By contrast, Nick's suite at The Gritti Palace was large and opulent. Yet, he was more comfortable here.

The door to the bedroom was open. Nick glanced in and noted everything was as neat as if the maid had just serviced the room. Only a stole lay on the bed. Nick recalled when he was married, things were frequently scattered all over the bedroom when his wife was getting ready for a night out. He remembered how neat Christine was. A superficial thing, but...

Is that one of the things I liked about her?

Nick didn't sit, but paced the small room.

"You shouldn't leave the room door open," he said through the closed bathroom door. "You can never tell what strange man might get in."

Christine opened the door, dressed for the evening.

"You're the only strange man I'm expecting."

She dazzled Nick in her shimmering black dress. It was sleeveless, with a neckline that complemented her cleavage and a skirt which displayed her shapely legs. She had made up her eyes lightly, painted her lips an alluring red, and wore, suspended from her ears, tiny lengths of brilliant crystal.

Nick realized he had never seen the formal version of Christine. He liked it.

"Wow," was all Nick could muster.

"You like?"

"Very much."

"I have a long dress, but this one is more practical here. I'm always climbing in and out of boats."

"As we are tonight," said Nick. "Your taxi awaits."

"I just need to get my stole."

"I'll get it."

Nick stepped into the bedroom, grabbed the stole from the bed, and returned. As he draped it over Christine's shoulders, he enjoyed the light fragrance of her perfume.

Christine was conservative in the use of many things, including her scent.

"You know, you should take care. Leaving the door open is not a good idea."

Christine scoffed.

"Nick, Venice is one of the safest cities in the world. And the garden is enclosed with buildings on three sides and a twelve-foot wall on the other. The wall has a canal right up against it."

"Aren't you the one? You really know your surroundings."

"I've been living here for months. I'm getting to know each crack and crevice."

"OK, OK. Shall we go?"

"Let's."

Nick walked Christine out. As they passed the fountain, Nick remarked, "Natural name for your suite, Fountain."

"Actually, that's not where it came from."

"Oh?"

"No. When the pensione was a villa, my suite was an apartment. An architect by the name of Fountain lived there."

"Interesting."

Nick noted men working near the other suite in the garden. They appeared to be finishing up for the day. "What are they doing?"

"They are reworking the brick wall outside the other suite."

"The noise must bother you."

"I'm usually away when they're working. And the staff told me that if I was bothered while here, they would make the men take a break."

As they continued to walk the path to the hotel dock, Nick noticed a large wooden double door in the brick wall. One side was open, and Nick could see a narrow canal with a small barge. A workman was dumping a wheelbarrow of old bricks into the barge.

"There's a break in your so-called secure garden," Nick said.

"Look at those metal slides," she said, pointing to the large iron slides on the side and top of the door. "They're like the doors of a castle. They close those in the evening when the workmen leave."

Christine studied Nick. She didn't remember him being so cautious about such things.

"Nick, why the concern? What's up?"

Nick didn't know. He had an uneasy feeling and had no clue why.

"Don't know," he admitted. Then turning to Christine with a smile, "Let's forget about it. Tonight should be fun, right?"

They passed through the lobby and exchanged a *buona sera* with Michael.

Out front on the patio, Christine stopped and turned to Nick. Nick looked over her shoulder to see an old man and his wife. The man gazed at Christine in appreciation.

"Nick, this is a working event for me. I'm sorry about it, but I will be spending a lot of time escorting Nevin around and introducing him to people. You understand, right?"

"Sure, no problem."

Christine smiled.

"I know. You're a good mixer in things like this."

They continued on to the water taxi waiting for them. As the bellman helped Christine into the boat, she saw Guido Bartoli standing on the pier looking smashing in a tux. He took her hand and kissed it.

"Guido! I'm so glad to see you are joining us."

"I was both surprised and pleased to receive an invitation. Perhaps, you knew about this?"

"Nevin wanted the leading business representatives of Venice there tonight. Who would have more of a stake in this wonderful city than the man who moves us through its canals?"

"Well, tonight I have the rare opportunity to have one of my men drive me," Guido said as he put his hand on the shoulder of the young man to whom he referred. "And a beautiful woman to accompany me."

"Not so fast, Guido," Nick kidded. "She's my date."

"Well, I'm pleased at the attention, but as I told Nick, I would be a lousy date. I'm working the crowd for Nevin tonight."

"I assure you, just the ride there and back is a pleasure in and of itself."

As Christine took a seat on one of the soft-upholstered benches, Nick walked by Guido with a grin for his old friend and whispered, "How do you Italians get by with that over-the-top stuff?"

"You American men may have something to learn, no?"

Christine wandered to the back of the taxi where it was warmer and where she could sit down. She positioned herself on the couch across from Nick and Guido. As the taxi pulled away from the dock and into the Grand Canal, Guido led the conversation, asking Christine about her life. Nick learned a few things.

Guido did not delve into how Nick and she met. Nick already had told him and talk of a failed business was not a good way to start an evening. Instead, he asked how she came to work for Nevin Dowd.

Christine was the one who brought up the business that she and Vanessa founded, but only as a point of reference. She told Guido how she started her own public relations company after the partnership ended. She had several top clients and a staff of seventeen. This, Nick did not know, and he considered whether he'd been listening closely enough.

The water taxi entered the lagoon, and the driver accelerated as they made their way to the Lido.

Christine continued her story: Nevin Dowd had appeared with an attractive checkbook. He wanted her to handle the PR for his work on Mose. The work he described would bill out half her staff, but he didn't stop there. He wanted one hundred percent of her time, and he wanted it on site. She protested that her Italian was not good, and that she didn't know the Italian market that well.

Christine said she would never forget Nevin's response. 'We're not working on an Italian stage, but on a world stage.' Dowd was not a humble man.

What nailed the deal was when he said that Vanessa Fabre, who worked for him, had highly recommended Christine for the job.

It surprised Christine. Vanessa and she did not leave on good terms. Perhaps they could patch things up.

Nick's expression told Christine he thought that wasn't likely.

The driver slowed as he approached the island.

Venice is located in a marshy lagoon separated from the Adriatic Sea by a strip of barrier islands. The central one is the Lido di Venezia. *Lido* is Italian for 'beach.' This word is used for everything from a nightclub in Paris to the lido deck of cruise ships. Part of the elegance associated with the name was the hotel located there. The Excelsior was built over a hundred years ago as a resort for the rich and famous. It had been maintained over the years and kept up to date with modern conveniences and superior service. The Venice Film Festival started there in 1932, the first golden age of the cinema.

Tonight, the hotel would not be showered with movie stars but with business moguls. Christine had made sure of that.

She was unaware it would also be a gathering of suspects.

Chapter 5

THEY BUILT THE EXCELSIOR on the Adriatic side of the Lido. In order to reach it directly from Venice, they built a special canal. The driver guided the water taxi into that canal. As they went, the surroundings became lush with palms and vegetation that seemed more at home further south. Fine homes and apartment buildings dotted the landscape. The hotel appeared before them on a rise. The boat headed to a dock, where bellmen tied it up, and helped everyone out and onto a red carpet leading to the hotel entrance.

The hotel was a pale, red brick affair with arabesque windows, towers, and balconies stretching its four stories along a full block of beach front. The architect, influenced by the Doge Palace, expanded that edifice by ten, and added architectural whimsey.

The hotel was new to Nick, but not to Guido, who took the lead. Taking Christine by the arm, he gestured, "This way, please."

Nick followed behind as Guido walked Christine along the red carpet as it continued through a long underground hallway beneath the street and to the hotel lobby.

"You've chosen a fine venue for this event," Guido said to Christine.

"It has the space we needed. Most hotels in Venice are nice, but small."

Guido passed a sly look toward Christine. "And it does not hurt that everyone wants to come here, does it not?"

Christine laughed. "No, it does not."

They walked up the steps to the lobby.

Nick's Gritti Palace was a luxurious renovation of a Venetian home, but rooms were small. The architects of the Excelsior had no such space limitations. The lobby was vast. A fountain with a statue of three nymphs occupied the center of a park-like area covered with marble rather than grass.

"Excuse me," said Christine. "We're early and I have to check on a few things."

With that, Christine walked over to the concierge desk.

"You have quite a woman there," Guido said to Nick.

"*Have* is the operative word. I never possessed Christy."

Guido couldn't understand Nick's comment. "You mean... you and her… never…"

Nick understood the direction Guido was going.

"Of course, we had the most intense, ah…, connection, I've ever had. But there was something that's hard to put into words."

"Try."

Nick looked at Guido. He saw a man who was truly interested.

"I've been with many women. But somehow, I always sensed a release on their part, somehow giving in to me. Not with Christy. She was in control, always challenging me."

Guido paused, studying Nick, seeing he was reliving one of those moments. "And?"

Nick was at a loss to express it and reached back to a 60's term.

"It blew my mind."

Guido laughed. "Ah, my friend. You are, what do you call it, smitten?"

Nick considered his friend's comment.

"Maybe. Maybe re-smitten."

Christine returned to the men. "They assured me that all is in place. Let's go to the ballroom."

Perhaps, because Guido had just heard Nick's story and understood his relationship with Christine, he relinquished his escorting duties to Nick and motioned them to take the lead. Nick took Christine's arm and walked toward the ballroom. There was no problem finding the way. A large sign on a tripod announced, *Mose Festa.*

The entry to the ballroom passed beneath an arch befitting a memorial to an ancient Roman dignitary. Above the center of the room was a giant dome adorned with round windows and a long crystal chandelier. The room gleamed in pearl white. Tall windows overlooked the Adriatic on one side and the garden on the other. Five tables, each seating six, were arranged around the room. At the far end of the room, was a dais with a large video display behind it. The word Mose was projected on the screen with a background representing undulating blue ocean waves.

Since she was helping arrange this soiree, Christine had arrived early. Only a few guests were present. Wait staff, dressed in black, were passing Prosecco and hors d'oeuvres. At the end of the room near the dais, Preston Smith talked with Vanessa Fabre and a woman Nick did not recognize.

"Excuse me," interrupted Christine. "I need to talk to Preston. Our table is that one beside the dais. You'll see name cards at your places."

Christine was all business, but she took a moment to tell Nick and Guido, "Enjoy!"

As she walked toward the dais, Guido turned to Nick.

"So, you enjoy such affairs?"

"Not much, how about you?"

"It's part of the business," said Guido as he shrugged. "I'm not the only boat on the water. I have competition."

"See any tonight?"

"Not yet. But the night is young," Guido said. More people filtered in and he surveyed the crowd as though competition could arrive at any moment.

"Ah, but here is a familiar face," he continued.

The familiar face turned out to be Commissario Bruno Russo, who noticed them from across the room and walked over to the men. Russo looked the quintessential kindly grandfather. He stood about five-five in a rumpled tux. His curly hair, more gray than black, was in need of a trim.

"Bruno!" said Guido. "What brings you here? Official business?"

Russo gave Guido a warm handshake.

"Always," said Russo.

"I would like to introduce you to my friend. Mister Nicholas Foxe, Commissario Guido Russo."

As Russo shook Nick's hand, he looked serious and said, "I know of your unfortunate introduction to our city. We do not welcome people who attempt to kill our visitors."

"Yes, if not for Guido, I would not be standing here. Any word on the man who tried to kill me?"

"We have some information. I have gotten involved in the investigation. We will talk again, yes?"

"I appreciate that."

Nick saw a look of suspicion on Russo's face belying the friendly affirmation. The Commissario need not say anything. Nick knew what he was thinking.

What was Nick into that made a man want to kill him?

Guido and Russo walked away greeting other mutual friends. A slim, young man with a pale complexion approached Nick. Nick had always referred to such ivory skin as 'English schoolboy complexion.' The first words out of his mouth, in perfect Oxford English, confirmed that nationality.

"Mr. Foxe," he said. "Allow me to introduce myself. My name is Robert Morrison. I'm from the British consulate office here in Venice."

They shook hands.

"Some hardship post you have, Mr. Morrison," Nick quipped.

"Please, call me Robert," the man said grinning at Nick's joke. "Yes, it has its pluses. I heard about the unpleasantness that greeted you upon arrival. Do you think it had anything to do with your discovery?"

"Discovery?"

Morrison returned a 'don't play dumb with me' look.

"Mr. Foxe. Everyone has heard of your discovery in New Mexico. Few people know where that discovery led."

"Well, you know how it is. After a news cycle or two, people lose interest."

"Not everyone, Mr. Foxe."

The conversation was interrupted when Christine returned with a tall, slender woman dressed in a striking long, gray gown, her hair straight and to her shoulders. The woman struck Nick as someone who would have had it in a sensible ponytail outside of this formal affair.

"Nick," Christine said. "I would like to introduce you to Elena Zago. She's my public affairs coordinate at Mose.

Nick shook the hand Elena offered.

"It's a pleasure to meet you. This is Robert Morrison from the British consulate."

Elena and Morrison shook hands. Morrison seemed annoyed by the intrusion.

Christine continued.

"Elena has been great to work with."

Elena returned Christine's smile and, as a tribute to the man Christine worked for, said, "Mr. Dowd has been so instrumental in Mose. His contributions of time and capital are greatly appreciated."

Nick looked toward the dais. Vanessa and Preston were in conversation, but there was no sign of Dowd, even though the room was now full of guests as the appointed hour of the dinner approached.

"And where is the illustrious Nevin Dowd?" asked Nick.

Christine and Elena exchanged amused, knowing glances.

"Nevin likes to make dramatic entrances," offered Christine.

The two women laughed. Each shared the same opinion.

As though on cue, Nevin Dowd burst into the room. Although dressed the same as all the other men, Nick thought

Dowd's tux classier, appearing fresh from a fitting on Savile Row. Dowd, all smiles, worked through the crowd like a politician with strong handshakes and first names uttered. He paused by Christine and Elena with a kiss in turn on each woman's hand.

"Thank you for putting this together. It looks smashing. Doesn't it, Nick?"

"Indeed, it does."

Turning to Morrison, Dowd appeared to find the one man in the room he didn't know.

"I'm sorry," he said as he put his hand out. "I don't believe we've met."

"Robert Morrison," he said as he shook Dowd's hand.

"Good to meet you, Robert."

Addressing the group, Dowd said, "Hope you enjoy the evening." And then he was off to work the crowd on the way to the dais.

A voice came over the room from an unseen speaker, first in Italian and then in English. "Ladies and Gentlemen, our dinner is about to begin. Please take your seats."

Christine walked ahead and led Nick and Guido to their table at the foot of the dais. Bruno Russo shared the table with them, but Robert Morrison sat at one of the tables far away. Nick appreciated it. Morrison bothered him.

Too inquisitive, and not in a good way.

On the dais, joining Dowd, was Elena and Vanessa. Nick asked Christine, now seated beside him, "Why aren't you up there?"

Christine gave Nick a playful punch in the arm and a smile.

"Because I'm with you."

Nick noticed Preston Smith standing off to one side.

"Why isn't Preston seated. Doesn't he eat?" Nick thought it fitted Preston's appearance to be one who feeds only in the dark of night.

Christine did not have the same reaction. Although Preston was unsettling, she had grown used to him as one might a friend's mongrel pet.

"He's working the presentation."

"Working the presentation?"

Christine smiled. "You'll see."

Caprese salads were served all around as Dowd took his place on the dais, engaging in an animated discussion with Elena Zago, seated to his right. To his left, a sad-looking, middle-aged, slightly balding, man seemed neglected as he picked at his caprese.

"Who is the man beside Dowd?" he asked Christine.

"That is Vittorio Musolino, the head of the Mose project."

"He looks forlorn."

"Vittorio was under huge pressure and criticism. Mose was over budget and behind schedule. He took the hit for it, although much of the delay was beyond his control."

The salads were swept away and replaced by veal and lobster. Servers refilled wine glasses. Nick paused as the wait staff performed their duties. He studied Musolino.

"Dowd swept in and saved the project, right?"

"Well," said Christine hesitantly, "much of that was the force of personality of Nevin Dowd, and some good PR."

Nick smiled.

"Of course," he said as he raised his wineglass as if to toast. "PR. You're the best."

"It's easy with Nevin. He's larger than life."

Guido, following the conversation between Christine and Nick added, "But of course, he is part Italian."

"Is he? One would never guess it by looking at him," Nick said, noting Dowd's Chinese background.

"His adoptive mother was Italian," said Christine. "Venetian, in fact."

It was Guido's turn to raise a glass.

"And that is good enough for everyone in Venice," he said. "It keeps him from being the outsider coming here to save the city."

"But not enough to wipe the dour expression from Musolino's face," added Nick.

"This is Nevin's event," said Christine. "He's footing the bill. Vittorio will begin the evening and introduce him, but I know Nevin will give credit where credit is due."

As the guests consumed their veal and lobster, Dowd turned to Musolino and spoke a few words. Musolino took his cue and stood.

In Italian, Musolino thanked everyone for attending. He then switched to English to introduce Dowd.

"As you may know, Mose is a project long in its realization. You have all heard about the project, but few know the details. We will change that tonight. Dessert is coming, but we first want to provide an overview. To do so, I would like to introduce the man who has provided the project with his time, his talent, but most of all, his money."

Musolino smiled for the first time at his little joke. Dowd shared in the laughter from the crowd.

"So, how much money?" Nick asked Christine.

"Only his banker knows," she responded.

"Does he get naming rights?"

Christine hushed Nick. "Hey, I worked hard on this presentation. Just watch."

Musolino paused a moment for the gathering to enjoy his joke and then announced the special host.

"Ladies and Gentlemen, Mister Nevin Dowd."

Dowd rose while the guests and those on the dais provided generous applause. Were the applause not enough, recorded boisterous music played from an opera Nick did not recognize. The screen behind Nevin whirled the name Mose in computer graphics worthy of a football game introduction on American television.

Dowd returned the applause to the crowd and to Musolino and Zago. He allowed the applause to subside before beginning.

"Thank you, *Signor* Musolino. Thank you, *Signorina* Zago. And thank you all for coming tonight. It has been my pleasure to be a part of this important project and to contribute my time and," he turned to Musolino. "My money."

Chuckles rippled through the crowd.

"Let me take you on a journey, a journey back in time," he said as the lights dimmed and the screen flashed pictures of Venice going from current day back in time until nothing appeared but a marsh.

"Venice first occupied a marsh for protection. But it was not to remain an isolated outpost in a lagoon."

Pictures moved forward, showing drawings of early buildings, then cutting away to a map of the region.

"As trade between Asia and Europe increased, Venice found itself at the doorway of the silk route. Explorers like Venice's own Marco Polo extended the trade."

A painting of Marco Polo appeared as buildings in Venice began rising in stone behind it.

"Venice and its Republic became a major power in the world. A rich power. And with its riches, rose magnificent palaces. But Venice was unique in the world as the city of water with its canals and as important today as ever.

"The fortunes of Venice have come and gone, but the city's glory continues."

The Doge Palace, Saint Mark's, and other landmark sites appeared on the screen as triumphant music rose in volume, but then abruptly stopped as the screen went dark.

"But changes on this globe we occupy challenge us."

The screen showed a glacier calving with a thunder of sound flooding the room. It was followed by cars in a major city traffic jam, then forest trees being felled.

"Climate change… and the seas are rising."

Videos showed flooding in the streets of Venice. Tourists walking on platforms above the water covering Saint Mark's Square. Diners in a restaurant wearing wading boots. Then, more severe flooding entering swank hotels. Nick recognized the lobby of the hotel where he was staying, the Gritti Palace. The sitting area had water over a foot deep. Expensive carpets were stacked on sofas.

"The *acqua altas,* the high tides, are coming more frequently and more severely each time."

The video went dark.

"Introducing Mose."

The word Mose did another football graphic on the video screen accompanied by dramatic music.

Below the name 'Mose' appeared what it stands for. *Modulo Sperimentale Elettromeccanico.*

"This is a case of backing into an acronym and finding words that fit. But what I like is the imagery of the name. Mose is like *Mosè*, the man we call Moses in English. The man who parted the sea."

Dowd looked away.

"I can see Charlton Heston doing just that."

The crowd snickered, with several younger people asking their companions "who?"

A satellite view of the lagoon and barrier islands appeared on the screen.

"The Venice Lagoon is one of the Mediterranean's largest and most important wetlands. It is a fragile environment. The lagoon is separated from the Adriatic Sea by narrow strips of land, one of which you are seated on right now. The Lido di Venezia."

The Lido was lit on the map behind Dowd.

"There are just three inlets to the sea, the Lido, the Malamocco, and the Chioggia."

The three inlets lit in turn from north to south as Dowd names them.

"The tide flows in and out of the inlets twice a day. Master these three inlets and you master the tides of Venice. How do we do this?"

The screen showed a huge gate, much like one found in pairs on either end of a canal lock, but thicker and painted bright yellow. The gate dwarfed the specially built truck on which it rested much like a Saturn rocket dwarfed the mobile transport taking it to a Cape Kennedy launch pad.

"Gates. We control the tides with gates."

The video turned to a drawing in which one of these gates is positioned underwater. The gate tapered to a pair of hinges at one end. Beneath and to the right of the hinges were sealed walkways forming an underwater tunnel. The cross-section of the tunnel contained silhouettes of people the size of gnats in relation to the gate.

"When inactive, the gates are full of water and lie invisible in special foundation structures in the inlet's bed. When a high tide that could flood the city is anticipated, water is pumped out of the gate and air is let in, allowing the gates to float into place. We have a system to allow ships to enter and exit, even when the gates are up.

"There is more, much more, but dessert awaits."

A round of light laughter filled the room.

"You may ask, "What role did you play in all of this, Mister Dowd?" Let me be clear, this design, this functionality, and most of the work, are to the credit of *Signor* Musolino and his brilliant team."

Dowd began a round of applause for Musolino who, for the first time that evening, warmly smiled. He stood to acknowledge the compliment and waved to the crowd.

Dowd continued.

"My role, besides the aforementioned money, was technology help to enhance the system. I provided a newly developed paint that will last far longer than what we originally used. Don't worry, it's still the bright yellow of the original."

Light laughter.

"We designed hinges to last longer as well. And, in association with Fabre Robotics, we are supplying a fleet of underwater craft to work on the system in ways that are more flexible and versatile. I would like to introduce Miss Vanessa Fabre, head of Fabre Robotics."

Fabre stood smiling, acknowledging the applause.

Nick couldn't hide his disdain for Christine's former partner. "Guess every dog has her day," he sniped.

Christine was not amused. "Nick, don't do that. It's cruel."

Nick shrugged as Dowd continued.

"But what I'm particularly proud of are the new pumps we are putting in place. They are of an advanced design that operate faster and more efficiently. Even though tides are predictable, it doesn't hurt to get those gates up faster than the half-hour it now takes. The pump installation is finishing up and we will test them soon."

The screen showed iconic and romantic scenes from Venice as soft music prevailed.

"Mose. Protecting the city of history and culture, and yes, romance, for generations to come. Thank you."

Dowd received a standing ovation as he returned the applause to the gathering and to the others on the dais. As the applause died, wait staff began serving tiramisu and coffee.

Guido and Russo turned to Christine, acknowledging the part she played in tonight's affair.

"*Brava*," said Guido.

"Very impressive," added Russo.

Christine's face expressed relief that the evening went well. "Thank you."

She turned to Nick. "And what did you think?"

"I think you are remarkable."

"I meant about the evening."

"My statement stands."

Nick felt the vibration of his phone in the inside pocket of his jacket. He pulled it out and looked to see who was calling.

It was the Gritti Palace. Being presumptuous as to how the evening would progress, he had asked the concierge at the Gritti Palace to arrange some special treats in his room.

"Would you excuse me? I have to take this."

He answered the call and began to speak as he left the room. A man seated at the rear table, hidden in a corner, examined Nick, taking stock of the man.

"So, that's the famous Mr. Nicholas Foxe," the man said with a detectable Texan accent. Where others were drinking wine, the Texan drank bourbon.

"You've never met?" asked a gentleman to his left.

"No, but I feel that I know him."

The young man to his right said in sycophantic tones, "Sir, I could have gotten you a better table. We need not be back here."

"No. I know that. I like it back here. Like to take in the whole room."

"Do you want to meet Mr. Foxe? I mean, I'm sure I can arrange it."

The Texan brushed aside the idea.

"No need. I've got a feeling Mr. Foxe will be working for me soon. Whether he knows it or not."

Chapter 6

BOSCH WAS THE FIRST MAN to enter the dark alley. Vermeer, Steen and Rembrandt arrived in stealth from different directions, and assembled behind him. Frost had thought of everything, including the warehouse with the replicated rooms. Only Rembrandt, using his skills with locks, had seen the inside of the actual targeted room. He confirmed that Frost had duplicated it accurately in the warehouse model. This would go according to plan.

Each man had a pistol in hand with a silencer, but Vermeer also carried an AK-47 on his back like a ninja sword.

The alley went off a small street that had little foot traffic. No cars around during the day, let alone at this late hour. But Bosch took no chance and kept watch as Rembrandt worked on the lock, a simple keypad beside a nondescript door that anyone would pass without a second thought. No one would suspect that one of the most valuable treasures in the world resided behind it.

Tom Littleton was working late. Tom was a computer scientist by trade, but his first love was caving. As a slight, agile man, he was perfect for exploring tight spaces deep under the earth.

Tom had been the caver who discovered an encoded metal slab that eventually led to the Omni, which now occupied a glass cage before him. As he worked with the Omni, he often reflected on how an Army Ranger had set him on the path to discover The Tablet, the name given the metal slab by the public, and how that man had saved everyone's life deep in a cave in New Mexico.

That Ranger was now a close friend. The Tablet led him and his friends to a chamber below a castle in Italy, to a secret lab in Rome, and then to the final prize, the Omni.

The Omni, with its pulsating glow, no longer occupied an obscure grotto on the Adriatic. It was Tom's constant companion, housed near him in a glass enclosure behind a door locked with a thumbprint scanner. The Omni was wirelessly connected to a supercomputer in Germany. Tom talked to it through that supercomputer.

'Talk' was a loose term for how they interacted. The Omni housed more advanced knowledge than seemed possible. Already, directions for gene manipulation had been extracted. Scientists were well on their way to fighting a variety of viral diseases.

Of all the advanced information it held, the Omni remained mute on one item. It is the first thing anyone would want to know.

Who left the Omni Scientia for us?

Whoever left The Tablet left the Omni, and The Tablet was 10,000 years old. The Omni was a vast encyclopedia, and like one, held little information on its creator. Or, if it did, that information lurked deep within it, hidden from view. Tom searched for it, but other valuable discoveries surfaced first. Now, he was working on one of them.

Tom had an intriguing but daunting challenge. The Omni clearly spelled out the feasibility of drawing energy from seawater. When they discovered the Omni, it was in a grotto near seawater and they suspected it used that water to light the cave. Now, housed deep below the streets of Basel, no one knew how. One of many secrets to discover.

From what the Omni told them, they knew the ancients had built a model that demonstrated this theory in action. But where was this model? Just as with The Tablet, the ancients had set in place another puzzle to be solved. Tom was determined to solve it.

However, at the moment he was taking a break, having a phone conversation with Rachael Friedman. (Rachael was on the team who had discovered the Omni.) As a professor in physics at MIT, her interest was in what the Omni could teach them about time and space.

"So, how is your work going?" asked Tom.

"It's exciting, and it's frustrating. The Omni uses formula notation of its own. I've been spending most of my time translating it into what we use today. Just working with imaginary numbers now. The ancients seemed to have a way to make sense of them in a way we cannot."

Rachael paused. "Tom, I sense your blank stare coming right through the line. I don't need a video feed."

Tom laughed. "Guess I skipped imaginary numbers on the way to becoming a computer programmer."

Tom had a strong peripheral sense. Just as one might feel some unseen person is looking at them, Tom could feel unseen people in a much wider space. That sense was activated at that moment! Rachael noticed the pause.

"Tom, what is it?"

"Somebody's here."

"You have guards on duty, don't you?"

"Yes, but it's someone else. There are more than one. Just a minute."

Tom set the phone down.

The intruders had been silent. The guard never saw Vermeer, who put a silenced slug through the man's head. Bosch came next and shot the guard through the heart as he lay on the floor. The others looked stunned. Did Bosch want to make sure he was dead, or did he like it as sport? They moved down the dark hallway to the next entry point. The door had another keypad. Rembrandt made short work of it.

Now the Dutch Masters stood on a ledge overlooking the work area. On the far side was the Omni in the glass cage. In front of that, was the workstation where Tom now stood looking up at them. A guard working the main floor jumped in front of Tom and aimed his pistol at the intruders. Vermeer took him down with a short burst from his AK-47. Tom was able to get behind the workstation for protection. He saw the guard's pistol on the floor close by, and grabbed it.

The invaders ran down the steps as Tom rolled over with the guard's pistol in hand. He knelt and fired a shot at Bosch, aimed for his head, but just clipped his left ear. So close…

"You bastard!" Bosch yelled as he grabbed his bleeding ear with his left hand and fired off a shot with his right, hitting Tom in the torso. Tom fell back, hitting his head on the console, knocking him unconscious.

"No!" yelled Rembrandt. "We need him!"

Rembrandt ran to Tom as he lay unmoving and put two fingers on his neck.

"We just need his thumb," groused Bosch as he continued to hold his ear.

"We need his thumb, with a pulse in it, you idiot!"

Bosch reacted by pointing his pistol at Rembrandt who returned a defiant look.

Steen interceded as he stepped between them.

"Cool it. We got to get back to the plan."

Bosch cooled down a notch as he took the lead again.

"Yeah, let's get back to the plan. Steen, get on the computer. Vermeer, get the Omni."

Rembrandt and Bosch dragged Tom over to the glass cage housing the Omni. Rembrandt lifted Tom's hand to the pad beside the cage's door and placed his thumb on it. There was a click and the door opened an inch.

Vermeer swung the door wide open and rushed in still holding his AK-47 as though assaulting a human target. Were it only human.

A second after Vermeer entered, an immense pulse emanated from the Omni. The Omni compressed the air around it and directed it toward Vermeer in one sonic blast. It bashed him against the glass, leaving deep cracks as he fell to the floor.

Bosch looked through the cage door, cautious about entering.

"Are you all right?" he asked Vermeer.

Vermeer could not move. "I think every bone's broken," he groaned.

"Can you get up?"

"No."

Bosch pointed his pistol at Vermeer and said, "Sorry," just before he put a bullet in the man's head.

Alarms went off. Red lights flashed all over the room. This was not in the plan!

Steen pulled a thumb drive from the console and held it up for the others to see. "I've got what we need. Let's get out of here."

Steen rushed by Bosch who paused to look at Tom, debating whether to put another bullet in him. But Rembrandt grabbed his arm and shouted, "Come on. Let's go!"

After the Masters were gone, from the phone receiver left on the console came Rachael's voice.

"Tom, Tom, are you there?"

Chapter 7

THE HOTEL DANIELI, located on the lagoon, beside Saint Mark's Square and the Doge Palace, boasted the best view in Venice. Nevin Dowd asked Nick to join him at the hotel's rooftop restaurant. Although the place sat over twenty diners, Dowd apparently booked the entire area. There would be only two for lunch.

Nick stepped from the dark hallway into the bright sunlight washing over the patio. A waiter greeted him. Nick saw Dowd sitting at a table at the far side of the restaurant. But before the waiter could escort Nick to Dowd's table, Dowd had walked to Nick and shook his hand.

"Nick. Glad you could make it."

Dowd led Nick to his table, from where they saw gondolas below on the lagoon waiting for passengers, and Saint Mark's Square where pigeons outnumbered tourists. Dowd paused as the waiter brought coffee. Once the waiter left, he continued. "I want to show you something."

He placed a leather satchel on the table and withdrew a manila folder. Even though they were alone, Dowd looked around to ensure there were no prying eyes. He opened the folder and passed three eight-by-ten photographs to Nick, who inspected each with some recognition. The photos were of an object, though covered by murky silt, sparkled like silver. It was a square stake bearing markings he could not make out. The metal reminded him of The Tablet, the coded slab Tom Littleton discovered in New Mexico.

Nick tried to see a connection with The Tablet. He reasoned that any shiny object might remind him of it since it had been such an integral part of his life.

But what if there was a connection?

Dowd had never seen The Tablet, so he wasn't making the association. He had invited Nick here because Christine had touted his reputation as an archeologist and cryptologist who might determine the origin of the stake.

"What do you make of it?" asked Dowd.

"Where is this?"

"When we were dredging for Mose, our team hit something, something unmovable, and we sent one of our divers down to see what it was. These photos are what he came back with. We have no idea where it came from and we don't know how far into the bottom it goes."

"I would like to take a closer look at it."

Dowd smiled. "I thought you might. Would now be a good time?"

"Now?" respoded Nick, surprised that Dowd was ready. But then again, Dowd had a reputation for not wasting time.

"Sure, I have a boat waiting. Let's go."

Dowd was already standing. Nick saw no reason to wait. He got up and said, "Lead the way."

Dowd led Nick to the elevator and down to the lobby level. Outside, to one side of the gondolas, waited a motor launch. It was not like the water taxi Guido operated, but more like a luxury tender for a yacht. Once inside, the pilot sped across the lagoon.

They headed toward the north end of the Lido where Mose gates had been installed. Once ashore, Dowd led Nick to a small building beside a canal which had been built for the project.

"I'll need a wetsuit and scuba gear," Nick said as they entered the building.

Dowd smiled.

"That won't be necessary. We'll be using this."

A few steps further and a two-man mini-sub came into view. Workers had suspended it just above the water by a crane beside the canal. "This is my design," Dowd said with obvious pride.

"You designed this?" asked Nick.

"Didn't get a degree in mechanical engineering for nothing," Dowd remarked as he moved toward a technician dressed in an orange jumpsuit. Nick remained behind, surveying the craft. It looked like a huge medicine capsule painted white with an aircraft cockpit on top. The cockpit reminded Nick of a vintage World War II fighter he once flew at an airshow. This was a different environment and, unlike an old aircraft or submersible, there was no sign of propellers. Small ducts appeared on the front with a nozzle positioned at the rear. A vertical rudder blade was attached to the lower back.

"What do you think?" Dowd asked, fishing for a compliment on his handicraft.

"What propulsion does it use?" asked Nick.

"Ah, that's what I'm proud of. Think of it as a water jet, but it's more like a maglev train for underwater. No moving parts."

"Impressive."

"Yes, it is, isn't it?" Dowd was not one to be shy about his genius.

"What's great is it doesn't disturb the water. You'll see. The diver who took the pictures stirred up more silt than this will."

As they spoke, the technician slowly swung the capsule over to a stand near Dowd and Nick, and lowered it in place with a soft thud. The technician pushed a control button on the remote he held. The glass dome opened.

Nick could not help but notice the nameplate on the side of the craft. It read 'Fabre Robotique' and below that 'Equipe des Sciences de la Mer.'

"Fabre Robotique?" Nick asked. "As in Vanessa Fabre?"

"That's right. Vanessa's company manufactured this craft under my supervision. She added robotic systems and controls.

"Shall we go? I'll sit in back and you up front where you can see best."

"Where are the controls?"

"They're duplicated front and back," said Dowd as he mounted the two steps on the stand and climbed into the cockpit.

Nick waited on the step while Dowd positioned himself and then stepped over the edge and lowered himself into the other seat. It was a tight fit. Before him were controls, not unlike those found in a small airplane. Before him was a steering yoke. He assumed that the yoke could be turned and pushed and pulled, just as in a plane. Two pedals on the floor completed the resemblance to an aircraft.

Dowd said, "Buckle up," as Nick heard him snap a shoulder harness across his chest. Nick found the straps for his and did the same. Dowd flipped a switch which lit up the control panels before him and in front of Nick. In the center, there was a square video panel similar to that of a jet's primary flight display. There was an attitude indicator, simulating a horizon with blue on top and brown below. A speed indicator appeared to the left and a compass at the bottom. Besides these somewhat familiar controls were small joysticks placed to the right and left.

Dowd clicked another switch. Hydraulic lifts lowered the glass cowl into place. Nick felt the air pressure change as the cowl sealed. Except for the noise of intermittent hydraulic pumps doing their job, the craft was silent.

The technician flipped another control on his remote. The crane slowly lifted the craft, swung it over to the canal, and lowered it into the water. When it floated on the surface, Nick heard the chains snap loose. Dowd pulled another switch and the craft began moving forward in silence.

"Nick," whispered Dowd, "what do you hear?"

"Nothing."

Nick, sitting with no choice in the tight space but to look straight ahead, could almost feel Dowd smile with pride as he said, "Precisely. It's my aqua-maglev at work."

"Aqua-maglev?" questioned Nick.

"That's what I call it. Got a copyright on the name and a patent on the process."

"I'm impressed."

"As they say, you ain't seen nothing yet."

Dowd pushed the yoke forward and submerged the craft under the murky water of the lagoon.

"And, now we dive the depths of the Venetian lagoon?" asked Nick.

"Not exactly. The lagoon averages a depth of just five meters, but the cruise ships follow a channel fifty meters deep. We're headed to a place forty meters down."

"Not quite the Mariana Trench," Nick joshed, naming the deepest part of the ocean.

"Nope. I designed this craft for just what we are doing today. If you tried to use this as a diving bell, it would likely be a short trip."

Dowd leveled off the craft as they continued silently through the water. Nick considered the silence remarkable. When Nick scuba-dived, the only sound was the regulator assisting his breathing. Here, there was not even that.

"Look forward," Dowd said as he switched on exterior beams lighting the bottom. "We are following the furthest reach of our trenching in this area. To the right are the gates we will raise into place."

The muddy bottom of the lagoon looked as if a giant had taken a hoe and dug a ten-meter trench. To the left, the bottom rolled by. Nick saw trash one would expect at the bottom of a busy waterway. To the right, lower down, was a bottom as smooth as a plaza. Dowd moved to the right and down into the fresh bottom. The trench wall glided by on their left.

Nick felt the craft slowing. The yellow gates and floor reflected light. As Dowd advertised, the maglev system of the craft stirred up nothing, keeping the field of vision as if they were looking through the glass of an aquarium. Out of the brown seascape, an object ahead sparkled, reflecting the light from the craft like a mirror.

"Here it is," said Dowd. "I'm going to circle to the right and pull up to it from that side, so you can get a good look."

As Dowd maneuvered the craft, Nick saw they had excavated the area around the object such that the craft could approach it from any direction. He could examine the stake up close and all around.

Dowd pulled up to the stake so close that the craft's nose practically touched it.

Is he going to hit it?

As though Dowd could read Nick's mind, he said, "Don't worry. The craft has radar sensors much like those on a car that keeps it from colliding with an object in front of it. So, what do you think?"

Nick said nothing. The thing captivated him.

The Tablet they slaved over in New Mexico was covered with pits similar to those encoding a DVD recording. This stake was not like that. The metal had the shine of The Tablet. It was likely the same metal, impervious to aging over millennia, but the markings were more like Japanese kanji characters.

"I'm moving to each side," said Dowd.

Nick could utter only an "OK," as various possibilities occupied his mind.

The exposed part of the stake was the length of a man's arm, but perfectly square. Each side bore similar marks, three on each side.

They spent a half-hour looking at the stake. Dowd inspected Nick's face reflected in the cowl. Those few images told him it had him captivated.

Nick will sort this out! I need to know what we're looking at.

"Have you seen enough?" Dowd asked.

"You have photos? Besides the ones you showed me?"

"Sure, and don't worry. You can come back."

Both men were quiet during the return trip. Nick continued considering the possible significance of the markings. Dowd tried to read Nick's facial expressions. Nick was careful not to reveal his gut feeling that this stake was indeed related to The Tablet. He remained charmed by Dowd's style, but something about the man begged for caution.

Back at the dock, the technician reversed the process, pulling the craft from the water and setting it back on its resting place. The cowl unsealed and lifted. Nick stepped out with Dowd right behind. Dowd wasted no time in continuing the conversation.

"What was it, Nick? How did it get there?" he asked. "Why would someone put it there, and leave it so deep? We've checked with experts on war relics. It looks like something from World War II, but the markings are code we can't figure out. You're a cryptographer. Seen anything like it?"

"The markings? No. I've got some work to do."

Nick's phone buzzed in his pocket. He pulled it out and saw he had a new text message.

"What is it?" asked Dowd.

"I've got to get back."

"Back where?"

"To Switzerland."

"What's up?"

"There's a friend I've got to see."

Chapter 8

NICK'S JET had him on the ground in Basel by midnight. Waiting for him on the tarmac was a familiar, black Suburban SUV. Beside it, stood an even more familiar man, one who still bore the ramrod straight posture of a former Army Ranger.

Nick smiled and walked directly to the man. "Tanner! It's great to see you again!"

They had the hearty handshake of brothers-in-arms.

"You, too!" replied Tanner. "Although I'd rather it be under different circumstances."

"How's Tom doing?"

"Hop in," Tanner said as he opened the passenger door for Nick. "I'll get you to the hospital and you can see for yourself."

The pilot brought Nick's overnight bag to the vehicle and handed it to Tanner. Nick could not help but notice how the pilot seemed intimidated by his friend who resembled a linebacker.

Nick climbed into the front seat and Tanner took the wheel.

"I think my pilot was taken aback by your size," said Nick.

"Yeah, I get that a lot," was Tanner's simple reply. He put the Suburban in gear and headed away from the landing strip and southeast onto Rue du Printemps toward the University Hospital.

"Fill me in. What happened?"

Tanner briefed him on what he knew. He had seen the surveillance video and described it to Nick, adding, "Our man Tom is a gutsy guy. He shot one of the attackers. Tom almost took his head off, but ended up clipping the man's ear."

"That should help ID the man."

"You mean someone walking around this town with a piece of his ear missing?"

"Yeah."

"The police put out an APB to look for a man like that, but no luck. These weren't local guys. They were pros and they disappeared back to wherever they came from."

Nick considered what that might mean. He knew his team had enemies. That became clear when they obtained the Omni. But the threat came from a preacher's son who made clumsy attempts at killing them.

These guys were on a whole different level. Who was behind this?

"Oh," said Tanner as he grinned. "I didn't tell you the best part."

"There's a 'best part' to this?"

"There is. Seems the Omni has teeth."

"What do you mean?"

"Tom was unconscious. They dragged him over and used his finger to open the cage where the Omni is. One of the men stepped inside and the Omni crushed him."

"Crushed?" asked Nick, not sure that he heard right.

"Yeah. Literally. The Omni generated a pulse that knocked the man against the glass and broke bones."

"What happened to the guy after that? Did the others take him with them?"

"No, they didn't," Tanner said, practically spitting out the comment. "They shot him."

"What? Why?"

"I think they were afraid to go into the cage. The Army takes their wounded and dead with them. They should have. If for no other reason that no one could ID the guy."

"Then we have someone who could be ID'd."

"They're working on it."

"Sounds like they got away with nothing," Nick said.

"Unfortunately, not. One man was working the computer at Tom's workstation and walked away with a thumb drive he said was what they needed."

"But the contents of the Omni hardly fit on a thumb drive."

"True, but that's what we heard on the surveillance recording."

Nick pondered this for a moment. "They were after something specific. What could it have been?"

"Tom might know. Maybe something he was working on at the time the guys broke in. He's not talking much. Pretty sedated. Maybe Rachael knows."

"Rachael? Rachael Friedman? Why would she know?"

"Rachael was on the phone with Tom when all of this happened."

"She was?"

"Yeah. In fact, she was the one who called the police."

"Rachael," Nick said. He repeated the name in a neutral tone, but Tanner could see Nick was pondering something more. Tanner knew Nick flew her back to Boston on his jet after they left Basel months ago. He hadn't talked to either of them after that.

Did something happen between the two of them?

"She's coming over. Should be here tomorrow," Tanner said, studying Nick to see if there would be a further reaction.

There was not.

Nick replied, "Good." Then he changed the subject. "How's Lizzy?"

Lizzy Rodriguez, a sassy redhead Latina, was Tanner's girlfriend. Nick missed her streetwise wit and wisdom.

"She's good. She's at the hospital with Tom."

Nick noticed Tanner smiling at the mention of her name.

"I look forward to seeing her again," Nick replied.

The Universitätsspital Basel was a modern hospital of light gray modern design. It had a fine reputation. Tom was in good hands.

Tanner pulled into the hospital parking lot and stopped near the entrance. They were soon outside Tom's room where a policeman stood guard. Apparently, the police thought Tom was still in danger.

The policeman, a man with a sturdy alpine physique, acknowledged Tanner with a smile and stood aside to allow them in.

"Hans," said Tanner to the policeman. "This is Nicholas Foxe."

"It is good to meet you, Mr. Foxe. I've heard much about you."

"Well, if it's from Tanner, I would believe only half of it."

"No, no. It is from the news."

"Then believe *less* than half of it."

Nick's comment elicited a laugh from Hans and a snicker from Tanner.

"So, how's the patient?"

"That is for the doctor to tell," replied Hans.

"Well, let's see for ourselves," said Tanner as he pulled the door open and walked in with Nick behind him.

Tom lay in the hospital bed, his upper body slightly elevated, with a variety of tubes attached to him, monitors pulsing. His eyes were closed. In a chair beside him sat Lizzy. She focused on Tom as though he would speak at any moment. Then she spotted Nick.

"Nick!" she exclaimed as she leaped from the chair and raced over to Nick to give him a big hug.

"Good to see you, too, Lizzy," said Nick as the redhead continued to hug him. "How's Tom?"

Lizzy released him and looked at Nick with worried eyes.

"Not good."

"Come on, Lizzy," said Tanner. "The doctor said he would make a full recovery."

Lizzy frowned at her boyfriend.

"Yeah. Well, Tom's not going anywhere, anytime soon. That's for sure."

Nick walked over to Tom.

"Tom," he said. "It's Nick."

Nothing.

Nick worked with Tom over the years. Until Tom discovered The Tablet, it had all been computer work. With that discovery, Nick had entered Tom's world of caves. Tom led the way to the discovery of The Tablet deep in the earth.

He was first into the secret room under Castel del Monte. It was Tom who first knew the location of the Omni. After all of that, it touched Nick to see his robust friend so helpless.

Lizzy stood beside Nick.

"Has he said anything?" he asked her.

"Just a few things. Kind of like he was talking in his sleep."

"Was it anything that made sense?"

"Not really. He kept muttering "energy." Crazy, huh?"

"Have you talked to Rachael?"

Lizzy brightened at the mention of Rachael. Lizzy was very guarded the first time she met 'the brainiac' young physics professor. But in time they became good friends, texting each other often.

"Yes, she's coming tomorrow!"

"The two of them were talking when Tom was shot, so I understand."

"True, but I didn't get into details."

"I want to talk to her," said Nick.

Lizzy offered a sly smile.

"Oh, I bet you do," started Lizzy, but Tanner signaled her to stop with a short shake of his head.

Nick, lost in thought, hadn't noticed Lizzy's remark. His focus was on what information Rachael could add.

Hans stepped in and whispered something to Tanner. Tanner nodded affirmation and walked over to Nick.

"Director Birchmeier wants to see you," Tanner told Nick.

"Who's that? Hans' boss?"

"Not exactly," said Tanner with an air of mystery. "I got the address. Come on. I'll tell you on the way."

"You're leaving?" asked Lizzy.

"Yep. Duty calls." Tanner gave Lizzy a hug and a kiss on the cheek, a tender moment that required him lifting her off her feet. Lizzy wasn't short, but Tanner was much taller.

Back in the Suburban, Tanner punched in an address on the GPS, pulled out of the parking lot and headed away from the hospital.

"OK. So, who's this Director Birchmeier?" asked Nick.

"To answer your earlier question, Hans doesn't work for him. Hans works for the canton. If Switzerland were a state in the US, a canton would be a county. So, Hans is the county police."

"And what about Birchmeier?"

"He works for a national group. It's one nobody even knew about until 2009. They're called the Einsatzgruppe TIGRIS. The French speakers here call them Groupe d'intervention TIGRIS and the Italians, Gruppo d'intervento TIGRIS.

"And what would the US equivalent be?"

"There isn't one," said Tanner. "They're kind of CIA, FBI, and counterterrorism SWAT team rolled into one."

"Sounds impressive."

Tanner glanced at Nick with a grin and said, "You know those Swiss Guards at the Vatican who dress funny?"

"Yes."

"Well, these ain't them."

Nick couldn't help but laugh, but then asked, "They suspect terrorism?"

"They suspect something beyond their borders at play. Like terrorists, but only better trained and organized."

Nick remained silent, trying to make sense of all of this.

"We had some bad guys after the Omni before, you know," Nick finally said.

Am I trying to convince myself that we've been here before and came out OK?

"Yeah," Tanner said, as though he could read Nick's thoughts. "But they were amateurs. These are the real deal."

The two men said no more. The destination was just ahead, but both began to question whether the GPS had led them to the right place. Nothing but old warehouses bordered the street. Up ahead, one had two unmarked, simple sedans parked out front.

Police cars.

They were at the right location.

This was not anywhere on a tourist's map. No charming old-world homes here. It appeared to be an industrial park, long abandoned. Dark and grimy came to mind.

Nick saw a large man outfitted in black standing guard: black helmet, black flak jacket, shirt and pants, in addition to a black Heckler & Koch MP5 submachine gun.

This guy looks serious. What are we into?

Tanner led the way up to the man. "We're here to see Director Birchmeier."

"Your names?" he asked.

"Tanner and Foxe."

"Your full names."

Tanner paused as though providing his full name hurt. He hated his first name. Nick, knew it and took over.

"Walter Tanner and Nicholas Foxe."

Tanner expanded with "Nicholas B. Foxe, the Third," and smirked at Nick.

Saying nothing further, the guard pulled a large door open and allowed Nick and Tanner to enter.

What they saw surprised them since they both instantly recognized it. It was a replica of the underground room which housed the Omni and the work area around it.

Two men in white jumpsuits were working around the area as though it was a crime scene, and actually, it was the duplication of a crime scene. One man held up his hand to keep Tanner and Nick from advancing further.

"They do not want anyone jeopardizing the scene," said a man who seemed to come out of nowhere. He was a tall, muscular man in a tight khaki tee and black pants. Nick thought he looked like the fifty-year-old version of Tanner, not as tall, but having a similar build and the unmistakable bearing of the military.

He thrust his hand out to Nick. "I'm Director Birchmeier."

Nick shook his hand and as the director did the same with Tanner, he added, "You may call me Lukas." He said it as though he was granting permission.

"You recognize this?" asked Lukas as he pointed to the scene.

Nick replied, "It's a good reproduction of our work area where we keep the… ah."

"Omni," said Lukas, finishing Nick's statement. "It's OK, Mr. Foxe."

"Just call me Nick," interrupted Nick.

"Very well, Nicholas," said Lukas as though he could only meet part way toward informality. "We know the Omni is housed here in Basel. Your little ruse fooled most people to believe it's in Germany. But we know the truth."

Tanner frowned. "Someone else knew as well."

Lukas smiled at Tanner's appraisal. Nick felt he was standing between a father and his son. He broke the precious moment.

"I assume the bad guys were practicing their raid here."

"That is our belief," said Lukas. "This shows that these men were well financed to create this."

"Do you know who they were?" ask Nick.

"Yeah, how about the guy the Omni smashed?" added Tanner.

Lukas added to Tanner's comment. "*Smashed* is close to accurate. The coroner thought he was working with a bag of loose bones, but we got fingerprints. He was Josip Horvat, a Croatian. Interpol has a long history on this man. He dealt in weapons."

"Weapons? What kind of weapons?" asked Tanner.

"Seems his favorite was submachine guns, much like the ones we use, but he sold them to every dictator he could. He was an expert in their use. Authorities cornered him in Caracas, Venezuela. Shooting his way out, he left four police officers dead."

"But he died here," said Nick, still reticent to talk about the Omni being lethal.

"Yes, because of your Omni."

Nick cut Lukas a questioning expression.

"We've seen the surveillance tapes, Nicholas. Quite a defense mechanism you put in place to guard it."

Nick glanced at Tanner. They had the same thought.

He thinks we put the defense in place. He doesn't know the Omni did the deed itself.

Nick thought a moment.

"Lukas, you said that these men were well financed to do this. Have any idea who's behind them?"

"We do not, but I have something that may help." He motioned to a man in white sweats to bring him something. The man picked up a clear-plastic evidence bag from a nearby table and walked it over to him. Lukas handed it to Nick with Tanner looking over Nick's shoulder. "The men were meticulous in cleaning up after themselves, but we found this. It slipped behind the console table and into a space where they would not have spotted it. It appears to be a message."

In the bag was a slip of paper on which was handwritten in block letters FROST and below that a phone number.

"A phone number?" asked Nick.

"It's a burner phone, long since discarded. What about the name?"

"FROST? Is it an acronym?" asked Nick, more to himself than to the others. There was something about the name that sounded familiar, and it wasn't Jack Frost he was thinking of.

It reminded him of something he had seen recently, but he couldn't place what it was.

"Is Frost a code name for someone?" asked Tanner.

"That is what we believe," responded Lukas. "Interpol ran it through its database. They came up with nothing. We intend to find this Frost, whoever he is."

Nick studied Lukas Birchmeier. Tanner had bonded with the man. That was clear. But Nick sensed something about the man beyond his obvious competence. Perhaps, it was how he said they intended to find Frost. Lukas seemed to take it personally.

Why?

Nick's cell phone began buzzing in his pocket. He took it out and looked at it. It was a call from Guido Bartoli.

"Excuse me," Nick told the men. "I need to take this."

Nick stepped away a few feet and answered the call. "Guido, what's up?"

Guido was emphatic. "Nick, you've got to return to Venice."

"Return? Why?"

"It's Christine."

Chapter 9

NICK SAT IN THE POLICE STATION across from a very different Vanessa than the one he left. This Vanessa was tearful, as if suffering a great loss. The police inspector, ever the gentleman, had provided her with tissues to dab her eyes. Used ones littered the table.

"Nick, who could have done this? I know you never cared for me and I know I rub people the wrong way. But this should have been me, not Christine. Everyone loved Christine!"

Nick was at a loss for words. He agreed to what Vanessa said, especially the part about it should have been her. That was a petty thought. He was not a big fan of Vanessa's, but he didn't want her dead.

Even more puzzling was why someone killed Christine.

Nick's jet returned him to Venice in response to Guido's call. Guido was standing by to water-taxi him to the city. On the way, Guido furnished more details. The cleaning lady at the Pensione Accademia made the discovery. Someone had strangled Christine to death. The police arrived at the crime scene promptly to gather evidence. Police Commissario Russo wanted to see Nick.

"Does he have a lead on who did this?"

"I do not know," answered Guido. "But I do know he is, let us say, perplexed by what your connection may be. He knows all about the attempt on your life in my boat. Now someone you are close to dies. He's a man who, as you Americans say, connects the dots."

Nick understood. "I guess that having one dead guy on my first day here and then this..."

Nick couldn't make himself say it, that Christine was dead. Guido saved him from having to complete the thought. "Yes, the circumstances are troubling," he said. "Bruno told me the homicide rate here was near zero until Mr. Foxe arrived."

Nick fumed. Christine was no mere statistic to him. She had been very close at one time and now had become close once again. He wanted to strangle the man who did this. He snapped back at Guido. "Well then, Russo can pay more attention to this death since he has nothing else to do."

"Nicholas, I told him you are an honorable man. He is following procedure in talking to you."

Nick stewed for the balance of the trip.

The police station, the Questura di Venezia, is on the upper edge of the Grand Canal. Like most of Venice, it has water access, but it also can be reached by car. The motor entrance appears at the boundary of the Piazzale Roma, the first and last stop for motor traffic into Venice, allowing access from the greater Venezia region it serves. Guido steered Nick to the water entrance.

Nick told the policeman working the front desk they had a meeting with Commissario Russo. Russo appeared in a minute. He took Nick's hand with both of his and looked him in the eye with sympathy.

"Mr. Foxe," Russo said. "I'm so sorry for your loss."

Nick did not expect Russo to have made it so personal, as though Christine was a member of the family. It disarmed him. He could only utter, "Thank you."

"Thank you for coming. We have been talking to Miss Fabre. You met her at that event we both attended, did you not?"

Nick realized that he was being interrogated right here in the hallway. Vanessa was probably still in the building. Russo was checking to see if their stories matched.

"Yes, Vanessa first came up to us at the opera."

"Us?" said Russo, intentionally not filling in blanks.

"Yes, Christine and I attended Madama Butterfly..." began Nick.

"Ah, my favorite!" Russo interrupted. "But it has been very popular. You were lucky to get tickets."

It put Nick off pace by this man's mix of personal and procedural, but he continued.

"Christine had them. We were guests of Nevin Dowd."

"I see," said Russo. "Mr. Dowd, the man who is working magic with water to save Venice. Quite a show he put on for us."

From the way Russo said this, Nick doubted the police inspector was a Dowd fan.

Russo continued. "Miss Blake worked for Mr. Dowd. Correct?"

"Yes, she did."

"So, we understand. Mr. Dowd was here earlier and gave us a statement."

Then why are you asking me? Nick thought.

"Mr. Foxe, may I ask you. What was it that took you away from Venice?"

Nick figured Russo likely knew something about the events in Basel, so he responded with the truth, but as little of it as he could.

"We had a break-in at a work location in Basel, Switzerland."

"A break-in?" exclaimed the wide-eyed Russo. "Was anyone hurt?"

By the very nature of the question, Nick understood Russo knew the answer, but he would give only so much.

"Yes, one person was injured."

Russo's expression turned solemn. "You poor man. Unfortunate events seem to follow you, do they not?"

Nick thought about it: a death by concussion, a shooting, and a strangulation within a few days would lead one to that conclusion.

All this led to Nick sitting in a room with the heartbroken Vanessa. Although Nick always considered her a cold fish, he knew Vanessa was once Christine's best friend. Business can ruin a friendship, and it did so for these women. Nick didn't jump for joy seeing Vanessa again, but he could tell that she wanted reconciliation.

"Nick, they had me identify the body," Vanessa said between sobs. "Do you know how difficult that was?"

"It must have been awful."

"She looked so peaceful. Asleep, as though she could wake at any moment. The only evidence of anything wrong was the fine line around her throat."

"Fine line?" Nick asked, suspecting the answer.

"Yes, they said the killer garroted her."

"Oh?" Nick didn't say it, but this spoke of a professional killer.

What was Christy involved in?

"Nick, I was the last person to see her alive."

Nick thought, strictly speaking, the killer was the last person to see her alive, but it was no time for such details.

"I wanted to talk to her. We met in her hotel room. She had a bottle of wine brought in. Here we were in Venice and working on the same project. It was like old times."

She noticed Nick's raised eyebrow.

She amended her statement. "It was like the best parts of old times. We talked and decided we would be friends again. I had to leave. If I had just stayed, maybe this wouldn't have happened."

She broke into sobs again. Nick wasn't prepared for this side of the ice queen. He handed her the box of tissues.

Commissario Russo entered the room. "*Scusate.* Would you please walk with me?"

"Both of us?" asked Vanessa.

"*Si*"

"What's up?" added Nick.

"We have a surveillance video from the hotel. We may have a picture of the killer."

Nick and Vanessa followed Russo to a room filled with electronics. On a rack to the left was a monitor with a black-and-white image of a hallway. A young man sat near a control panel ready for instructions from Russo.

"We have taken the video from the surveillance camera in the garden outside of Miss Blake's hotel suite. We have isolated the time around the events in question.

"Matteo," Russo said as he turned toward the seated man. "Please play it."

Judging by the angle of the shot, a camera in a corner of the garden filmed the video. First Vanessa and Christine came into view. There was no sound, but the two women were smiling and chatting with each other. Arm in arm, they headed down the brick path through the garden.

"First, we have Miss Blake and Miss Fabre enter Miss Blake's room," said Russo. "Or, at least, we assume they entered the room. The door to the room is just off camera behind the hedge. Then fifteen minutes later," he said with a nod toward Matteo who fast forwarded the video. "We have a woman from room service with a bottle of wine in a cooler. Someone must have accepted the wine and the woman leaves.

"We questioned that woman, and the rest of the staff. They did not see anyone they could not account for that night. No strangers. Just guests and staff. It is a small pensione. They know everyone by sight. Which raises the question 'how did our suspect arrive?' We will see him in a moment.

"An hour and eight minutes pass." Mateo advances the video. "As Miss Fabre leaves, we see her turn to someone at the door we cannot see. The hedge blocks the view of the door itself. Saying goodbye to your friend I assume?"

"Yes," replied Vanessa. "That's right."

Returning to the video, Russo nodded to Matteo to advance to the next scene.

"Seventeen minutes later, this man enters the garden."

On the screen appeared a rough-looking man, someone who looked like a boxer past his prime, but who you would still not cross. He was dressed in a turtleneck and dark pants.

"Note that he pulls out a key card as he heads to the door. How he came into possession of this key, we are still investigating. We have no sound, but we might believe that Miss Blake was in bed. Miss Fabre, you told us she said she was turning in for the night, is that not so?"

"Yes. Too much wine, and the hour was late."

"Only three minutes pass, then the man leaves the room. Matteo, please advance the video and stop, here!" The frame captured the best view of the man's face, although it was at an angle. "Do either of you recognize this man?"

"No," said both Vanessa and Nick. But Nick noticed something about the man. He was surprised that Russo did not mention it. However, Nick thought it was a significant link.

Russo shrugged. "It was worth a try, but it does not surprise me that he is a stranger to you."

"Have you made an ID on him?" asked Nick.

"We are working on it now."

"Did the hotel staff identify the man?"

"He did not enter the garden through the lobby."

Vanessa looked confused.

"How would he have gotten in there?"

"You cannot see it in this video, but the service gate on the canal beside the pensione was left unlatched. He must have gained entry by that means. Miss Fabre, did you notice it being unlatched?"

"No," said Vanessa, beginning to tear up again. "I wish I had."

Russo pulled a tissue from a box and handed it to her.

"We believe the men doing work in the garden may have left it unlatched. They tie up the barge there that handles their debris. We have talked to them and they swear they made sure it was closed. Too bad the *pensione* trained no camera on it. We would then know."

Vanessa controlled her sniffles as Russo finished with them.

"I want to thank you for your help today. Let me walk you out."

Nick was more sympathetic toward Vanessa than he ever imagined he could be.

"Can I give you a lift?"

"You came by boat?"

"Yes."

"Thanks, but I have a car picking me up. I have some business to take care of on the mainland."

Russo led Vanessa and Nick out of the room. He handed each his card.

"If anything at all occurs to you that you think might help, please do not hesitate to call me."

With that, Russo walked Vanessa to the roadside entrance to the building. Guido was standing in the hallway in the opposite direction. Nick headed over to him.

Guido waited until Vanessa was out of sight. He took Nick aside and told him, "You know I have friends in the police."

"Why does that not surprise me?" responded Nick.

"They tell me nothing in the room where your friend died was disturbed. There was no sign of a struggle. For someone who was attacked and strangled, that would be strange, would it not?"

"Yes, it would," said Nick. "But Vanessa said Christy was going to bed. The killer may have snuck up on her while she was asleep."

Guido gave Nick a puzzled look.

"But the bed was still made."

"How do you know that?"

"I was told that the bed was made, and Christine was still dressed."

"Interesting," Nick said. "But I saw something equally interesting. I've got to call someone. Excuse me."

Nick pulled out his phone and punched in a frequently called number.

"Tanner," Nick said.

"Hey, Nick, I heard about Christine. I'm sorry, man."

It surprised Nick that Tanner knew, but bad news travels fast among friends.

"Tanner, the police just showed me a video that caught the killer on camera. Do you know where Tom winged the intruder?"

"Yeah, he shot a piece off of the upper part of his left ear."

"Christine's killer had a big bandage on the same part of his ear. Looked fresh."

Tanner didn't hesitate.

"I'll be right there."

Chapter 10

TANNER SAT AT A CAFÉ TABLE on the edge of Saint Mark's Square, passing time by tossing crumbs from his biscotti to the pigeons. Big mistake. More birds immediately flocked around the large man who had to shoo them away.

The scene amused Nick.

"Having some trouble with the birds?" he asked as he walked up to the table.

Tanner, his avian annoyance obvious, stood and gave Nick a firm handshake. Tanner looked Nick in the eye and said, "I'm sorry about your friend getting killed. You think it was the same guy who shot Tom?"

"Let's walk," Nick said, "and get away from these pigeons."

"With pleasure."

"How did you get here? I offered the jet, but you didn't take it."

"I appreciate the offer, Nick, but the train was just as quick, once you consider the ride to and from the airport. The train let me off right on the Grand Canal."

"I kind of expected Lizzy would be with you."

"She wanted to stay with Tom and with Rachael, who's coming in today."

Tanner studied Nick's face for a reaction when he mentioned Rachael. Nick's expression was noncommittal.

Is he avoiding any talk about Rachael?

Nick began another line of conversation as they walked along a narrow street passing shops filled with tourist trinkets.

"We're going to see a friend of mine who can help."

"A friend?" asked Tanner.

"Yes, you would have met him were you coming from the airport. He runs most of the water taxis and gondolas here. His name is Guido Bartoli."

"So, we need a water taxi?"

Nick smiled. "No, not yet. In addition to running water taxis, Guido knows everyone. He has friends in the police department. He said he has some information for me."

"You mean for us," Tanner said. "Nobody messes with my friends and gets away with it."

Nick was not sure whether Tanner was talking about Tom's shooting or Christine's murder. Tanner never met Christine. Nick didn't ask. He was just glad to have Tanner on his side.

"Here we are," announced Nick upon arrival at a shop, windows filled with carnival masks. The shop wasn't different at first glance from dozens that dotted the streets of Venice. They entered and found Guido at a desk talking with the proprietor, another person Guido knew in his network. Guido noticing Nick and Tanner's arrival, turned to greet them.

"Ah, Nick," he said, "this must be the famous Tanner."

Tanner scoffed at the 'famous,' but the man at least got his name right. Tanner, just Tanner. Not Mr. Tanner, and certainly not Walter Tanner. A man once called him Walt and Tanner strongly dissuaded him from doing so again.

Guido dispensed with pleasantries. He didn't shake Tanner's hand, but said, "Let's go to the back room." He led the men through a curtain of masks hanging everywhere. The back room was the workshop with his friend's tools lying about. There were no windows for prying eyes. On the workshop table was a folder. Guido turned to the men to discuss its contents.

"I've been talking to my friends in Commissario Russo's office," said Guido. "They've told me some interesting things. Nick, I brought a picture from the video you saw, the one that shows the killer. I thought your friend would like to see it."

Guido pulled from the folder a black-and-white photo Nick instantly recognized. It was a screenshot of the man he told Tanner about.

"See," Nick told Tanner. "He's got a wound on his ear about where Tom shot the guy. He appears to be the right size and shape of the man we saw on the surveillance video in Basil."

Tanner did not equivocate. "It's him," he said. "Who is he?"

Guido smiled. "I thought you might ask."

He pulled a page from the folder and showed it to the men. It was a data sheet with a mug shot in one corner, and miscellaneous stats on the rest of the page. Most important was the name of the man.

"Branko Bosak," announced Guido. "Interpol has a red notice out for this man."

Nick held the sheet where he and Tanner could see it. The photo was of a brute of a man who resembled an old heavyweight fighter. He had a buzz cut, and a nose broken several times over. Even though now he'd be missing a piece of his ear, there was no doubt he was the man on the surveillance video.

Guido continued. "He's wanted for the assassination of an English consul in Istanbul. He killed the woman with a garrote."

"So, this bum enjoys strangling women," said Tanner. Nick thought he heard Tanner cracking his knuckles at the thought of a man having such a vile proclivity.

"The Brits must have their people tracking this guy," said Nick.

"Word has it," started Guido as he looked around as though someone might hear, "that MI6 is on this case."

Nick understood. "Then this consul was not just some diplomat. She was a spy."

Guido nodded.

Tanner asked, "Nick, was Christine involved somehow in the spy business?"

The question caught Nick unaware.

"No way," he said. "Christy is the last person I would suspect to be a spy."

"Then she would be perfect."

"Knock it off, Tanner. I'd bet my bottom dollar on it."

Nick pondered, the shared something else. The dots were so wide apart, he couldn't possibly connect them, but his gut said there was some connection. So, he forged ahead.

"Tanner, you remember The Tablet, both yours and the one Tom discovered?"

"How could I forget?"

"What if I told you that the people who made The Tablet put something in the Venetian lagoon?"

Tanner, wide-eyed, asked, "There's another tablet?"

"No, it's not a tablet this time. It's a large stake made of the same metal. I'm sure of it."

Guido, a man who knew everything about Venice, could not believe this. "How could such a thing be in the lagoon, undiscovered for hundreds of years?"

"It was deep, Guido," replied Nick. "It wasn't until Nevin Dowd did his dredging that it was uncovered. Dowd took me in a submersible yesterday to see it."

"What does it mean?" asked Guido.

"I don't know, but something tells me this discovery was why Christy died."

"Well, that makes little sense," said Tanner. "You said Dowd showed it to you himself. He's not making it a secret?"

"He's not exactly telling the world about it either."

"Why did the man who tried to get the Omni, and shot Tom to get to it, also kill Christy?" asked Tanner. "There has to be a connection. Is it possible Christy knew something Dowd's not telling you?"

Nick thought further on this last point.

"Or, perhaps even Dowd didn't know."

The slim man walked onto the balcony overlooking Santorini. He wore heavily tinted sunglasses against the glare of the intense sun on the bleached white of the buildings around him. The man had developed a deep tan on this holiday from work in London and dreaded the thought of returning in a week. He'd grown accustomed to wearing light-colored linen and never needing an umbrella.

The phone rang, the one that should never ring during his holiday. His girlfriend, sunning herself on a chaise, observed him holding the phone, just looking at it and considering whether to answer. Finally he answered with a simple, "Yes?"

His girlfriend heard just one side of the conversation.

"They have? Where? Istanbul?

"Venice? Who was she? Not one of ours, I'm guessing.

"Where's he now?

"I see. OK."

The man ended the call and turned to his girlfriend.

"Daddy's got to leave, I'm afraid."

The woman scowled. "Why?"

"Duty calls."

About the same time this man received a call in Santorini, Nicholas Foxe placed a phone call, one he should have made long before.

The phone rang twice, and she picked up.

"Rachael?" he said.

Chapter 11

NICK AND TANNER were back in Basel at the hospital, greeted again by Hans, who seemed always to be keeping guard at Tom's room. The scene was like the one they had left. Tom in bed, hooked up to a variety of monitors and Lizzy at his bedside. This time, Rachael joined them. But best of all, Tom was finally awake. Rachael looked up at Nick. The temperature of the room cooled by Rachael's flat acknowledgment of "Hello, Nick."

"Hi, Rachael," Nick responded.

Still the same Rachael. Hair pulled back in a ponytail, wearing athletic shirt and pants like she was going for a jog. But those deep green eyes sent no love in my direction.

Nick turned his attention to Tom.

"Hey, great to see you awake."

"Thanks," said Tom. "Great to be awake. But I've a got a chest pain that won't quit."

"That'll get better," said Lizzy with a smile.

"Thanks, Nurse Rodriguez," said Tom. Then looking at Tanner, "She's quite the caregiver, you know."

Tanner allowed himself a grin.

"I know."

"Have the police talked to you?" asked Nick.

"I've had the pleasure of meeting Director Birchmeier. I understand you've met already."

"Yeah. Tanner and I talked to him. Met him at a warehouse where the bad guys had practiced their attack."

"So I hear. Guess they wanted to get it right. I understand the Omni provided a little surprise for them."

"That it did," said Nick. "Birchmeier thinks we put in a security device that killed the man. He doesn't know it was the Omni itself. That's one little feature that surprised us all."

Tom smiled. "Just glad we were on its good side when we found it in the grotto."

Nick wondered what the police did and didn't know. "Did they ask you about what the men copied to the thumb drive?"

"Not really. The surveillance camera showed I was unconscious. I didn't know they took anything, but Rachael did."

Nick could not help but express confused curiosity. "Rachael?"

Tom turned to Rachael. "Tell him."

"Tom and I were talking on the phone when all of this happened," she said.

"What about?" interrupted Nick.

Rachael shot Nick a disapproving glance. "Hey, I'm telling this. Don't interrupt."

Nick backed off. "OK, OK."

"It may be a coincidence, but I believe they took data that pertained to what Tom and I were discussing. You remember that one of the major areas of expertise the Omni possessed was about energy, right?"

Nick, after having been chastised, responded with a gruff "Yes."

"I know what was on the computer," she continued. "I was following the session Tom opened from my office computer so we could both see the same thing. When the men broke into the room, I saw the flow of data they took away. I know what it was about."

"And what was that?"

"Nick, it was all about the model."

"The model?"

Nick's reaction annoyed Rachael.

Has he already forgotten?

"Data from the Omni outlined a method in which seawater can be changed into energy. The physics looks a little sketchy, but then again, we're still working to correlate the math functions the ancients used to our own. Our math doesn't use them in the same way. Nevertheless, what is clear is that they left a working model. Were someone able to find it, with the math we do know, and a little reverse engineering…"

She stopped to let the potential set in. Everyone in the room got it.

"So, what did the data they took tell them?" Nick asked.

Tom finished Rachael's story. "Nick, it tells them how to find the model."

Nick could only look to Tanner to see if he felt the same shock, but the large man wore his usual impenetrable expression.

Rachael mitigated Nick's unease.

"But it's not exactly a treasure map. From the data, it's clear that the device is somewhere under the ocean."

"But the translation reads that 'it is invisible,'" added Tom.

"We think," said Rachael, "the device may use some stealth technology that would make it invisible to most detection systems."

"So," Nick said, "Just how is one to find an invisible device, in some ocean, not specified?"

"They left poles," said Rachael.

"Poles?"

"Pole is one interpretation," added Tom. "Stake, spike, or something stuck in the ground."

This time, when Nick glanced at Tanner, he got a knowing look and a nod.

"What if I told you I've seen one of the stakes?"

Tom and Rachael exclaimed in unison, "What?"

"Nevin Dowd, the guy working on tide control in Venice took me in a submersible to see one. They uncovered it in their dredging."

"And why did he do that?"

"He said he brought me there to determine what the markings on the side might mean."

"Markings!" exclaimed Tom. "What could you make of them?"

"Could not make hide nor hair of them. But I have photos from all four sides. Rachael, you're good in finding clues in photos."

Nick's reference to her code breaking in the past may not have broken the ice between them, but it chipped it.

Lizzy carefully listened to everything. The group remained silent for a moment, and then she put her slant on things.

"So," she said, "a team of bad guys break in and steal info on this energy machine. It includes the lowdown on stakes in the ocean. Nick's new buddy Nevin asks Nick to see what he could make of one of said stakes. The guy who tried to kill Tom killed Christine Blake, who worked for… Nevin Dowd.

"Do I have all of it straight so far?"

Lizzy precisely laid out pertinent points, but it was clear by the blank expressions around the room, no one had an idea how to connect them.

Nick now realized he had to be careful around Dowd.

Chapter 12

ONCE AGAIN, Nick and Tanner were meeting with TIGRIS Director Lukas Birchmeier. This time it was in Birchmeier's office. When they arrived at the address, they thought it must have been a mistake. It looked like a small, quant inn set among neat shops, nestled in an old Swiss neighborhood. They entered a small lobby containing two easy chairs and a desk with keys hanging behind it. A petite woman in her later years, with short gray hair and a grandmotherly smile, welcomed them. When they told her who they were looking for, she picked up the phone and announced, "Your guests are here,." She hung up and told them, "He will be right down."

The door to the right of the desk opened and Birchmeier stepped into the lobby. "Thank you for coming," he said as he shook their hands. "Please come to my office. I have someone I want you to meet."

The lady behind the counter pushed an unseen button and a door buzzed open. Birchmeier held it for Nick and Tanner, then led them along a short hall with numbered doors, presumably guest rooms. They entered the lift. Birchmeier placed his thumb on a security pad and pushed the button for level five.

When the door opened, a stainless steel, no-nonsense office area greeted them. Agents walked about, some pausing at desks to confer with colleagues. Only one or two of them looked their way, as though two strangers arriving with Birchmeier was a common practice.

"Step this way," said Birchmeier as he led them to an office door at the opposite end of the room. Nick and Tanner followed. Birchmeier had a simple desk: sleek, modern stainless, similar to the ones in the area outside. Behind the desk was an Aeron office chair placed in front of a window that was covered by a mesh screen. Nick recognized it. They designed these screens to let light in but block any radio waves from leaving. It was secure.

There were two armchairs to the left and one to the right. A man Nick and Tanner had never seen before occupied one of them.

Birchmeier walked around to his side of the desk, remained standing, and said, "Nick, Tanner, I want to introduce Paul Allerton."

Allerton stood and offered his hand. He was dressed in a gray suit that fit him like a second skin: a starched white shirt, pale-blue tie neatly done in a double-Windsor knot, French cuffs, topped off with a white pocket square. He had short dark hair trimmed as though he just left the barber. As he shook hands, he delivered his "pleased to meet you" in a proper English accent. Nick noted his steel-blue eyes. They did not look at you casually.

This guy is sizing me up.

"Please take a seat," said Birchmeier, as he sat down behind his desk. "Paul here is with MI6."

"Just like that?" joked Nick. "First thing we know is you're with the secret service? No 007 secret identities?"

Allerton made the grimace of one who'd heard this many times. "Afraid not. I don't put it on my name tag at parties. But we're among friends here. Just as we all know Tanner is with the CIA."

"What?" Nick exclaimed.

After all, they'd been through, something like working for the CIA hadn't come up?

Then it was Tanner's turn to grimace.

"I don't work for the CIA," he told Nick. "I've *done work* for the CIA."

"Tanner has told you about his exploits in Afghanistan," said Allerton. "That was a CIA operation."

"The CIA wanted the guy we were after, but it was an Army operation," corrected Tanner.

"You're splitting hairs," said Allerton. "We both know how things worked in that war. I was serving in Her Majesty's Marines on the ground while you were in the Rangers."

This got Tanner's attention. He squinted at Allerton. "Have we met?"

"Afraid we haven't had the pleasure. Seems we went our separate ways. Me, to intelligence and you, to solving mysteries in caves."

Tanner wasn't sure he appreciated that summation.

Nick, turning to Birchmeier, asked, "So what brings us together this time?"

"Branko Bosak," was Birchmeier's simple response.

Nick and Tanner both knew this was the name of the man who shot Tom and murdered Christine Blake, but they already knew this from backdoor information gleaned from the Venice police. They doubted the other men in the room knew they knew. Nick thought it better they didn't. He delivered a simple, "Who?"

"Branko Bosak," repeated Allerton. "He's the man who killed Christine Blake."

"MI6 is investigating Christy's murder?" asked Nick, his expression incredulous.

"No," responded Allerton. "You see, Bosak murdered our consul in Istanbul. The consul, she was one of us."

"MI6?"

"Yes. I cannot tell you why she was targeted, but I can tell you we want Bosak. I've been tasked with getting him."

Nick directed his attention to Birchmeier. "Lukas, why are you involved in this?"

"We believe Bosak was the man who shot Mr. Littleton."

Tanner remained stone-faced, no way acknowledging he already knew this. "Then, I want this Bosak, too," he said.

"Good man," said Allerton. "Because your CIA wants you on the case with me."

Tanner shot Allerton a puzzled look. "Why?"

"First," said Allerton, "you have the right training in black ops."

"Lots of guys have that," said Tanner.

"Second," continued Allerton, "you know what they may have been after when they tried to steal the Omni."

"Tom knows all that."

"Yes, but Tom is in the hospital, isn't he? Hardly in any position to travel."

"How about Nick?" asked Tanner.

Allerton looked toward Nick with slight discomfort.

"The CIA did not want Mr. Foxe."

Nick smiled knowingly.

Yep. No clearance. No patience. Not good at following orders.

Allerton stood and addressed Tanner.

"We have good reason to believe Bosak is in his native Croatia. I have a transport leaving for Dubrovnik at 2200 hours. Will you be on it with me?"

Tanner looked at Nick who returned a nod. "I'll be on it."

"Good," said Allerton "and here are directions to the plane."

Outside the TIGRIS offices and at a small café nearby, Nick and Tanner spoke.

Nick was dumbfounded. "CIA? Why didn't you tell me?"

"Like I said in there, I didn't work for the CIA. I worked on an operation for them."

"And they remembered it."

"They remember everything," said Tanner, wishing they didn't.

"I can see how they could ID Bosak from the surveillance camera in Christy's hotel, but how did they connect him to Tom's shooting? He dressed in black from head to toe with his face hidden.

"Maybe they had the same idea about the piece of ear missing."

"Maybe," said Nick. "But I feel something is off. I don't think the CIA is showing all their cards."

Tanner sneered. "They're not the only ones, are they?"

Nick laughed. "Yeah. We're not offering much, are we? We know what they took from the Omni. I've seen one stake that may tell us the location of the 'energy machine,' as Lizzy puts it."

"Know a better name?" said Tanner.

"Guess not. So, Energy Machine it is."

Nick paused to consider Lizzy and Tanner.

"Have you two been separated since I last saw you?"

"Naw, she'll be OK."

"Oh, I'm sure she will."

"What are you going to do?"

"Me? I will be Nevin Dowd's best pal."

Chapter 13

LIFE CHANGING MOMENTS may last but a few seconds. The glint from a razor-sharp blade laid against his daughter's neck was one for Lukas Birchmeier. Birchmeier witnessed the inch-long cut the knife made by the slightest of motion, the tiny drop of her blood. It played back in his memory as seen through a telescope. He would never forget it. Neither would his daughter.

The Swiss tasked TIGRIS with combating terrorist activity. When Aton Mlakar entered the country, Director Lukas Birchmeier put his men on high alert. There could be no mistaking his identity. The airport surveillance camera showed a weasel of a man passing through security. The Slovenian Mlakar was coming from his hometown of Koper under a bogus name. Lukas studied the still shots from the airport and shook his head. How could such a lovely seaside town produce such a blot on humanity? The man stood only five-five, wore a ridiculous black mustache as a disguise which matched his greasy straight black hair.

Mlakar was the worst of terrorists, a gun for hire. In his case, a bomb for hire. Birchmeier was accustomed to amateurs radicalized for a cause. In their minds, they were noble. In the eyes of the law, they were inept, prone to give themselves away before they harmed anyone. Mlakar was a different breed. He made few mistakes. TIGRIS was lucky to get a match on him at the airport.

Birchmeier put Chris Batz on Mlaker's tail. Although Batz was young and not his most senior agent, he was amazing at being unseen. In training, Batz was assigned to tail Birchmeier and Lukas never saw him. To prove he was there, Batz produced photos of Lukas doing everyday chores around his neighborhood. He was the right man. No question about it.

Birchmeier was a family man with a wife and two kids. His work often kept him away from home, but he tried to spend as much time as he could with them. He made a point of leaving work behind when he walked through the front door. But work caught up with the family in a very cruel way.

Birchmeier had a son and daughter. The son, Liam, was ten years old, smart as a whip, and split his time between science books and video games. The daughter, Laura, was the polar opposite. Lukas thought being a sixteen-year-old had something to do with it. She was all about who liked who, particularly who liked her. She was a cute blonde, just like her more serious mother, Lisa. Lukas loved them both, even when Laura would roll her eyes when someone remarked how cute it was that the family were all L's: Lukas, Lisa, Liam, and

Laura. Lukas was not into 'cute' and gave the credit for this alliteration to Lisa.

Birchmeier and his wife differed on whether he was keeping a tight enough rein on his daughter. He thought he was being generous, allowing Laura to go to her friends' homes without an escort. Laura thought she should be able to go to clubs. Strictly off-limits ruled her dad. But Laura would go to a friend's home and then off to a club, her teen logic justifying bending the rules. This game was her undoing.

Batz did a good job tailing Mlakar. He soon found the nondescript house to which Mlakar carried several small suitcases over a matter of three days. Batz witnessed Mlaker picking up luggage from several sources – the train station, a passing van, a car parked along a street two blocks away. When Batz reported to Birchmeier, they concluded the bomb maker was collecting components. TIGRIS shared intelligence with agencies such as MI6, Interpol, NSA, and the CIA. When a terrorist event was being planned, there was lots of chatter on monitored channels, but in this case, nothing. This operation was under the radar. Yet why did Mlaker allow himself to be tracked? Birchmeier knew the operative word was 'allowed.' Mlaker was too clever to enter the country via an airport and in a simple disguise. Something was wrong.

Delaying action on a gut feeling was not Birchmeier's option. He had to raid Mlaker's little shop before it led to a regrettable outcome. He would assemble a team and do it that night.

Birchmeier called his wife in the late afternoon before the planned raid and told her not to wait up for him. Not an unusual request. His wife told him their daughter was begging to go to her friend's house to study. Again, not an unusual request. Birchmeier's gut was better attuned to what bad guys might do than to what his daughter was up to. So, he said that it was okay to let her go.

What he didn't know, until too late, was that Mlaker had evaded surveillance. He had returned to his apartment, but Batz never knew he had left. Batz would never live it down.

That night, Birchmeier and two men met Batz at the house where Mlaker was working. Batz confirmed that Mlaker was inside. Birchmeier told the two men to cover the exits to the house. He and Batz would confront Mlaker.

Birchmeier and Batz crept up a flight of steps to Mlaker's apartment, pistols drawn. They stood at the top on either side of the door. Noise came from within the room. Mlaker was no doubt inside. Birchmeier took the lead and kicked open the door with Batz following.

Inside stood Mlaker, smiling and calm as though he was expecting the men for tea. There was no sign of the suitcases. No bomb materials to be seen. Birchmeier knew something was wrong.

Mlaker lured me into a trap, but for what purpose?

Mlaker welcomed the two men and then from behind a screen he rolled out an old, clunky office chair. Seated on the chair with her arms strapped to the sides and a piece of duct tape over her mouth, was his daughter, her eyes wide with fear. Mlaker kneeled behind the chair with a knife to his daughter's throat. Birchmeier realized Mlaker's target was not a building. It was Birchmeier. It was a trap to dispose of him. Mlaker demanded the two men lay down their guns. The choice was to sacrifice his daughter's life or his own. Mlaker was sure to kill him.

Birchmeier had only a moment to think this through. Mlaker made sure the only target was his daughter. He was behind the heavy chair, using it and his daughter as a shield.

Sometimes, training that teaches caution cannot tame the impulsiveness of youth. A man will go against all instruction and do something wrong, imprudently risky, but ends up saving the day. So it was with Batz as he fired a bullet into the center of Mlaker's head. He could have easily missed and hit the daughter. Mlaker could have sliced Laura's throat open as he fell. Neither of those things happened.

Batz ran to the body to be sure Mlaker was down. The bloody mess of a head left no doubt Mlaker was dead. Birchmeier untied his daughter and ripped the tape from her mouth. She leaped into her father's arms, sobbing. Birchmeier comforted her as he had when she had a bad dream as a child and said it would be all right.

But it was not all right. That night haunted Laura. She was never as carefree. It may not have been noticeable to her friends, but it was clear to her mother and father. Birchmeier knew it affected his relationship with his wife. Lisa would look at him in a way that said, "how dare you let that part of your life into ours."

The incident made Birchmeier swear that he would never let someone in his care suffer again. Which explained his actions later, when another young woman went missing.

Chapter 14

COMMISSARIO RUSSO ruminated as Matteo sat attentively in his office.

"So, we now have a suspect for Signorina Blake's killer?"

"Yes," responded Matteo. "We have a report from Interpol. The photo matches the one from the surveillance video."

"And who is he?"

"His name is Branko Bosak, a Croatian."

"Where is this Branko Bosak now?"

"Interpol believes that he has flown to Dubrovnik."

"Ah," said Russo, "Back to the safety of his mother country. Extradition from Croatia is difficult, if not impossible."

Then Russo smiled at the fresh-faced young colleague.

"Matteo, I must confess. Before you came in here, I knew all of this."

Matteo's expression was one of both disappointment and embarrassment.

Russo continued.

"I received a call from Director Birchmeier of TIGRIS in Switzerland. He identified Bosak first."

"But why would anyone in Switzerland be involved in this murder?" asked Matteo.

"They had an incident there where someone was shot, and they believed the shooter to be the same man who murdered Signorina Blake."

"Who was shot?"

Russo leaned back in his desk chair and smiled.

"It was a colleague of Signor Nicholas Foxe."

Matteo was not a detective. Besides being a sometime video technician, he was a regular cop. But Russo saw more in the man than someone who just scans reports and video. Matteo validated Russo's opinion when Matteo saw the connections immediately.

"So, a man tries to kill someone close to Signor Foxe and then succeeds in killing a woman close to him. Not to mention someone trying to kill Signor Foxe himself in a water taxi."

"That's true, or at least the person who Foxe said tried to kill him," added Russo.

Matteo wrinkled his brow.

"Guido was actually the one who did the man in. He was trying to save Foxe from being shot. There were plenty of witnesses who support this. They saw the man taking aim at Foxe."

"Yes, but who was that man who tried to kill Foxe?"

It was Matteo's turn to smile. Russo knew what the grin from ear to ear meant.

"You have his identity, do you not?" Russo said.

"Yes, it just came in. The man's name was Marko Bosak."

"Bosak?" exclaimed Russo.

"Yes, he was the younger brother of Branko Bosak."

"Interessante," ruminated Russo as he tented his fingers, tapping them together as he pondered the information.

"So, we seem to have Croatians running around trying to kill Foxe and people associated with him. Why would that be?"

"Sir," said Matteo, "Interpol reported that each of these brothers were hired assassins. It is unlikely they were acting on their own."

"Then, who hired them?"

Matteo shrugged.

"Matteo, we must understand who would have a connection to Foxe that would make Foxe a target. I must learn more about him."

Russo was lost in thought for a moment.

Does this man attract death like metal attracts lightning?

Matteo wondered the same thing.

Russo dismissed Matteo by saying, "I'm calling Director Birchmeier. He and I have much to talk about."

Birchmeier had taken ownership of protecting everyone who had anything to do with the Omni while on Swiss soil. Birchmeier confided in Nick that the leaders of their government considered the Omni a national treasure, but like the gnomes of Zurich, they kept it secret. Officials made it clear to the director to keep it both secret and safe.

Tom Littleton was being discharged from the hospital. Birchmeier sent Chris Batz to be his driver. Batz picked up Nick first. Wearing a knit shirt and jeans, Batz looked little like a policeman. One would not guess the loose cotton jacket covered a shoulder holster and pistol.

Nick realized the advantage Batz had.

He could blend into any crowd without drawing suspicion. Guess that's the point.

Nick rode up front with Batz on the way to the hospital and started a conversation. It seemed to be casual chit-chat. "How did you wind up in TIGRIS? Where are you from?" But Nick was trying to figure out the young man.

Could he trust him?

There were reasons that made Nick believe trust was in short supply.

Batz stayed with the car while Nick went into the hospital to check Tom out. Nick found Rachael was already there completing the necessary paperwork.

"So, are you checking Tom out?" he asked.

"Yes, almost done," she responded, annoyed, letting Nick know she still held a grudge.

"Thought they would need a next of kin."

"They thought I'm his partner," she said without looking up from the paperwork.

Nick laughed, and Rachael turned her gaze to him.

"What's so funny?"

"Nothing. I just…"

"You just thought no one would think we were together. Why?"

"Look, Rachael, I don't know why it struck me that way."

Nick thought he was in a hole he dug and was only digging deeper.

Rachael set him straight.

"Did you know that Tom and I talked almost every day? It's a lot more communication that I could say for some people."

She turned back to her paperwork.

Nick never realized Rachael thought twice about the two of them losing touch. That ride back to the States on his jet began it all. Nick spent several nights in a row at Rachael's place in Cambridge. It made him feel like a man in his twenties again, being with a young woman in a modest apartment. He had resigned himself to rich, divorced women in New York where the supply was wide, but the depths shallow. Rachael challenged his mind as well as his body, sometimes the latter struggling to keep up.

Nick assumed Rachael thought their time together had been no more than a short vacation. Before long, the mysteries of the Omni once again absorbed her, just as they did when they first discovered it. Nick wasn't surprised she talked to Tom every day. She started that while Nick was still living with her.

Nick had to return to New York, although he had a great last night with her. They ordered in Chinese food. The empty boxes and chopsticks were strewn across the bedroom floor the next day when Nick left Rachael peacefully sleeping.

Did he call Rachael after he left? He couldn't remember. Apparently, she could.

Rachael finished the paperwork. "Done. Let's go get the patient."

The nurse had Tom sitting up with Lizzy at his side giving him encouragement in her own style.

"There we go," said Lizzy as Tom sat up. "You'll be crawling in caves before you know it."

"Thanks, Lizzy," replied Tom. "You've been great, but it may be awhile before I'm back in caves."

A nurse wheeled him out for procedural reasons, with Hans for protection. Hans' chief had told him that the person picking them up at the hospital would provide protection from that point on. It didn't take Hans long to figure out that it must be TIGRIS.

Batz got out of the van to assist and Nick introduced him to the group. As he shook hands and names were exchanged, Nick said, "Chris is a trusted resource for us." That was his signal they could speak freely around Batz.

Tom stood up from the wheelchair, showing he was more stable on his feet than anyone expected. Batz slid the side door open and helped Tom into the middle seat of the van. Lizzy and Rachael took the back seat and Nick rode shotgun.

As they pulled away from the hospital, Batz asked, "Where to?"

Nick turned around to look at Tom.

"I think we want to take you to your apartment where you could get some rest."

"No," said Tom. "I've had plenty of rest. I want to go to the Omni."

"All right," said Nick as he turned to Batz. "The Omni is located…"

"I know where it's located," said Batz with a smile.

Everyone confined their conversation to general banter since none fully trusted Batz, yet. The trip didn't take long. They soon were outside the building where the Omni resided. They took the alley that led to the basement entrance. As they unloaded, Nick walked around to Batz and said, "I thought TIGRIS was going to have extra guards on site."

Batz' perpetual smile broadened.

"You're looking in the wrong direction."

He looked up across the street to a third-floor window and tipped his hat to someone vaguely seen behind the glare of the glass. The man there waved and Nick could make out a rifle on a tripod before him.

"There's another officer inside. I'm taking the van. You have my number when you need me."

Nick said, "Thanks," and Batz drove away.

Tom led the group to the door of the work area at a pace faster than Nick had expected.

He seems raring to return to work.

Tom opened the door and, as Batz promised, another guard stood just beyond the entrance. She was an expressionless young woman in Kevlar black holding an assault rifle. Nick wasn't sure he felt all that safe. But Lizzy broke the tension when she told the guard, "I see you know you can never go wrong with basic black." The guard allowed her a slight smile.

The group walked past the guard and down the steps where they could be alone with the Omni. Perhaps it was Tom's close work with the glowing Omni, or perhaps it was its self-defense mechanism that made Tom consider the Omni an organic thing that created a pet-master relationship. But Tom wasn't sure who was the pet and who was the master.

Alone with his trusted allies, Tom could be open with his thoughts.

"Nick, did you send me the digital photos of the stake you found in Venice?" Tom asked.

"Yes, they should be in your secure file area."

Tom turned to Rachael. "You examined the photos. See anything?"

He hoped Rachael would have the same luck with the stake she had when she found a key clue to The Tablet code.

"No."

He turned to Lizzy. "Any ideas?"

Tom had long ago learned Lizzy was one sharp customer.

"Thanks for asking," said Lizzy. "All I can say is that you can't hold down a tent with just one stake."

Tom turned to Nick who shared a smile with him.

Turning back to Lizzy, Tom asked, "Meaning?"

"Meaning: there's probably more than one."

"At least three is what I figure," said Tom. Then he looked at Nick. "If there was something under the one stake we were shown, I'm betting your man Dowd would have already found it."

"He didn't say so, but I'm sure he's tried every way to find what may be under it."

"Except digging it up," said Rachael.

"He's smart," answered Nick. "If there's something it points to, he wants to leave it exactly where it is."

"Well, there is someone we can ask," said Tom.

Everyone knew what Tom meant as all eyes turned to the Omni.

Chapter 15

TANNER AND PAUL ALLERTON sat on the patio of the Nautika Restaurant, carved from the ancient battlements of Dubrovnik. Tanner admired the evening view overlooking the sea and the line of sailboats docked below. But he didn't enjoy trading his camos for a golf shirt and pleated pants. Maybe it was the respect for rank Tanner had baked into him. Paul was a colonel in the Royal Marines in Afghanistan the same time Tanner was there. Sure, it was the Brits; not the US Marines, but that respect was still there.

On the transport over to Dubrovnik, Tanner and Paul traded war stories. Paul was not a desk colonel. He led troops in some heavy fighting. He earned Tanner's respect.

Here, they were far away from fighting, although this city showed its battle scars. The hotel where they stayed had bullet holes in the exterior stucco from the Bosnia War. Tanner thought they would have resurfaced the marks after all these years. But the marks provided a memory of war, not to be forgotten.

Tanner felt comfortable in Dubrovnik. He had never been to Croatia before and could not help noticing how he was no longer a giant among men. Many Croatian men were his height, and some women too. Although none had his bulk.

Paul was relaxed here, as he seemed to be in most places. To the American eye, he was close to the James Bond model. He reminded Tanner of Nicholas Foxe with a British accent.

"We're taking a tour tomorrow," Paul said after finishing his dinner of cuttlefish in vinegar and garlic sauce. Tanner had a meal of beef and potatoes. Tanner seldom ate light.

"Oh?" Tanner responded.

"We are going is inland, to farm country. There's a dune buggy 'adventure' excursion all the cruise ship tourists take. I thought it would be a good way to blend in if we joined them. A contact is meeting us at the farm where we'll have lunch. The word we have is Bosak is staying with family in that area. Our contact will lead us to him."

"Aren't we putting civilians at risk? I mean, riding with a bunch of tourists?"

"We have no reason to believe Bosak knows we are here. Everyone should be safe."

Those words rang hollow to Tanner. His last assignment for the army, the one that took him out of commission from a military career, was well planned. It all went to hell in practice.

"You're the boss," he told Paul who didn't disagree.

Paul studied this man with only one name. He was accustomed to using the last name in the military. Every man or woman reporting to him used last names. The first name was their rank. He was Colonel Allerton or 'Sir' to the men reporting to him. Colonel or Allerton to the people to whom he reported.

Tanner broke the silence.

"So, how did you get involved with MI6?"

"Please," said Allerton, "we prefer SIS, Secret Intelligence Service. MI6 was a cover name, long abandoned. Just like your CIA, everyone knows about it. I understand that at the height of the cold war the location at Langley was as secret as possible for such a large installation. Now road signs point to it."

"And you put your headquarters squarely in London on the Thames."

Paul smiled.

"Yes, we did."

Tanner grinned, a man who had done his homework.

"But you're not located there, are you? You're in the SRR."

Paul's face betrayed nothing, as one would expect from a member of the Special Reconnaissance Regiment.

"Perhaps."

Tanner knew about the SRR. Although they reported to the British defense department, they conducted what the Americans call Black Ops. They were rumored to be the best shots in Britain. They used concealed weapons, wore civilian clothes, drove like Formula One racers, and might be experts in explosives, scuba diving, and parachuting.

If James Bond were real, he'd be in the SRR.

Paul asked, "Does it matter who I work for?"

Tanner continued his grin.

"I like to know who I'm partnered with."

Paul then broke his stone face with a smile.

"Well, as you Yanks say, I would tell you more, but then I would have to kill you."

How Paul expressed himself seemed to Tanner to be too close to the truth. He decided he knew all he needed to and returned his focus to the mission.

"Who was this agent that Bosak killed? Some woman in Istanbul?"

"The 'some woman' was Priscilla Westly. She was one of us."

Tanner was not the most sensitive guy on the planet, but he could tell that, to Paul, 'one of us' meant more than a colleague in SRR.

"Why was she targeted?"

"Well, my friend, that appears to be where our paths cross and one reason you have joined me."

Tanner could not imagine the connection.

"What?" he asked.

"Priscilla had in her possession a letter from an old Arab scholar containing a fanciful story, one that told of a machine that could turn seawater into energy."

Tanner tried to show no reaction, but Paul was a master of reading faces.

"Your Omni knows of such a thing too, does it not?"

"You know the answer to that already."

Paul grinned.

"The person who killed Priscilla took the letter, but she had made a photocopy and put it on a thumb drive."

"And where is the thumb drive?" asked Tanner.

"It's with top translators at headquarters."

Paul stopped and looked away. Tanner thought his mind was wandering to an unpleasant experience.

"Someone went to extremes to get the letter from Priscilla, probably to no avail. My translation specialists tell me the ancient Arabic it's written in, is conversational and difficult to make sense of. Whoever has that letter now is not likely to have the translation specialists at their disposal that we do. Stealing it might have been a waste of time."

"Nick would no doubt like to see the translation when it's complete," Tanner said.

"I'm sure he would. But nobody gets to see it until I do."

"And where does Bosak fit in?"

"Simple," said Paul. "Bosak stole the letter, and I was there when he did it."

"So, you've met the man."

"Only for a few moments before he pushed me down a flight of steps."

"Ouch," replied Tanner.

"Well," said Paul, "going after Bosak is not a matter of seeking revenge. He can lead us to whoever planned the attack on the Omni; what they know, and what they plan to do with it. If this feat of energy science is real, it cannot fall into the wrong hands."

The evening sun was setting as Paul finished filling Tanner in. "I don't know about you, but I'm exhausted, and our little tour begins early. I'm headed back to the hotel. How about you?"

"Sure," replied Tanner. "Guess it's about time."

They left the restaurant as the modern lights of the medieval city came to life, illuminating the cobblestone streets leading to the hotel. As they walked, the discussion turned casual and personal.

Tanner asked Paul, "Do you have any family?" He wasn't sure why this was the first thing he asked.

"No."

"Married?"

"No."

"Girlfriend?"

"Well," Paul said, "I left a lovely young thing on a Greek island to join this mission. I suppose one could call her a girlfriend. How about you?"

"There's Lizzy," he said. Maybe he started this line of discussion because he wanted to talk about Lizzy.

"Lizzy?"

"Yeah. Lucinda Rodriquez."

" A Latina lass?"

"Well, the dad she never knew gave her the family name and the olive complexion. She got the bluest eyes you've ever seen from her mom."

Paul saw that Tanner's affection toward this Lizzy person was unmistakable. "Guess you really care for her."

Tanner returned to the unexpressive soldier. "Guess so."

They reached the bullet-pocked hotel, now a Hilton. The desk clerk on duty when they checked in had been friendly and welcoming. The evening clerk now on duty was less cordial. It was as if he knew who they were but was trying not to show it. Tanner looked at Paul. His expression told the tale.

Something was up.

They took the elevator to their rooms, one across from the other.

"Goodnight," said Paul.

"Night. See you tomorrow," returned Tanner as he entered his room.

Paul opened his room door, slid his room card into the holder by the door, and the lights came on. He would later curse himself for being so careless. Why hadn't he seen the man before a garrote appeared in front of his neck?

At least Paul had not lost his reflexes. He put a hand between his neck and the garotte. Luckily, the device was tough leather and not a wire or else he would have lost fingers saving his neck. He used the situation to his advantage by backing into the attacker, bending forward, and launching him over his head.

The man was huge and ugly. As Paul pulled out his pistol, he found the man was also astonishingly agile. He bounced onto his feet and kicked the gun from Paul's hand. The man launched a left toward Paul's face. Paul blocked it with his right arm. The man swung his right. Paul blocked it with his left. This syncopated attack repeated a half dozen times before Paul ducked and hit the man with his shoulder knocking him back toward a glass coffee table. The man was too massive to fall from Paul's ramming, but he had the air knocked out of him. A swift kick from Paul sent him crashing into the table shattering glass everywhere.

The man was wedged into the metal frame of the table unable to get out, kicking and struggling like a turtle on its back. However, the man could reach a pistol in his shoulder holster. Paul, seeing his own pistol lying across the room, planned to roll to it and pick it up. If only he could do it without being shot first.

Tanner interrupted that split second of decision-making by kicking the room door open. The surprise on the face of the man lodged in the coffee table was clear. He hesitated. Tanner did not. Tanner entered the room with his pistol out and he unloaded two shots into the man. With both hands on his pistol, Tanner walked to the dead man and kicked his gun away, as though this huge man pouring blood from his wounds remained a threat.

Paul looked beyond the busted door and across the hall to Tanner's room. Another large man rested on the floor with his head twisted in an unnatural position, blocking the door.

"You OK?" asked Tanner, still focused on the dead man bleeding out.

"Yes," Paul said. "Yes I am." Paul studied Tanner in a new light. He had walked back to the hotel with what he considered to be a gentle giant, sweet on a woman with blue eyes. Now, before him, was an awesome killer who could snap a large man's neck and a moment later take out his partner.

Tanner put his pistol away. "I was bothered by a guy who shouldn't have been in my room and figured he may have had a partner messing with you, too."

"You figured right," said Paul.

"Damn," said Tanner, as he surveyed the damage in his room and in Paul's. "Now we have to clean up this mess."

Paul said only, "I'll take care of it."

Tanner wondered what he meant.

Chapter 16

PAUL DIDN'T PROVIDE TANNER all the detail about the theft of the letter. He focused only on Bosak and his role. He thought that was sufficient, but there was more to the story.

"Good morning, Miss Moneypenny," said Paul to Priscilla, to which she shot Paul a middle digit concealed behind a legal pad.

Priscilla Westly, like M's secretary in the James Bond series, fit the part of the highly efficient, unassuming British secretary. She wore sensible dresses fitting her trim figure. Her black hair was styled in a short bob that flipped up at the ends. It was Jackie Kennedy retro. Priscilla had worn her hair that way beyond the time it was fashionable. She flirted lightly with Paul which probably aided his image of her as Moneypenny. To the casual eye, she appeared to be an ordinary professional who worked at the British Embassy in Istanbul. What was not evident was that she was the only one among them trained in martial arts and who could shoot a fly off an apple at a hundred paces.

The CIA has a spy or two in embassies around the world. Priscilla was the British secret service equivalent there in Istanbul. She was Paul's contact. It was Priscilla who was responsible for his being there. It all started with a bizarre story Priscilla pondered before reporting it to her superiors.

Pricilla was the first to notice the man. He was old, dressed in shaggy robes and a turban that appeared to be as old as the man himself. He had just stepped into the lobby of the embassy pleading with the marine to let him pass. Priscilla saw the commotion from a distance. Why she intervened, she never knew. Just instinct.

The old man was animatedly arguing with the marine that someone should know what he had found. Priscilla told the marine that she would take care of this and she escorted the man to a visitor's office. After calming the man, offering him tea, which he graciously accepted, she heard his story. Tea, and someone who would listen, put the man at ease and he told his tale.

The man claimed to be a descendant of an Arab scholar employed by Federico Secondo in the 13th century. The scholar had a son who settled in Constantinople. That son became a rich merchant and a close ally of Emperor Andronikos II Palaiologos. Federico was so pleased with the scholar's work, he presented him with a gift of sixteen matched swords. Those swords eventually became the son's property.

At that time, there was a large Italian expat population living in Constantinople. Those were the days of city-states on the Italian peninsula. Citizens from one city often held hostilities toward those from another. The Genovese didn't like the Venetians and they attacked the Venetian population, killing many. The emperor took the side of the Genovese and arrested many of the surviving Venetians, blaming them for the trouble. This did not sit well with the people back home in Venice, so they declared war on the emperor. Venice prevailed. As part of a peace offering, the old man's ancestor provided the emperor with the swords to give to the ruler of Venice for his palace.

Priscilla thought it a nice tale and her expression said it was nothing more. That is when the man returned to his excited state.

He said the swords were a family legend. They contained the key to unlocking immense power, so much power, that it could alter the face of the earth. He repeated the legend that the Black Sea was once dry land populated by people. The unlocked power of the sword caused a great flood.

Priscilla knew of the theory. In fact, explorers discovered foundations to buildings at the bottom of the Black Sea dating back 7,500 years. Some scholars point to these foundations as evidence of the great flood depicted in lore and religion. The Jewish version of the story is of Noah and the ark.

The old man said he discovered a manuscript hidden away in clay pots the family thought worthless. He pulled the manuscript out from his robes and carefully laid it before him on the table, asking Priscilla if she could read Arabic. She could not. He told her it used an ancient form of Arabic, but he could piece it together. This was the document the scholar sent to his son along with the swords. The scholar told his son there was a code on one sword that would unlock the source of tremendous power from the sea. The scholar didn't know where the source, this thing, was located that produced this power, but he knew from his readings it needed this code.

The old man looked kindly toward Priscilla as a grandfather would gaze at his granddaughter. He explained he had no family. His wife had passed away long ago. His only son died recently from cancer. He had no one to continue the legend. He wanted her to have this document.

Great Britain was a mighty nation. It would have the means to protect this information.

The old man left, more peaceful in his exit than his arrival. Priscilla put the document away in a safe place and tried her best to continue with her day. Everything changed when she walked home. Up ahead were police cars with their lights ablaze. Something had happened in an alley. She looked across the police tape to see the old man, dead. The means of death was clear. Blood trickled from the straight gash across his neck made by a garrote.

Priscilla turned around and returned to the embassy to contact headquarters. HQ dispatched Paul and he arrived the next day.

There was clear chemistry between Priscilla and Paul. Perhaps it was that of colleagues who worked in the shadows and could relax with each other in daylight. Maybe it was just two people whose single status caused background noise of possible intimacy. For now, Priscilla was happy to play the Miss Moneypenny game.

Paul reviewed the scroll. It was old, but that was all he could add to its authenticity. Paul could read some Arabic, but experts would have to do the translating. Even if the scroll lived up to the story the man told, there would be more questions than answers.

What machine was the writer talking about?

The power to change the face of the earth seemed an embellishment. The whole thing could be a fantasy, except for the fact someone murdered an old man for it.

"This is something we need to make a copy of," Paul told Priscilla pointing to the scroll.

"Already done," replied Priscilla with a smile. She pulled open a side drawer in her desk and removed a thumb drive and held it up for his inspection.

"Well done," said Paul as Priscilla returned the thumb drive to the drawer.

Priscilla's phone rang. She answered. Paul heard only Priscilla's part of the conversation.

"Hello. Who? She didn't say. Oh, she did? Put her through.

"Priscilla Westly here. Yes. I guess that could be arranged. What's the address?"

She picked up a pen and wrote an address down on a pad of paper.

"Yes. OK."

She hung up and turned to Paul. "Well, that was interesting."

"What was it?"

"It was a French woman, or at least she sounded French. She said she had heard about the discovery of the 'scroll of the sword' as she called it. She believed I had possession of it."

"News travels fast."

"Except it wasn't news. Only you and I know I have it and I doubt you've been telling random French women about it."

Paul smirked. "No, haven't even had the chance."

"She said it was an important find and she knew what it meant and how it could be used."

"Do tell," said Paul, "and what else?"

"I'm meeting her tonight?"

"I can't wait."

Priscilla frowned. "She said come alone."

"And bring the scroll, right?"

Priscilla sarcastically stated the obvious. "How could you guess?"

"And what was this woman's name? She gave you a name, right?"

Priscilla snickered before giving the answer. "Miss Glaçage."

"Glaçage?" Paul laughed at the meaning of the name in English. "Miss Frosting?"

Priscilla joined him in laughing at the obvious alias. She added, "Well doesn't that take the cake!"

"Well, I'm sure you know the right people to alert to this meeting," Paul said, turning to the serious business at hand.

"I'm not alerting anyone," she said.

That idea flummoxed Paul. "Why the devil not?"

"This is Istanbul. I'm never sure who I can trust," she said before adding, "Present company excepted."

Paul nodded as though paid a compliment. "But I'm going with you."

"Why Paul, is this our first date?" she said slyly.

"I won't be bringing flowers, you know."

"But you will bring this," she said as she opened another desk drawer and pulled out a ball-point pen and something that appeared to be a small flip-phone. "I'll carry this," she said holding the pen, "and you'll carry this," pushing the flip-phone across the desk to him.

Paul held the phone in his hand studying it.

"If I arrive and find there is anyone besides her in the room, or if things get ugly, I will click my pen." She clicked the pen as though she was about to take a note and the phone in Paul's hand vibrated and a light on it blinked red.

Paul smiled.

Miss Glaçage picked a location for the meeting in a place devoid of people, a hard trick to pull off in bustling Istanbul. Priscilla and Paul dressed like tourists taking in the city in the late evening. Paul wore a blue blazer to conceal the pistol he carried. Priscilla was unarmed. She reasoned a gun would be the first thing Glaçage would look for. Priscilla carried the scroll in a yoga mat bag. She had her pen, which she pulled out and clicked. Paul could feel the phone in his pocket vibrate. He pulled it out to show Priscilla the blinking light.

"OK," she said to Paul. "Wish me luck."

As she turned to leave, Paul stopped her. Priscilla turned to face him.

"Be careful," he said.

Priscilla smiled. "I bet you say that to all the agents."

Her calmness eased Paul and reminded him she was a professional, just like him. But he didn't like the situation.

Priscilla entered the apartment building, not unlike others in the area. The building showed no sign of occupants. She had heard of a block due to be torn down and replaced by a modern office building. She realized this was that block. That Glaçage had chosen such an isolated location gave her pause. Priscilla was a woman who could take care of herself, but if weapons appeared, she would be on the ballpoint quickly.

Her instructions were to go to the apartment on the second floor immediately off the stairs. She climbed the stairs to the second floor with the bag in hand. There was no ambiguity which apartment it was. The old wooden door was the first thing you saw at the top. The apartment building was dank, gray, and dimly lit. This door looked fresh and new as though they hung it yesterday. She knocked.

"I'll be right there," said the voice she had heard on the phone.

A young blonde woman, her blue eyes sparkling, opened the door.

"Come in," she said. "Please."

The woman led her into a room that Priscilla had not expected. It was freshly done in red damask. Two oversized sofas faced each other with a Louis XIV style coffee table in between. She felt she had entered a Russian tearoom. She noticed a stuffed armchair in one corner. A side table with a stack of books. No weapons within sight. Priscilla relaxed just a bit.

"Please come in," Glaçage said. She led Priscilla to the sofas. She sat in one and pointed to the other. "Please have a seat."

Glaçage said, "I would offer you tea, but they cut the water off just yesterday. I'm the last holdout in this building."

"Is this the block that will be demolished?" ask Priscilla.

"It is. They will be building a modern monster in its place. Pity."

"I have to ask you why you thought I acquired this scroll you seek?"

Glaçage wrinkled her nose. "I've learned Istanbul has many eyes where you least expect."

"Excuse me," said Priscilla as though she forgot something important. "But who are you?"

"I am Essa Glaçage, professor of Latin studies at the Sorbonne."

Priscilla paused and Glaçage could tell what she was thinking.

"Yes, I know. The last name. People have fun with it."

"Sorry."

"Never mind," said Glaçage. "Let's talk about the scroll."

Priscilla had been quickly charmed, but she had a question or two. "What is your interest in the scroll?"

"Certainly," said Glaçage patiently. "It has to do with Frederick the Second. I am writing a book about him. I've been doing research off and on for years. He had a scholar working for him who translated a code found on a tablet into Latin. I learned that this scholar had a son here in Istanbul. That is why I am here. I've been tracing the family through the generations. I understand that a man who may have been the last of the line had a document from Frederick's scholar. That would be immensely important to me in my work. Completes the story, if you will."

"I see," said Priscilla. It all seemed plausible, but she wasn't totally convinced.

Glaçage displayed her excitement.

"Did you bring the document with you?"

"Yes, I did."

"May I see it?"

Priscilla took the yoga bag and unzipped it. She handed the scroll to Glaçage who reverently unrolled it onto the coffee table.

"Yes, this is what I've been after."

Then Glaçage looked at Priscilla as though transformed into a different person. Evil intent is not easily hidden.

"Thank you, Priscilla. Your work here is done."

Priscilla stood, unsure of what to do next, and backed away.

The huge man moved more silently than Priscilla would have expected.

When did he enter the room?

She didn't know of his presence until she felt the garrote around her neck. Priscilla attempted to pull the man over her shoulders, but he was too massive to move. She pulled the pen from her jacket, pushed the point down and stabbed at the unseen man's face.

The phone in Paul's coat vibrated. He didn't hesitate to take it. Paul ran toward the apartment building. He dashed up the stairs and arrived at Glaçage's apartment at the moment the door swung open. Paul stood face-to-face with a huge man. Neither made a move for a brief second of surprised encounter until the large man pushed Paul down the steps.

Paul did a controlled roll like the paratrooper he once was and arrived on the landing bruised, but not broken. He caught sight of the back of a blonde woman dashing down the hallway followed by the large man. Paul stood and rushed back up with his pistol out. He got off two shots at the two before they disappeared behind a fire door. He sped to the door only to find it jammed closed by the departing couple.

Paul ran back to the apartment. Through the open door, he saw Priscilla lying on the floor. He walked in and knelt beside her placing two fingers on her throat. No pulse. The cause was clear from the mark on her neck.

Paul was a professional. He didn't have time to mourn the loss of a woman who had become a fast friend. He headed to the embassy. The marine in front examined Paul's credentials carefully and let him pass. Paul made his way to Priscilla's office and to her desk. He pulled the thumb drive from the drawer and held it up to address it as if it were alive.

Why do people kill for you?

Chapter 17

TOM SAT AT THE CONSOLE outside the Omni chamber with Nick, Rachael, and Lizzy looking over his shoulder.

"You sent me the digital photographs of the stake," said Tom. "I uploaded them to the supercomputer in Germany. We always talk through that computer to the Omni and I haven't shared the files with it yet."

"Remind me why we do that," said Nick.

"Why we do what?"

"Talk through the supercomputer."

"You might remember," Tom said to Nick, as though the man had missed class that day, "we really don't know how to talk directly to the Omni. It formed its own connection to the supercomputer, and it uses that computer to translate for us."

"So, you can hold information in a separate file that the Omni hasn't seen?"

Tom displayed the grin of a proud parent and one who never underestimated the Omni.

"Well, I'd like to think so. But I suspect the Omni knows more of what's on the supercomputer than our German colleagues would like."

Tom paused a beat and looked at everyone. "But let's not share my speculation with our friends there."

Something puzzled Nick. "Why didn't the Omni tell us what the markings on the stake mean?"

"Because, we didn't ask."

"Then, by all means, let's ask."

"I'm doing it now."

Tom began a series of requests to the Omni. In the short time Tom had worked with the Omni, he had developed a natural language query system. As he began doing so, the teacher became the pupil as the Omni took over and provided language Tom could use. What surprised everyone was, that now, the Omni could speak.

"Omni," said Tom. "I want you to look at a recent file."

"I will do that right away," said Omni in a pleasant female voice. The sound emanated from speakers positioned over Omni's enclosure. Although the connection was from the supercomputer in Germany, it appeared the device before them was speaking.

All, but Tom, were astounded to hear Omni speak. Tom displayed the sheepish smile of a boy at a junior high science fair showing off his project.

"Wow," said Lizzy, "I didn't know you had a babe. No wonder you've spent so much time here."

"I am not a babe, Lizzy," replied Omni.

Lizzy did a double take. "She knows who I am?"

Tom replied, "I fed recordings of you guys into her to try out voice recognition. Guess it works."

"Ah… yeah," said Lizzy. "I would say so."

Rachael tried it. "Omni, do you know who I am?"

"You are Rachael Friedman, a professor at Massachusetts Institute of Technology. You were the person who recognized the octal nature of the code Tom discovered. You had a personal relationship with Nicholas Foxe, who is standing to your right."

Lizzy gave Rachael a playful nudge and grinned at Nick at the mention of 'a personal relationship.'

Nick was both stunned and confused. Stunned that Omni knew of a 'personal relationship,' but confused how she knew he was there and standing to Rachael's right. He asked Tom, "How does she know that? I haven't talked to her."

It was Omni that answered Nick.

"You have been speaking, Mr. Foxe, if not to me. Tom installed directional microphones, so I knew your position."

Nick said, "I need to watch what I say."

Omni asked in a confused tone, "What device will you use to view what you say, Mr. Foxe?"

Tom interjected, "I haven't taught her a lot of idioms."

Omni responded. "So, Tom, that was an idiom? I assume that 'watch' in this case was a personification of being careful, correct?"

"Yes," said Tom.

"So noted."

"Omni," Tom said, getting down to business. "I am directing you to the files I uploaded."

"Was this the last upload you made?" asked Omni.

"Yes."

"This is a *spica,*" she reported.

"In English, Omni."

Tom turned to everyone to explain Omni's choice of terms. "We still have Latin expressions remaining from the original translation work we did."

"Very well, it is a stake," she said.

"Tell me its origin."

"My creators left it."

"What does it designate?"

"My creators left such stakes to locate gifts they left behind."

"What do the markings mean? We cannot decode them."

"These markings would be difficult to translate into the manner in which you communicate. They use my basic codex."

"Does that mean you understand what they mean?"

"Yes."

"Can you put it in terms we can understand?"

"Yes."

Tom looked at his teammates to explain why Omni seemed like a smart aleck.

"I'm still working on getting her to act on questions beyond answering them literally."

Then readdressing Omni, "What do the stakes designate?"

"There are three stakes. This is one of three. The other two are identical. The gift they locate is the machine that converts seawater into microwave energy. The machine is in the center of the triangle made by the three stakes."

Nick could not help but interject himself into the conversation.

"Omni," he said, "how do we find the other two stakes?"

"Tom," Omni began, "do I have your approval to answer Mr. Foxe?"

Tom turned to Nick with what Nick thought was a smirk. "She uses voices as a password."

Then, without turning away from Nick, Tom answered, "Yes, you have my permission. You can talk freely to Rachael and Lizzy as well.

"Each stake is a beacon using light in the infrared spectrum."

"Is each stake emitting this light now?" asked Nick

"No."

"How do we turn them on?"

"Turn one on and it will signal the other stakes to turn on."

"We've really got to get Omni to carry on a better conversation," Nick said to no one in particular.

"Would you like me to be more effusive, Mr. Foxe?"

"Yes," replied Nick noting her choice of words. "Please be *effusive*."

"It appears you have identified one stake," said Omni. "The stake has a harmonic frequency of 440 cycles per second. Subject the stake to that frequency. It will turn on the beacon and turn on the beacon of the other two stakes. They locate the machine in the center of the beacons."

Nick grinned, satisfied, but Tom had another thought. "Omni, how long will the beacons stay on?"

"The beacons remain on for one revolution of your planet from the moment they are lit."

Nick turned to the others. "So, all we have to do is focus a 440 hertz sound at this stake."

Lizzy asked, "Why 440 hertz?"

Rachael answered.

"It's an A in music. The note used to tune the orchestra." Then she paused. "Nick, don't you remember the first note you chose for The Tablet, when we tried to correlate the code to music?"

Nick wrinkled his brow. "Of course. It was an A." Nick couldn't believe the coincidence. "Is this a joke?"

Omni answered.

"It is not a joke, Mr. Foxe."

Nick forgot that Omni was still listening.

"It's just odd. But we can talk about the philosophy of that another day."

"I would be happy to discuss this later," added Omni.

"Omni," said Nick. I appreciate your help, but let me talk to the others."

"Certainly," said Omni before she went quiet.

"So," Nick said, "seems we need to play an A note for the stake…"

"I can bring my slide whistle," joked Lizzy.

"Thanks," said Nick. "I think I'll pass on that."

Rachael added, "And scan the ocean for infrared beacons within one day."

Nick frowned. "Yeah. That's a problem."

Tom smiled. "But I think I have the answer."

Chapter 18

THE TEAM AGREED WITH TOM'S PLAN on how to locate the stakes, although Nick harbored some doubt that Tom could really pull it off.

Nick was confident, however, that Tanner and Allerton would track down Bosak. He wanted to join them in Croatia and take Bosak to task in person for Christy's death, but that could wait. Now it was time to find the Energy Machine. Nick considered what Bosak and his crew stole from the Omni site. Although he didn't know who they worked for, he was in a race to secure the ancient device.

Before everyone left the Omni lab, Nick handed out assignments.

"Tom, it's clear you need to continue to work here to locate the stakes. Lizzy, you've been a great caretaker for Tom. Could you continue to help him?"

Tom interjected, "I'm OK."

Lizzy did not agree. "Tom, you look like death warmed over," she said. "I'm keeping an eye on you."

"Hey, I'm here too," added Rachael, as though Nick had forgotten her.

"I'd like for you to return with me to Venice," said Nick.

Rachael gave Nick a wary eye. "And why would that be?"

"If we're to pull off Tom's plan, I'll need some help. Besides, I'd like for you to size up Nevin Dowd."

"You think he's the guy behind all this?"

"I'm not sure. I want your opinion. But I feel, at the very least, someone close to him is involved. Help me find out who he is."

Rachael didn't buy it. Her expression said so.

She was no super sleuth. Was Nick trying to patch things up between them?

"Please?" added Nick.

Nick's plea surprised Rachael.

So unlike Nick to do anything remotely like begging.

"Sure, I guess so."

Nick returned a smile. Too smug a smile Rachael thought, but she made the commitment, nonetheless.

Rachael noticed the roles between Lizzy and her had reversed.

Shouldn't she be with Tom since they were collaborating?

Then she caught herself. Lizzy didn't need a PhD to be smart and to be keenly intelligent at solving things.

Nick seemed pleased with himself. "It's decided then. Let's get out of here."

Tom looked like he was on his last ounce of adrenaline. "I'm staying here to do a little more work."

"No, you're not," said Lizzy. "You need rest."

"But..." Tom started, but Lizzy put a finger in the air in front of his face to close the argument down. Tom didn't object. He was exhausted.

"We'll get Chris to drive us," said Nick. "I'll call from the car to have the jet ready. Tom, your apartment has been secured by TIGRIS. We had maid service clean up, so it should be ready for you. TIGRIS will be guarding your place as well, Lizzy."

"What, no maid service?" joked Lizzy.

Batz had the van waiting for them. It was a short ride to Tom's place. The TIGRIS guard walked Tom to his apartment. Tom entered, headed directly to bed, fell into it, and went fast asleep.

Lizzy's place was two streets away. A TIGRIS guard was there as well.

"Take care of yourself," said Nick.

Lizzy said nothing but her expression was not the usual carefree look Nick was used to. Nick thought he knew why. It was the apartment she shared with Tanner, who was now gone and perhaps in harm's way.

"Don't worry," he said. "He'll be all right."

"Yeah. I guess he can take care of himself, right?"

"You bet," agreed Rachael.

Lizzy left the car. The TIGRIS guard joined her. Both walked silently to the lift. The guard punched three and they rose to the floor for Lizzy's apartment, which was just across from the lift. The guard opened the door for Lizzy and said, "Good night." He returned to his position at the entrance to the apartment building.

Lizzy looked around the small apartment, decorated in Bavarian traditional style. The cuckoo clock in the kitchen fit right in. It seemed spacious without Tanner lumbering about. She missed the big lug. The cuckoo clock began the cadence of eleven o'clock. She almost didn't hear the knock at the door.

Lizzy thought the guard must have forgotten something. When she opened the door, her first thought was Tanner had returned. But the large man before her was not Tanner.

A chloroform-soaked rag is an old, tried-and-true, method to render someone unconscious. Lizzy was soon dreaming.

Chapter 19

PAUL HAD MADE A QUICK CALL and a pair of men arrived in short order to clean up the mess and dispose of the bodies. It impressed Tanner that Paul had clean-up personnel at his beck and call.

"Forensics will have IDs soon for these two gentlemen," Paul said, as the bodies passed by them.

"Let's go down to the bar and talk."

On the way to the bar, Tanner noticed the desk clerk was not the one who was there when they entered earlier that evening. Paul could tell he noticed.

"We have people questioning the other desk clerk. Letting undesirables onto the premises is suspect."

No one else was in the bar save for a bartender. Paul told him they needed nothing, and the barkeep disappeared. They took two seats in the corner.

Paul reviewed what they would do the next day. "As I said earlier, our contact lives on a farm out in the country. He knows how we can find Bosak."

"Why are we going in this group?"

"The contact works as a part of the tour. His family owns the farm where we'll stop for lunch. He will be helping prepare the meal. It was his idea to come this way. He thought it would raise little suspicion if we were a part of a group that comes there almost every day."

"Well," replied Tanner, "it's clear someone already knows about us. Two men are being removed from our rooms right now that knew. I'm betting there're more."

"Guess we'll find out," Paul said.

Tanner and Paul dressed in collared knit shirts and khaki pants to blend in with the tourists. Neither one would go as far as shorts. Paul would never wear them outside of Bermuda and Tanner would never wear them. Period. Both had backpacks much the size and shape of the other tourists gathered for the back-road tour. Even though the contents of their backpacks would freak out a TSA agent were they in an airport, there were no such security measures here for this small group of eight people.

Outside the hotel was a line of four matching RZR XP 1000 dune buggies, each with a gray body, open sides, a small roof, and a red stripe running along the side. These buggies had become popular for off-road recreation and tours over rough back roads. Tanner cast a wary look at them.

"I know you're used to Humvees," Paul said. "But these buggies are highly maneuverable."

Tanner gave Paul a 'you've got to be kidding' look.

"OK, and they're a blast to drive," Paul admitted.

"Welcome, ladies and gentlemen," said a young guide wearing jeans, a tee shirt, and a broad smile. "We'll be getting started in a moment. First of all, will the person who plans to drive raise his or her hand?"

Of the eight people, two were staff, the guide and his assistant. The six left included two couples. One was a young man and a woman who looked to be in their twenties and could be celebrating their honeymoon. The other couple was a trim older man and his slender wife who looked like they went to the gym every day. Then, there was Tanner and Paul, the odd couple.

"You want to drive?" asked Paul.

"You said they were a blast to drive. Guess you've handled one before. You drive."

"OK," said Paul. Did Tanner detect a boyish delight in his acceptance?

After a few instructions from the guide on how to handle the buggy, the twosomes got into each of their assigned vehicles. Tanner and Paul had the one in the back. The guide came by each buggy and peered in to check if the driver was OK with operating the thing. When he reached Paul and Tanner, he asked Paul if he had any questions. He said "no." The guide returned a "very well" and a wink.

"What was that about?" Tanner asked Paul.

"What was what about?"

"That wink. Do you know the guy?"

"Never saw him before."

Tanner sensed Paul was being evasive.

"But you know who he is, don't you?"

Paul looked directly at Tanner and said in a low voice, "I've been led to believe that we may have one of our own on the trip. Maybe it's him. Or maybe he's just a man with a habit of winking at people."

"Paul," Tanner said, "if we're going to work together, you can't be holding back. I gotta know what you know."

Paul shot Tanner a moment-of-truth look.

"And do I know everything you know?"

"What do you mean?" asked Tanner

"Your little team is known to hold secrets to themselves. No one knows everything your Omni can tell us, except you and your friends."

Tanner was taken aback.

"Hey, I'm just the muscle. Tom, Nick, and Rachael are the brains."

"Yet," returned Paul, not letting Tanner off the hook, "you were the one who found the original tablet. You were the one who researched it for a year. You were the one who got Tom into the cave in New Mexico to find the mother lode that led to a grotto where the Omni was waiting for you."

"How…" Tanner began.

"How did I know all this?" Paul said finishing Tanner's question. "Our group's done its homework."

Tanner fell silent.

"But Tanner," Paul said, continuing in a less harsh tone. "I will try to give you a heads-up on all I know. Maybe you will too?"

Tanner smiled. "Sure."

The guide started his buggy and the others followed him out of the hotel plaza. The hotel was located on the edge of town and soon they were in the countryside. They took a road that was more of a rural tractor path through a flat plain. Rolling hills lined the distance. The group forded a small stream. On the other side of it, the guide stopped the procession under a stand of trees. He told everyone to take a stretch break. They had been on the road about an hour. The guide said the farm, where they would have lunch, was another hour away.

Tanner and Paul got out and stood in the tall grass by the creek. The young couple were into each other and walked in the distance holding hands. The older couple approached Tanner and Paul. The man spoke first.

"Hi, I'm John," he said with his hand out to Tanner to shake, "and this is Dot." Dot smiled.

"Tanner," was Tanner's reply. The same interchange happened with Paul.

"So," said John with a British accent, "how about this weather? Beautiful isn't it?"

Paul laughed. "In London, I carried an umbrella with me everywhere. Nice not to have to here."

"At least, not today," said John.

Cell phone ringing came from a fanny pack Dot wore on her hip. She removed her phone and looked at the incoming ID. "It's the children," she told John before she put the phone to her ear and walked away.

"Even way out here, we can't get away," said John. "Excuse me." He turned to join Dot.

"Nice couple," Tanner said, scanning Paul's face for any trace of recognition. He got none.

"Yes, they seem to be," was all Paul offered.

"Are you Brits all over this country?" asked Tanner.

"Well, remember that we are a lot closer than you Yanks. The Dalmatian Coast is something of our new Riviera."

The guide asked everyone to return to their buggies and they were off again.

More rolling countryside passed. The buggies and their passengers entered a farm. It was a working farm with pigs and cows. Beside a stucco flat-topped barn off to one side and a modest farmhouse on the other, there were open brick cook areas where wood had been burned down to charcoal. Three large Dutch ovens simmered the lunch. A few feet away were picnic tables and benches for the guests.

The tour guide told everyone to stretch their legs, look around, and to be sure to take a look at the lunch being prepared for them. An old man, weathered and wrinkled, with a large white mustache stood by the fire. The tour group lined up to see what he was preparing, Tanner and Paul at the end of the line.

The old man took a long iron rod, poked it under the handle of the lid on a Dutch oven and lifted it to expose a simmering mix of vegetables and beef. The others viewed and sniffed and offered praise for the aroma. They left the area leaving Tanner and Paul with the old man. The old man set the lid back on the oven, then said as an aside, "So, you want to see Bosak?"

Tanner didn't expect this.

So, this is our contact?

Paul responded. "Yes, we understand you can lead us to him."

"I can tell you how to find him. But is this something you really want to do?"

"We didn't come for the stew," snipped Tanner.

The old man maintained a deadly serious expression.

"Bosak is a very dangerous man, and he has very dangerous friends. He is not one to be played with."

"That's our problem," said Paul. "So, where do we find Bosak?"

"He drives a gray Range Rover. It is the only one like it around here."

The pop of a rifle was barely noticeable. The look of surprise on the man's weathered face was not. Before he could touch the wound on his side, another bullet hit him in the neck, his artery spewing blood.

Tanner and Paul dropped to the ground, looking toward the top of the barn where the shots came from. Both regretted leaving their weapons in the buggy.

The tour guide pushed the young couple to the ground behind a picnic bench. But John and Dot ran toward Tanner and Paul with pistols in their hands, shooting toward the roof of the barn. They pushed a nearby table over and Tanner and Paul did not hesitate to join them.

Paul seemed unsurprised by the fact this middle-aged couple were packing heat and knew how to use it. Tanner wondered why they were carrying a backpack around. Now he knew.

The shooter was now visible on the roof behind his sniper rifle. John and Dot were exchanging shots with him. As they did, a gray Range Rover bolted from behind the barn.

"Bosak!" yelled Tanner.

John told them, "Dot and I will cover you. Go after him."

With John and Dot firing at the sniper, Paul and Tanner ran to their buggy. Paul started it, put it in gear and they sped off.

The Range Rover was far away, but visible in the open meadow. Although Bosak's vehicle could run through rough terrain, the buggy could take shortcuts that minimized the distance.

Tanner held tightly to the sides of the buggy to keep from falling out as they hit one bump after another. He had to ask Paul, "You knew John and Dot were support right from the beginning, didn't you?"

"I thought they were, but was sure of it when we stopped by the river."

Tanner grinned. "I thought you were telling each other more than just a weather report."

"You're catching on. It may be a cliché, but we do use weather talk to verify each other."

"Now, what do we do when we catch him?"

"Well, he's not shooting at us."

"Somehow," Tanner said, patting the backpack with their weapons. "I wish he was."

"Easy, Tanner. We have to take him alive."

After a slight rise in the road, Paul and Tanner saw a cabin in a grove of trees which appeared to be little more than a small hunting lodge. Bosak was headed straight for it. He reached the lodge, stopped his Range Rover, got out and walked a few feet to the building. Without even looking back, he entered.

Paul stopped the buggy a hundred feet away from the lodge. He and Tanner stepped out with their pistols in hand pointed up. No one tried to stop them as they walked toward the door. That was worrisome. Paul took a position with his back to the wall with the door on the right. He nodded to Tanner, who kicked the door open. Both he and Paul ran in with guns at the ready.

Bosak, unperturbed, sat in a large leather chair facing away from the men, looking at a fireplace where a small fire burned. The single room made up the whole lodge with no place for an accomplice to hide.

"You could have knocked," said Bosak between puffs on his cigar, but not turning. Tanner had his gun trained on the back of Bosak's head as Paul carefully walked around to face the seated man. Bosak showed no sign of a weapon, but Paul kept his pistol trained on him.

"You're coming with us," said Paul.

"I don't think so," calmly replied Bosak.

Paul didn't expect this.

What did the man have up his sleeve?

"I believe that Mr. Tanner is the man standing behind me, is he not?"

Neither man said anything, but Bosak picked up a cell phone lying beside the chair on a small table. He touched an icon and held up the phone. "There is a guest of ours that would like to speak to you."

Paul lowered his gun and took the phone from Bosak. He held it so Tanner could see it as well. On the screen was a montage terrorist use for hostage videos. A brute stood with an assault weapon in hand and a hostage seated in front of him. The hostage was Lizzy Rodriquez.

Lizzy could see Tanner in this video session.

"Hi, honey," she said. "I'm afraid I'm in a bit of a jam."

Chapter 20

"YOU'VE BEEN TO VENICE BEFORE?" Nick asked Rachael as Guido sped them across the open water toward the city.

"My folks brought me here as a little girl. Mother loved the city. She was a violinist and we went to every music venue the city offered."

"So, you remember the music. Anything else?"

Rachael seemed embarrassed to share her comment, but went ahead. "The city smelled bad."

Nick laughed. "That was the complaint years ago, but they've kept the canals clean and they don't smell anymore. Odd things to top your memory list. Music and stink."

"Hey, I was eight-years-old."

Guido listened to the conversation with amusement. At first, he thought Rachael and Nick made an odd couple. She, so much younger than Nick, and so smart. A college professor. Guido knew Nick relished a challenge, and perhaps that was the attraction.

Guido asked, "Do you want to go to your hotel?"

Nick glanced at Rachael. "I think we should meet Dowd first, don't you?"

Rachael was eager to meet Dowd. She sensed he had a personal role in all that had happened: the break-in, the attempt on Nick's life, Christine's murder. Perhaps he wasn't the perpetrator, but she suspected some connection. She wanted to make her own assessment of the man. She nodded her head in the affirmative.

Nick beckoned to Guido, "Head over to the Mose project at the Lido inlet. You know the place, right?"

"Of course," returned Guido. "I'll take your things to your hotel after I drop you off. Does Signor Dowd know you are coming?"

"Yes. I called him earlier."

Rachael pondered.

So, Nick already set this up. The hotel first was not an option.

As the boat approached the Mose gates, it was as if space aliens had occupied the area with huge machines, far out of scale with any building across the lagoon. Among them was a red contraption resembling those used to load transfer truck sized boxes onto container ships, but twice as large.

"Impressive, isn't it?" Nick asked Rachael. Nick was among a few, select people who had been there before. It wasn't a tourist stop.

"That must be for placing the concrete caissons in place," said Rachael.

"I see you've done your homework."

"Of course."

As they neared the dock, Dowd walked toward them. Dowd wore dark gray, silk pants and a matching shirt. Rachael thought he looked like Doctor No.

Two men tied the boat up and placed a set of steps beside it. Guido stayed by the controls as Rachael and Nick exited. Rachael was first. Introducing himself, Dowd took her hand in a strong handshake, his left hand over hers as they shook. A generous smile lit Dowd's face as he said, "Doctor Friedman. Such an honor to meet you. I've read your papers on string theory. Fascinating."

Dowd instantly charmed Rachael.

No one outside of a conference has ever told me they read my papers.

Nick knew Dowd's reputation. Yes, he probably did read Rachael's work. And understood it as well. Nick stepped off the boat and stood behind the two with the quip, "Nevin, you never told me you read *my* stuff."

Dowd laughed as he released Rachael's hand and patted Nick on the back like an old friend.

"Nick, you are the least published archeologist I've ever met. But I've read your interviews. You were all over the papers with your discoveries in Brazil years ago, but not so much about the more recent work in New Mexico."

"Well, that was Tom Littleton's discovery, not mine."

Dowd saw through Nick's faux humility. He knew more than Nick realized. His smug expression let Nick know it.

"So, Nick, any news on the stake and its code?"

Nick put on his best poker face. "We're working on it."

Then Dowd turned to Rachael.

"Did Nick get you involved in his adventures, Doctor Friedman?"

"Please call me Rachael, and yes, to some extent."

"And it appears he has you in another. But let me show you around the project. I want you to see what we've done. Please follow me."

Dowd began walking the short distance down the pier.

Nick talked as they walked. "Mose was already a project when you arrived, wasn't it?"

"Yes, it was. It was a troubled project, to put it mildly. I didn't express it that bluntly when I made the presentation at the Excelsior, but it was."

Dowd turned to Rachael. "And you, my dear, did not have the pleasure of seeing the presentation. So, let me provide more information."

They reached a building similar to a trailer on a construction site, but four times as large. Built for temporary use, the rust and wear of the exterior showed it had exceeded its expected life. Dowd opened a door and Nick and Rachael walked in. He guided them to a table on which a model represented the project.

"The principle for this whole project can be thought of like this," said Dowd as he pointed to spots on a raised relief map laid before them. "There is one long peninsula and two narrow islands that stand in front of the Venetian lagoon like natural barrier reefs. They form just three openings to the Adriatic. The tides of the lagoon ebb and flow with those of the Adriatic because of these openings. Imagine if you wanted to block those openings to mitigate the tides, and you did so by placing steel gates across each of them. But you wouldn't want those gates there all the time. So, you make them hollow and sink them beneath the sea floor. When you need them, you pump air in and, like a submarine, they rise into place."

Dowd turned to another display as Nick and Rachael followed. "Here we have our concept of such gates." The table had a model of a cement caisson with a yellow block held to it by two large hinges. A cutaway of the caisson showed a walkway for worker access. The yellow block looked like welded steel used to make ships.

"This," said Dowd, "is a sample of one caisson and gate. There are multiples of these side by side. We fill the gates with seawater, and they lie flat on the lagoon bed." He looked at Nick. "Nick, the excavation you saw was for these gates. The stake was just beyond where one caisson would rest."

Dowd put a finger on the gate and slowly lifted it. "We pump air into the gate, and it rises on its hinges. Along with the ones beside it, we make a barrier preventing the Adriatic tide from raising the water level of the lagoon."

Rachael was skeptical. "And this really works?"

"In theory, my dear. In theory. It hasn't been put to the test."

"Why not?"

"The Italians had enormous problems. Hinges rusted far more quickly than expected, as did the gates themselves. That's where I came in. I worked in Holland on ceramic paints that preserve metal subject to seawater. I improved the lubricants on the hinge mechanism. And as for the pumps, I'm putting new ones in place. In fact," he said, looking at his watch, "it's time for a demonstration. Please walk with me."

Dowd strolled to a door across from where they entered. They followed him out and stood on a raised platform on the edge of one of the lagoon openings. Dowd gave a quick wave to a man below in orange overalls and construction helmet, a man who appeared to be waiting for him. The man nodded and disappeared.

"What are we looking for?" Rachael asked Dowd.

"Just watch."

Below the rolling waves, a large yellow object appeared under the surface. A minute later the edge of the gate began to surface.

"One of the gates?" Nick asked.

"Yes," responded Dowd.

"It's slow," surmised Rachael.

"Too slow," said Dowd. "Look for the second gate."

The same process began next to the gate just breaking the surface. However, this second gate broke the water and was soon rising higher than the first one.

"The pumps they were using were too slow. The first thing I did was to develop a faster and more efficient one. We've replaced all the existing pumps in the openings to our south and these are being replaced now. We will be ready to test the whole system in two days."

Nick had booked a suite at the Gritti Palace and kept it while he was away. He arranged to have a room for Rachael on the same floor. It was thought by many to be the best hotel in Venice, in spite of the fact the first level was heavily damaged in the flood. Extensive rehabilitation work was done, but traces of flood lines here and there on woodwork persisted.

Luckily, the palace was principally stone and marble, resisting the corrosion of the sea.

Nick and Rachael checked in and met later for dinner at the outdoor restaurant on the canal. Across the canal was an iconic view of the Basilica di Santa Maria della Salute. Sitting at the restaurant, one could imagine being a noble of this ancient city appraising his domain.

Nick ordered a fine Montalcino wine.

After ordering the wine, he asked Rachael, "Is your room OK?"

Rachael rolled her eyes. "More than OK."

"Was your luggage in your room?"

"Yes, Guido did a fine job getting it there."

It was not lost on Rachael that Nick had treated her to a gorgeous hotel and now what promised to be a fine dinner. It reminded her of their time in Rome. Although that hotel was far simpler, it was beautifully situated over the lights of the city which had kindled their affair. It was not long ago but now seemed a faint memory.

He's trying to make up.

Here she was in one of the most romantic spots on the globe. Her thoughts wandered, but they were quickly brought back to earth by Nick.

"So, what did you think of Dowd?"

Rachael paused for a second.

"He's charming. He's passionate about what he does. He's full of himself."

Rachael studied Nick as he smiled showing she confirmed his own impression.

Then she added, "He reminds me of you."

She knew Nick didn't expect this opinion, so he had only a lame rebuttal. "But he has more money."

"I never judge a man by how much money he has."

"Spoken by the woman with a trust fund."

Rachael fumed, and Nick realized he had said the wrong thing. He tried to reverse direction.

"Look, Rachael. I'm sorry. It's just all that's gone on has knocked me off course. Christy's death set me back."

"Oh, don't do that!" Rachael sniped.

"Do what?"

"Use the death of that poor woman as an excuse."

Rachael didn't understand the depth of feelings Nick had for 'that poor woman.' He set her straight.

Nick flared at Rachael and banged the table with his fist. Nearby diners took notice.

"I was in love with that woman. She may have been the only woman I truly loved."

Rachael sputtered her defense. "Nick, I'm sorry. I didn't realize…"

"You don't know me," Nick said. "I wouldn't expect you to. When something hurts me, I seal it off. I make it fireproof. When Christy was murdered, I just wanted to get the guy who did it. I wanted to do it in the worst way. I wanted to rip him apart. It was Tanner who brought me around. He convinced me I had too much 'in the game.' Emotion would cause me to jump when I should wait. That was the soldier in Tanner talking to me. I knew he was right.

"So, I put my rage in a fireproof box and set it aside. The mystery of the stake let me do that. I probably would not have been able to control myself otherwise. It's the distraction I needed."

Rachael put her hand on Nick's, still clinched in a fist. "I'm sorry," she said. "Can we start over?"

Nick appeared calmer although Rachael sensed his rage was sealed in a not-so-fireproof box and could re-emerge at any time.

"Sure," was his simple response.

Picking up the menu, she said, "What looks good?"

"Besides my dinner companion?" Nick said with a wink.

Rachael smiled.

The old Nick's back.

"Focus Nick. Food."

As Nick looked at his menu, Rachael studied the man. She thought his roguish compliment likely to be a knee-jerk reaction for a man who'd made such comments a million times. His time with her in Boston allowed Rachael to take peeks beneath the cavalier crust of the man, but only superficially.

Would he allow her in further?

She played to Nick's patrician instincts, at least for now.

"Everything looks great. Why don't you order?"

"You sure?" Nick asked. It was unlike Rachael not to take charge.

She nodded.

The waiter came by.

"We'll start with the black spaghetti, sea-urchins, candied peppers friggitelli and then the cuttlefish and veal tripes."

The waiter responded with a crisp, "*eccellente*" and "*prego*" as Nick returned the menus to him.

Rachael smiled at Nick's confident ordering. He knew he was being the man for her, something she usually disdained. But not now.

Maybe Venice is to blame.

The meal gave Nick a chance to learn more about Rachael's growing up. He already knew her father was an investment banker and her mother a violinist. Dad had passed away. Mother was still alive and doing well. However, this time she spoke about how she felt. Dad was loving but seldom there. Long hours, little home life. They never celebrated holy days and, knowing friends did, she missed it. She knew there were cousins out there, but she never met them. Her friends talked about their extended families, which made her feel more isolated.

The meal, the wine, the conversation relaxed Nick. He was about to suggest a tiramisu and expresso when a young man walked up. Nick recognized him from the event at the Excelsior. Robert Morrison wore a gray suit, a navy tie, and a white pocket handkerchief. He looked as though he had just walked out of an embassy. The leather briefcase he carried completed the look.

"Mr. Foxe?" he asked.

"Yes? How are you, Mr. Morrison?"

"I am fine. How good of you to remember me. I have something for you. Something from Mr. Allerton."

"What is it?"

"Could we go somewhere private? It's a translation. I think you will be interested."

Chapter 21

NICK LED MORRISON AND RACHAEL to his suite.

After passing through a short hallway with a coat closet to one side, they entered the living room. It was a corner room, decorated in masculine red tones, with views of the Grand Canal to the left. Two red plush chairs faced a renaissance style sofa. A desk was positioned between the two windows. Rachael went to the desk and picked up the letter opener laying there.

"Nice letter opener."

Nick cautioned her. "Careful. It's sharp."

Rachael laid the letter opener back on the desk. Nick chose not to share the origin of the opener, but momentarily felt as though Christy had entered the room.

Morrison placed his briefcase on a chair, brought out a laptop and set it on the coffee table. He took a seat on the couch. Nick and Rachael sat on either side of him. He opened the computer and, as he turned it on, he explained.

"As you may know, Mr. Allerton is on… an assignment. He had in his possession a photo image of a scroll. We've reviewed this scroll. Turns out it was a personal note. From a father to a son. The father, in this case, was a scholar who lived

800 years ago and was under the employ of Frederick the Second."

Nick looked at Rachael and said the name they both knew for this scholar. "Al-Muazzam."

Morrison glanced at Nick.

"We're familiar with your exploits at the Castel del Monte, Mr. Foxe."

Morrison was referring to the operation that led to the Omni. One that Nick thought few people knew about.

"Al-Muazzam performed scholarly work, most of it in Latin. This document is not one of them. Here it is," he said as he pointed to a photo image of the scroll that came up on the screen.

"As you can see, it is written in Arabic. Not only that, it is 800-year-old conversational Arabic in a dialect we had to decipher. However, we did it."

He turned to his briefcase, pulled out a document and handed it to Nick. It was two pages in neatly typed English.

"Although the translation is in English," Morrison continued, "it still holds a mystery or two. Most is chit-chat between a father and his son. Apparently, the father was proud of the son. He was sending him a gift of sixteen matched swords, probably provided to him by Frederick. A poor scholar would not have such a possession.

"Here is the unclear part: The father says the swords hold the key to unlock immense power. One sword contains a code that holds the key. But, he tells his son that the code is just a beginning. One must take it further. One must take it, as he puts it, 'as far as the sides of the Lord's towers.' That's it. No other information. What could the old man mean?"

Nick had a suspicion but did not express it. He did not betray himself and replied, "I have no idea."

Rachael thought Nick was playing it straight, but she believed they were thinking the same thing.

Morrison went on. "That is all we got from the scroll; however, the story continues in other historical records. In the Byzantine-Venetian war, the emperor presented the ruler of Venice with a peace offering of sixteen swords. They were 'for his palace,' wherever that might be."

"What else?" Nick asked.

Morrison shrugged his shoulders. "That's it."

He stood to face Nick.

"We think this is important. Allerton thought it important. He left instructions to bring this to you the moment we had a translation.

"Here is my card," Morrison said as he handed him a business card bearing contact information at the British consulate. "Please let me know when you have any idea what this all might mean."

"Will do," said Nick as Morrison shook his hand.

"Doctor Friedman," Morrison said with a nod.

Nick walked Morrison to the door and closed it. He turned to Rachael, this time, not concealing his excitement.

"Are you thinking what I'm thinking?" he asked.

"I'm thinking the 'enormous power' this code unlocks is one for the Energy Machine. But, Nick, how could that be? The Energy Machine wasn't mentioned on The Tablet. That's all al-Muazzam had to go on. It wasn't until the Omni that we knew about it ourselves, and al-Muazzam didn't have access to that."

Nick contemplated for a moment and responded, "I just feel it in my gut. I think you do too."

"Why don't we call Tom and discuss it?"

"Good idea."

Nick took his cell phone from his pocket and called Tom. He put the phone on speaker.

Tom answered on the first ring.

"Hi, Nick, what's up?"

"Tom, I have Rachael here. You translated The Tablet using al-Muazzam's lexicon we found in the chamber under the Castel del Monte. I didn't think we knew about the existence of an Energy Machine until we found the Omni, true?"

Nick and Rachael could hear the disappointment in Tom's response when he replied, "Nick, didn't you read the entire translation?"

"Well, did I miss something?"

"Yeah, you did."

"What?"

"The Tablet does not mention the existence of a machine that can change seawater into power. It's true we didn't know about that until the Omni. However… Wait, I'm here in the lab with Omni. Let me have her tell you.

"Omni."

"Yes, Tom?" came the female voice Nick and Rachael heard in the lab.

"What does the original tablet say about converting seawater into energy?"

"While The Tablet does not state it, it references a code that will transform matter into power."

Rachael was dumbfounded and asked like the physicist she was. "That sounds like nuclear power."

Omni heard Rachael and replied, "It is not atomic power. Yet, it can be powerful."

Nick had to ask an obvious question. "Omni, what is the code?"

"I do not have that information."

"Don't you have all the information in the world?"

"Did you discover me only after you had passed tests?"

"Well, yes," admitted Nick

"This is another test."

"So, you know the answer, but you're not telling?"

"No, I do not. My creators left blanks that you must fill in."

Nick looked at Rachael. "So, they are putting us to the test once again. I hate it when that happens."

Tom asked, "What's this all about anyhow?"

Nick filled him in.

When Nick finished, he announced to Rachael, "We're going on a tour."

Preston Smith waited in a sidewalk café near the Gritti Palace. Nevin Dowd's henchman wore a tan suit with a matching fedora. He looked like a character from a Humphrey Bogart movie, but not a heroic one. Morrison came and sat down on the other side of the table. Smith continued to sip his *café americano* unperturbed. Without acknowledging Morrison, he asked, "Did you deliver the package?"

"Yes."

"And?"

"I think we'll get what we want."

Chapter 22

THE DOGE PALACE is the iconic anchor in Saint Mark's Square and the symbol of Venetian power. For centuries, ships entering the city passed by the palace. It housed the representatives of the republic and their elected leader, the doge. Today, this masterpiece of gothic architecture is the first stop for day trippers, second only to feeding the pigeons in the square.

Guido joined Nick and Rachael in front of the palace. Nick filled in Guido about what they were looking for and asked Guido to book them an extended tour the next day. They asked for the 'extended tour' because the general tour wouldn't do. What they needed to see was accessible only on the more exclusive tour. Guido pulled strings and booked Nick and Rachael on the next one. Nick thanked Guido and told him he would catch up with him later.

The tour began in the basement of the palace, in the prison cells, and worked its way up into the rafters, the suspected resting place for what they sought.

Nick had taken this tour years ago during a private event. However, this time was new for Rachael. Nick took pleasure in seeing things through her eyes.

The prison cells, though not exactly in the basement, were near water level and were likely filled with seawater during flooding. The walls were composed of cold, damp, stone blocks. Rachael had seen worse in medieval castles. The quality of the cell reflected the social standing of its occupant. As they reached the next level, they came upon a room within a room. Beneath a ceiling supported by heavy wood beams, a wooden cabin was built against one wall. This cabin had thick iron bars across its one window and heavy wooden slats locking the door from the outside. The guide said this was the cell of Giacomo Casanova.

Nick added some of his own commentary for Rachael's enjoyment.

"Casanova led the good life in the 18th century. That was when Venice was the center of trade in this part of the world and rich with night life. It was a must-do stop on the grand tour for young English noblemen."

"So, you know a lot about Casanova? Why am I not surprised?"

"It's just a part of history."

"And his history got him into this accommodation, apparently."

"True," said Nick, "and he was only thirty years old."

Rachael could not help but notice how Nick punctuated that statement with an exhale reserved for admiration.

"And here you are, and none of your exploits have yet landed you in jail."

"Not yet."

The tour continued through the upper reaches of the palace to a large room where the ceiling edges were adorned with portraits of past doges hanging side-by-side.

"Which one received the swords?" Rachael asked.

"That guy right there," Nick said, pointing to the portrait of a sharp-nosed man with a pointed black beard dressed in the red robes of his office. "Pietro Gradenigo. He was the doge when things settled down with Constantinople in 1302. Most likely he received the swords."

"And according to the history we know, al-Muazzam's swords wound up in the ruler's palace."

Nick smiled. "And that would be here."

The tour moved along into one fabulous room after another, adorned with magnificent paintings. Despite seeing all this for the first time, Rachael was eager to get to their final spot.

The tour ended in the attic. Not called that by the tour guide, this area, nestled beneath the rafters of a wooden roof, was the armory. For a huge palace of marble and stone, Rachael was surprised to see so much made of wood. Huge wooden beams supported the roof. She thought it more like a grandmother's attic. One in which granny kept armaments.

There were dozens of sword displays, each set in fanned arrangements of sixteen. It overwhelmed Rachael. She whispered to Nick, "How can we possibly find the right one? There're hundreds here. They're all alike."

Nick said nothing. He focused on each case as he roamed the room.

Rachael joined him.

What is he looking for?

Nick stopped. "It's one of these."

Rachael saw no difference. "How can you tell?"

"I'll let you know later," he whispered.

When the tour ended, the participants dispersed into the courtyard flanked by the palace on three sides and facing the San Marco Cathedral on the fourth. Guido and Commissario Russo waited near the fountain in the middle of the courtyard. Nick thought them to be an odd couple. Guido had remarkable reach into police business, but Nick doubted it was through official sources like Russo. Rachael had never met Russo nor knew of the information Guido provided, so she was curious to know who Guido's friend was. Nick escorted her to them.

Guido spoke first. "Doctor Friedman, I would like to introduce you to someone Nick already knows well, Commissario Bruno Russo."

Russo took Rachael's hand. "Doctor Friedman. So good to meet you."

"Please, call me Rachael."

"Rachael. So smart, I expected. So beautiful, I did not."

Nick envied how Italians could blandish compliments that would make an American woman roll her eyes if they were uttered by him.

Russo's charming, but why is he here?

Guido answered Nick's thoughts. "Commissario Russo has some information he wants to share with you."

"Should we be headed to the police station?" asked Nick.

"No," responded Russo. "It is unnecessary. It was a nice day. I wanted to get out of my office. There is an office here we can use. Step this way."

Nick didn't buy it, but followed Russo.

He wasn't out for fresh air. He wants to tell us something where no one's listening.

Russo led them to one side of the piazza where a huge wooden door lay open. He led them past a man in a guard uniform at a desk who nodded to Russo in recognition before returning to his paperwork. They entered an office furnished with a wooden desk dinged from countless small injuries and four side chairs covered in green leather, nicked and torn at the edges. Guido pulled the chairs together facing each other. Russo took one of them with a '*prego*' to Guido.

Russo pointed to the other chairs. "Please sit."

Guido took the chair beside Russo. Nick and Rachael took the ones opposite them.

"How did it go, your tour? Good, yes?" asked Russo.

"Very good," responded Nick who figured Russo suspected someone like him didn't do tours. So, he added, "Rachael had never been through the Doge Palace."

Staging a wide-eyed response, Russo asked Rachael, "No? Did you enjoy it?"

"Yes, very much."

"It is the gem of our city. Much history there."

Russo's last remark was directed to Nick supported by a suspicious look.

Nick evaluated that look.

Does he know about the sword? What did Guido tell him?

Nick soon learned that Russo's visit had nothing to do with his search for an antiquity.

"Mr. Foxe, we have news about Miss Blake's death."

Nick expected nothing new about Christy's death.

Don't we know everything? Aren't Tanner and Paul hunting down the killer?

Russo continued. "We have the results from the autopsy. Normally we have no surprises in a case like this one. The cause of death was clear. And this is unlikely to be a cause, yet…

"Mr. Foxe, we found a high quantity of benzodiazepine in Miss Blake's blood."

"Benzodiazepine?" Nick asked. The drug meant nothing to Nick, but Rachael's expression of surprise told him she knew.

"A date rape drug," she said.

Nick studied Rachael who seemed to recall a bad memory.

Russo continued. "I am no expert in these things, but I was told that it has no taste or smell, and it is colorless when dissolved in a drink. People who take it can feel very sleepy and confused, and forget what happens after its effects take hold. It can cause weakness and make it difficult to move one's body. The effects can be felt within a few minutes and can last for several hours."

Russo looked Nick in the eye. "Mr. Foxe, do you know who gave her this drug?"

"What? Of course not! Now that I know what it's for, I'm offended that you asked."

Russo put his hands up to deflect Nick's anger.

"I know. I know. But I had to ask. I must admit that I thought of you first when the report came in. But you were out of the country at the time."

He's not ruling me out. He suspects someone did this for me. But the person who last saw her did not work for me.

"Have you talked to Vanessa Fabre?"

"Unfortunately, she is unavailable."

"Unavailable?"

"Yes. She is on her research ship and her office said they were having trouble themselves in reaching her. You can be sure that we will talk with her soon."

Russo rose, signally the end of their conversation.

"It is a delicate question I must ask of Miss Fabre. If she gave the drug to Miss Blake, or if Miss Blake took it of her own accord, I must ask why. I expect that would get into a personal matter. It is clear the drug did not kill her, but loose ends are loose ends and we must address them.

"Doctor Friedman," he said as he shook her hand.

Nick caught Guido's eye and mouthed, "Talk to you later."

Nick walked out with Rachael. Although Rachael had never met Christine or Vanessa, she appeared lost in thought about what she had just heard. Nick broke the silence.

"Rachael, I know you never met Christy or Vanessa. I knew them both from years ago."

"I know."

"I thought of an angle. When someone has a terminal illness, the family tells the doctor they don't want the loved one to suffer."

Rachael didn't see the connection, but humored Nick.

"OK. And?"

"And I think there may be another explanation."

Chapter 23

SHADOWS PLAYED on Saint Mark's Square as Nick and Rachael once again strolled toward the Doge Palace. The palace was closed at this hour. Their entry would be surreptitious.

Guido waited for them near the office where they had met Russo. They exchanged a few whispered words.

"I convinced a friendly guard to let us take an unscheduled tour of the palace. He had to gain cooperation from two men on the night shift," said Guido. "This is an expensive tour my friend."

Nick reassured him. "I'm good for it. You know that."

"I told them nothing would be taken. Was I correct?"

"We need to see something on a sword. We will put it back in its place."

Nick paused. "We may have to open a case. Pick the lock."

Guido smiled. "Perhaps not." He held up a ring with a set of five keys on it.

"They open everything?"

"Of course."

"Guido, you're amazing!"

"I know. Now follow me."

Guido led them along an abbreviated route of the tour they had previously taken. They bypassed the lower cells but walked once again by that of Casanova's. Rachael stopped to appraise it as Nick and Guido continued on. Nick turned and whispered, "Rachael. Come on."

After crossing one of the large sitting rooms, they entered a winding stairwell, one that would take them to the attic. At the top, walking beneath roof beams, they arrived at the armory.

"I'll wait outside to stand guard," said Guido. "Be quick."

Nick had to bend his tall frame to avoid hitting his head on the pitched roof. Although the palace had other armaments on display on lower levels, this is where Nick saw the sword they were after.

To one side, were display cases. Fortunately, the lights were left on as Guido said they would be. Three cases stood side-by-side, all locked. Nick examined each of them but returned to the one in the middle.

"Here they are."

Rachael continued to be puzzled. "How did you know these were the ones?"

"All the others are Venetian swords. These are 13th century crusader swords. Look at the handle and the knob at the top and look at the others over there to the right. See the difference?"

"Ah, yes. It is slight, but there is a difference."

"It's likely al-Muazzam received the swords from his mentor, Frederick the Second. So, when I saw swords like the ones Frederick would have, I knew they had to be the ones. Let's take a closer look."

Nick examined the ring of keys Guido had given him. Most were obviously too large for the lock on the case.

"Looks like it has to be one of these three small keys."

Nick inserted the first one. He did not force it, but it was not right. He tried the second. No luck. He held the third and paused. He held it up to Rachael who shared his thoughts.

All this work. Getting so close. This has to be the key.

Nick put the last key in the lock. It turned. They shared a sigh and a smile at their continued luck.

Nick pulled the glass door open. The case held sixteen swords. Iron rails held the crusader swords so they would fan out. He slid one from the rails. Rachael and he examined the blade as Nick held it. Then, they repeated the examination on the flip side. Nick put the sword back and extracted the next one.

By the time they had gone through twelve swords, Nick had doubts.

"I'm not liking this," he said.

"Maybe what we're looking for isn't on the blade."

Nick came to the last sword. He shrugged and stated the obvious.

"Well, this is the last one."

He pulled it out. Nothing on the first side. He flipped it over, expecting nothing there. But Rachael saw it first.

"There!" she said, pointing to an area close to the hilt. Numbers appeared, less than an inch in height. Nick read them off.

"31415"

"There's a space between the three and the one," Rachael said.

Nick took his finger and rubbed the area. A decimal point became clear. "3.1415"

Rachael knew instantly what the numbers represented.

"Pi."

"What?"

"It's the value for pi, or at least the first few decimal places."

"Oh," said Nick, his disappointment clear.

There must be something more.

Rachael pondered the meaning. "I guess al-Muazzam was waxing poetic when he told his son the code would unleash a great power. I mean, pi is powerful. It's more than just helping you figure the circumference of a circle. In physics, it is a central construct in many formulas."

Rachael continued on with her recitation on pi. Perhaps it was Rachael's mathematics monologue or Nick's focus on the mystery that prevented them from hearing the slight creak of steps on the wooden floor. Maybe they were too at ease knowing Guido stood guard. They did not expect the unwelcomed guest who entered the room.

Nick, lost in his own reasoning, had an ah-hah moment. It made perfect sense.

"Rachael," he said letting her come to a rolling stop in her monologue.

"I have it. I know what it means. How we can use it."

A new voice in the room interrupted him.

"Well, do tell."

It was Robert Morrison. He had a revolver trained on them.

Nick stood, holding the sword slightly raised, a natural reflex from his college fencing days.

Morrison smirked. "Well, my friend, it appears you've brought a knife to a gunfight."

Then Morrison smiled wickedly as though some hideous idea just popped into his head.

"Back away," he said.

Nick and Rachael moved back. Morrison pulled another sword from the display with his left hand and returned to where he had been standing. He now had the sword in his left hand and the revolver in his right.

"To make this fun, I will give you a sporting chance," he said as he slid the revolver into his shoulder holster and took the sword in his right hand. He struck a pose. *"En garde!"*

"I can't believe I'm doing this," Nick told Rachael.

Nick lifted his sword and advanced with a stomp of his foot to distract his opponent. Morrison was not distracted.

The two executed a series of advances and parries, moving back and forth and soon came body to body. Morrison's smug expression disappeared. Nick pushed him back.

Rachael could not stand by. She took a third sword from the display and advanced into the fight. Morrison sneered at the sight, but Rachael advanced with a series of thrusts. Morrison could see this woman was a threat.

Nick smiled, keeping his eye on Morrison, but working in tandem with Rachael.

"I see someone else took fencing in college."

Rachael embellished. "Took trophies, too."

Morison was good. Very good. He was alternating expertly between his two opponents. Nick was rusty in his form. He had fenced with the *épée* in college. This sword was a saber. Morison used expert, slashing moves for which that weapon was designed. Nick knew it was a matter of stabbing

Morrison in the lungs or heart before Morrison slashed Nick's throat.

Rachael was spot on. She matched Morrison's saber moves with those of her own. Morrison would normally have enjoyed one or the other, but not both. They were getting the best of him. Rachael followed a feint with a lunge. The feint, a false attack, startled Morrison. He'd underestimated the woman before him.

Morrison's expression turned grim. He had been cavalier, enjoying his sport. Now, he appeared determined to kill. He clumsily pulled his pistol from the holster while continuing his attack. When he pointed it toward his opponents, Nick slashed across Morrison's wrist, drawing blood. Morrison dropping the pistol, advanced toward both of them.

Morrison's slashing became wild, hitting the display case. Nick glanced at Rachael. Each knew what the other was thinking.

He's lost his finesse. Let's finish this.

Nick and Rachael had learned each other's rhythm. They attacked in an oscillating series of lunges, backing Morrison to where he first surprised them.

Morrison never saw Guido, who held a large brass bucket above him with both arms. Guido came down on Morrison's head with the bucket. The brass rang like a bell, and Morrison collapsed in a heap.

Nick and Rachael rushed up to him. Guido was swaying as though he had too much to drink.

Nick smiled. "You're getting good at bashing people's heads in."

Rachael put her fingers to Morrison's neck.

"He's alive. The slash on his wrist is hardly bleeding."

"Guido, what happened? Where were you?"

"This bastard," he said, pointing to the unconscious Morrison, "snuck up behind me and put a chloroform rag on my face."

"Knocked you out?"

"Not quite. I held my breath and fell down. I got enough to make me lose my senses. By the time I cleared my head, you all were playing with the swords."

"Not exactly playing," Nick corrected.

Guido, now clearheaded, acted the father of naughty children. "Have you finished here?"

"Yes, we have what we need."

"Well, put things back the way you found them and let's go."

"How about him?" Rachael said, still kneeling beside Morrison.

Guido took charge. "I'll take care of that on the way out."

Nick carefully returned the swords to the case and re-locked it.

They followed Guido out the same way they came in. This time, when they walked through the grand room, there was a guard at one corner.

"Wait here," said Guido who then walked over to the guard. He said something in Italian to the man who looked at Nick and Rachael and turned back to Guido. They could tell that the guard asked if he was sure about them and Guido confirmed that he was. The guard left and Guido returned.

"Did you ask him how he let Morrison in?" Nick asked.

"No, I trust the man. There are several ways up to the armory he could have used."

"Then what did you tell him?"

"I told him there had been a break-in in the armory, and he must call the police.

"Now, let's make our way out."

Nick and Rachael sat at a restaurant table on Saint Mark's Square across from the palace. Guido left to follow-up with the police on the reported break-in. Nick had ordered a Spritz for each of them.

Nick reflected on what happened. "Guido is great at taking care of loose ends."

He lifted his glass to Rachael. "Here's to Guido."

After a sip, Rachael set her glass down. She wanted to clear up what Nick had said earlier when he saw the numbers on the sword.

"So, how is a simple depiction of the value of pi such a valuable clue?"

"Just those five digits, nothing. But when you put it together with what al-Muazzam told his son in the scroll, it's everything."

"What do you mean?"

"Let's call Tom. I want him to hear this too."

Chapter 24

RACHAEL RETURNED WITH NICK to his hotel room to call Tom. His holding back on what pi was all about annoyed her.

Why all the drama? This better be good.

Nick reached Tom by phone and put the call on speaker.

"Tom, how's it coming with finding the other stakes?"

"I have what I need in place. All we need now is to have you and Rachael get near one of the stakes, the one you found, and play an A note."

"I'm working on that."

Rachael shot Nick a look that told him she didn't believe he had done anything in that direction.

Nick responded to her expression of doubt. "Well, I am. Really."

Turning his attention back to Tom, he said, "I have good news. I have the code that turns the Energy Machine on once we locate it."

"I'm all ears."

"It's pi."

"Huh?"

"The code left by al-Muazzam is the value of pi."

"3.14?"

"Actually, al-Muazzam left a fairly good representation of it to four decimal places, but it doesn't end there. He told his son in a letter that the code is just a beginning. It must be taken further, as far as the sides of the Lord's towers."

"The Lord God?"

Rachael now realized what Nick understood and why it was such a delicious puzzle.

"No, Tom," she said. "al-Muazzam's lord."

"Federico Secondo!" exclaimed Tom, who had been the team's leader at the Castel del Monte where they found al-Muazzam's translations. "The towers were eight sided."

"So," Nick summized, "the number of decimal places must be eight."

Rachael reflected on the elegance of the code.

"This makes so much sense," she said. "All along the way, the ancients who left us The Tablet, the Omni, and now, apparently, the Energy Machine, have been testing how advanced we are. The Greek symbol for pi wasn't used until three-hundred years ago, but we have known the ratio it represents at least as far back as the Egyptians. But it was never precisely known, certainly not when al-Muazzam was alive. He did well to represent it as four decimal places. Only modern mathematical theories have given more precision, especially when calculations were done by modern computers."

"Yeah, I knew that," teased Nick. Nick knew archeology. Rachael was the undisputed mathematician in the room. She punched him in the shoulder.

"So," said Tom bringing his teammates back to earth, "What do we do with the code? Swim down to the machine when we find it and turn some tumblers?"

"Maybe," said Nick. "But the code the ancients left us sounds like music. I'm betting if we produce the sound that represents each digit…" Nick paused. "We have a translation for digits, do we not?"

It was Rachael, who had been studying the formulas and counting systems of the ancients, who answered.

"Yes, we do. It's a base-eight system, not a base-ten like our own, but we can easily convert it. Isn't that right, Tom?"

"Sure. No problem."

"OK," said Nick. "Rachael and I will work on getting to the stake. We'll coordinate with you when we're ready to turn the beacons on. The Omni told us we have twenty-four hours to find them, but the closer we coordinate, the better."

"I'm standing by. By the way, something else. Have either of you talked to Lizzy today?"

Nick looked at Rachael who shook her head.

"No, why?" she asked.

"I called her. No answer. She usually likes to stop by, but I haven't seen her."

Nick thought nothing of it and blithely answered, "She's probably out sightseeing."

Rachael didn't like it. Her instinct flashed a warning. "Nick, I'm not so sure. With Tanner away, I think she may not be safe."

"Why do you think that?"

Rachael thought Nick was having one of his denser moments. "I don't know. Maybe it's Tom being shot, an attempt on your life, twice if you count our little sword play, Christine's death, Tanner being who knows where…"

"OK, OK," Nick said. "I get it."

Nick turned his attention back to Tom. "Tom, TIGRIS has a guard at Lizzy's place, don't they?"

"Yes, just like my place."

"Why don't you contact Director Birchmeier and have him check things out?"

"Sure thing. I'll do it as soon as we hang up."

"Which is now. Will talk again soon."

Nick disconnected.

"Don't worry, Rachael. You saw how the Swiss were all over things. They'll let us know something soon."

"Hope so."

"Now, let's go for a boat ride."

Chapter 25

LIZZY'S QUARTERS WERE TOLERABLE, for a dungeon. The walls were built of medieval stone, massive gray blocks mortared together, but the cell itself was furnished like Sherlock Holmes' study. A rich Persian rug softened the stone floor on which sat two comfortable overstuffed leather chairs. Behind one of the chairs stood a tall reading lamp, the glare muted by a Tiffany shade. A wooden bookcase holding a hundred classics, none published after 1940, stood against a wall. Over to one corner was a bed the size of a prison bunk covered with silk sheets and a comforter. The rest of the room was bare save for a partition behind which an 1890 Parisian belle would have changed clothes. The screen provided privacy for the toilet and sink behind it. On one side of the sink lay an embroidered toilet kit containing all the necessities a woman might want.

Looks like they were expecting me.

To the right of the incarceration toilet convenience was a window with heavy bars allowing outside air to drift through. Standing on her tiptoes, Lizzy could see a short vista to the sea. Waves rolled over rocks a hundred feet below.

Not getting out of here that way.

She felt like a caged animal in a habitat someone thought fit for a lady. The creature comforts of the cell ended at the bars in front. The bars were not medieval at all, but up to date with a rolling door opened by a magnetic card on a keypad. She saw it in operation when the guard came with her dinner. The man looked like Tweedledee saddened by the loss of Tweedledum. Tweedledee, dressed in gray overalls, waddled over to her cell and pulled a plastic card from a cord retractor clipped on his side pocket. He placed it on the keypad and slid the door to the left and entered the cell. He had a tray on a cart and placed it on the table beside the chair.

"Food," was his singular comment.

Lizzy tried to jolly him up with a volley of harmless questions.

"Hi, what's your name? Been here long? What's going on?"

Nothing in return from Tweedledee.

The food was fish and vegetables, well prepared, but Lizzy wasn't hungry.

After being snatched from her place in Basel, Lizzy snapped out of her induced snooze to find herself on a small private plane. She remained quiet, faking her continued sleep. Her captors said little, much to her disappointment. She had no clue who her abductors were. They removed her from the plane after an hour ride. No longer faking and fully awake, she was blindfolded, and her hands were cuffed behind her back. Someone pushed a gun between her shoulder blades and walked her to a helicopter. As the helicopter took off, Lizzy managed glimpses beneath her blindfold of the ocean below.

This is no two-bit kidnapper. Should I feel honored?

Still no communication, although Lizzy tried her best to start a conversation. They came to a stop and removed her blindfold. Lizzy found herself in an ancient castle on an island. It reminded her of Tanner's adventure with the others at a castle in Italy.

After an hour or two pacing around her limited surroundings and leaving her food untouched, a small, mysterious man entered the hallway accompanied by a tall guy in black carrying an AK-47. Lizzy loved old detective movies and the tall guy was ushering in a character from The Maltese Falcon. Even the tan suit he wore looked retro.

Tweedledee snapped to attention upon the man's arrival and hurried ahead of him to the cell. While Tweedledee pulled out the card key to unlock it, the small man smiled at Lizzy. It reminded her of the smile from a kid from the trailer park where she once lived. The kid liked to pull the legs off grasshoppers.

With the cell door open, the man and his guard walked in. The man extended his hand to Lizzy and introduced himself.

"Hello, I'm Preston Smith."

Lizzy looked at the outstretched hand with disdain and Smith withdrew it, wiping it on his coat as though Lizzy dirtied it.

"Have a seat, Miss Rodriguez," he said pointing to a chair.

Smith made himself comfortable in one while Lizzy remained standing.

Smith forced out a "Please?" and Lizzy took her seat.

"You may wonder why we brought you here."

"The thought crossed my mind."

Smith grinned as though he was about to let Lizzy know Christmas would be early this year.

"You have a part to play in one of the greatest discoveries of our age."

"Yeah?" Lizzy asked in her cavalier manner. "Been there. Done that."

It was not a small claim considering Lizzy's previous experience with Nick's team. However, Smith was not amused.

"I know your past, Miss Rodriguez. You've been close to greatness, but just a backup singer. When The Tablet was discovered in Carlsbad, you were keeping house for Mr. Foxe. I bet you never even saw it. When his team secured the codebook from the castle in Italy, you didn't arrive until later that night, after the deed was done. When everyone else found the Omni in that grotto, you remained behind on a yacht."

Smith's command of facts few people knew unnerved the usually nervy Lizzy. She tried not to let it show.

"So?" she said.

"So, you have a chance now to take center stage. We have a great opportunity for you."

"Like what?"

"Be patient, Miss Rodriguez. I work for someone who will make it all clear to you."

"Meanwhile, you'll try to make me accept this 'opportunity' by keeping me locked up in here?"

"A mere technicality. We cannot take chances until we're sure you're onboard."

The guard put his hand up to an earpiece listening to an unseen person. Smith looked at him expectantly. In a moment, the guard told Smith, "He's ready."

"Excellent!" cackled Smith. "Perfect timing."

He stood and asked Lizzy, "Won't you walk with me?"

Lizzy glanced at the guard and then at the AK-47.

"I guess I would be delighted, right?"

Smith led Lizzy down the hall with the guard behind her. At the end of the hall was a stainless-steel door with a small window. Smith opened the door and waved Lizzy in.

Central to the room was a dentist chair. Looking at the various unfriendly implements around the room, it was clear the work done here was not dental and likely without the benefit of Novocain. Lizzy had a hard time hiding her uneasiness. Smith noticed her concern.

"Don't worry. That chair is for bad little girls. Your seat is here," he said pointing to a simple office chair. The chair faced a small camera on a tripod with a tablet computer mounted beside it. Walking over to the chair, Lizzy took note of an item on the tray beside the dental chair that would come in handy.

"Please have a seat," directed Smith.

Lizzy did as she was told, noticing activity on the tablet screen. Someone on the other end of this little broadcast, carried a camera around showing the interior of a cabin. She noticed a deer head mounted on the wall. Then a rough-looking man with an ear injury appeared on the screen smoking a cigar.

"They're coming," the man said. "Should be here soon."

Then the screen went dark as though the man had laid the camera face-down on a table.

Smith adjusted the screen so that Lizzy saw a thumbnail video of herself in the lower right corner of the tablet screen.

They all waited patiently for a couple of minutes. Then they heard the man on the other end say, "There is a guest of ours who would like to speak to you."

It surprised Lizzy to see Tanner and someone she didn't know appear on the screen. Tanner seemed equally surprised to see her.

"Hi, honey," she said. "I'm afraid I'm in a bit of a jam."

"Who's got you?" asked Tanner.

Smith hit a switch before Lizzy could answer, and now the camera focused on Smith.

"You'll soon find out," said Smith. "Just do as Mr. Bosak directs and no harm will come to Miss Rodriguez. You will soon be reunited. We have an offer for you. Sorry we had to resort to these theatrics, but I assure you the offer will be worth it. That's all for now. See you soon."

Smith gave his bug-torturing grin.

"Won't that be delightful?" Smith asked Lizzy. "You and your boyfriend will soon be reunited."

Lizzy said nothing but returned Smith a vibrant look of disdain as the guard took her arm and helped her from her chair. As she walked out with the guard, she tripped near the dental chair and knocked the tray of instruments to the floor.

"Clumsy me," she said as she knelt and began to pick up items and put them on the tray.

Annoyed, Smith barked, "Never mind that!" and the guard lifted her from the floor. Lizzy shook off the guard's grasp and led the parade back to her cell at her own pace. Tweedledee pulled the cell door closed behind her.

Smith, now calm, smiled at Lizzy.

"Well, just sit back and relax. We have reading matter for you. Is there anything else I can provide?"

"Your head on a platter would be nice."

Smith's frown communicated his exasperation at Lizzy's absence of humility or fear. Lizzy knew the type. Smith had led his whole life being minimized. To an already disturbed person, such treatment can make a man dangerous. Lizzy couldn't help challenging his authority over her, and, yes, showing no fear. She knew she was baiting him.

With no other word, Smith huffed and walked away with the guard trailing behind. Tweedledee resumed his position in a chair and looked exhausted by the exchange. Lizzy walked behind the partition in her cell. She removed the item she took from the tray after she knocked it over and smiled.

Just what I need!

Chapter 26

NICK THOUGHT GUIDO favored this particular mask shop. It was the second time Guido wanted a private meeting here.

Did a cousin own it?

This time Rachael was included in the conversation.

Guido waited near the register where the shopkeeper was putting final touches on a Venetian mask. Rachael watched, with fascination, the extraordinary craftsmanship displayed by the shopkeeper who smiled at her interest in his trade. Guido and Nick stood aside, amused at Rachael's rapture.

Guido turned to Nick. "We need to talk about your friend, Mr. Dowd."

"Oh, what do you have?" Nick relished Guido's mastery of being in the know.

"Let's go in back."

Nick got Rachael's attention with a simple nod in the direction Guido was headed.

Rachael put her hand on the craftsman's shoulder and said, "*magnifico*." It may not have been a common Italian comment of praise, but the man appreciated it from this attractive woman and returned a "*prego*."

Rachael joined Nick and Guido in the back room. Guido looked around as if spies were everywhere.

"How well do you know Nevin Dowd?" he asked Nick.

"I hardly know him at all. Met him at the opera and the affair at the Excelsior. Took a tour underwater at Mose and later above water with Rachael.

Guido turned to Rachael. He was old school and trusted the instincts of a woman to see things about a man others may miss. She was brief.

"He craves adoration."

Nick raised an eyebrow. He never thought of Dowd that way, but he realized Rachael's succinct appraisal was on the mark. Guido smiled approvingly.

"He is also quite, what you American's call, a smooth operator, is he not?"

Nick snickered at the term. "Yes, I guess you could call him that."

Rachael shot Nick an amused look. "Takes one to know one."

Nick knew Rachael enjoyed placing the occasional barb in her conversation and took this one in stride.

"Do you mean smooth as in debonair or smooth as in con man?" Nick asked her, but Guido's interjection answered it.

"Some think it is the last one," he said.

"Con man?"

"What is it that Mr. Dowd is doing here?" Guido asked.

Nick knew the obvious answer, but Guido needed to lead him down a not-so-obvious path, so he played along. "He's saving the Mose project. He's using technology he developed in Holland."

"Hmm," Guido considered Nick's comment like a bad stage actor hearing this for the first time. "That must be very expensive."

"He has lots of money."

"But still, he is a businessman. He needs something in return, does he not?"

"The Italian government is paying him."

Guido quickly brushed off Nick's assumption.

"That is a myth. The Italian government is broke."

Nick continued to play Guido's game, but it began to bore him. "Then what?"

Guido wasn't finished playing his game and took an unlikely turn.

"How many people visit your Disneyland in California every year?"

Nick wrinkled his brow, continuing the game as though he thought they were playing poker and Guido changed suddenly to bridge. Rachael smiled. She knew where Guido was going and enjoyed Nick's confusion.

Guido answered his question without waiting for Nick.

"Eighteen Million. And how many tourists visited Venice the year before the pandemic?"

Nick shrugged.

"Twenty Million."

Nick quipped, "So, you've beat the Magic Kingdom."

Guido fumed. "We're not trying!"

"So," said Nick, "I know you have a problem. Too many tourists, but the pandemic dropped it to zero."

"We recovered. Like I told you at the airport, we got through the plague in the old days. We got through the virus. The cruise ships are coming back. We must prepare for them."

Where does Dowd come into this?"

Rachael spoke up. "I know the Cinque Terre had a similar problem with overcrowding. They started selling tickets to admit tourists."

Nick, who thought he was the expert on Italy, was surprised by Rachael's tidbit.

"How do you know that?"

"Keep up, Nick," she said and then turned to Guido.

"Are the Venetians considering doing the same thing?"

Guido had just met this woman, but her quick mind impressed him.

Nick has met his match.

"Indeed, they are," said Guido. "And the rumor is your Mr. Dowd will have a part of the action, you might say."

"Rumor?" asked Nick.

Guido modified his word choice.

"Better than rumor."

"So," said Nick, "Nevin Dowd is planning to turn Venice into his own personal Disneyland?"

Guido expressed his pain through a shudder, as his body ran cold at the concept.

"Please, I cannot imagine it."

"It cost over a hundred dollars a day to enter Disneyland," said Rachael eliciting a look from Nick.

How did she know that?

She responded to Nick's look. "My niece. I took her there last year."

Nick could do the math. "That would be over two-billion dollars a year. Not sure how much of that Dowd would get, but it should pay off his investment quickly."

Then Rachael considered something far darker. "Nick, do you think Christine knew about this?"

Nick had not thought of that possibility, and when Rachael led him there, his mood grew dark.

"What? Would Dowd have her killed?"

Guido added, "People have died for far less than billions of dollars."

Nick paced the floor, angry and confused. "I have to meet the guy in a couple of hours. I want to grab him by the throat and, and..."

Nick struggled to put into words what he wanted to do. Get the truth out of him? Assume the worst and strangle him? He wasn't thinking straight.

"Nick," Rachael said, "we're conjecturing too much. We don't know for sure that Dowd has a deal with the Italians. Did Christine know? So what? She would have to be threatening to expose him. We don't know that. Tanner is looking for the man who killed Christine. I'm sure he'll get him. He's our best bet to see whether or not Dowd hired the killer."

Nick calmed. "Yeah, yeah. Guess you're right."

"Look, we already suspect Dowd had something to do with the Omni break-in and that he wants the Energy Machine. Shouldn't we pursue that first?"

Nick refocused on the matter at hand.

"Which reminds me," he said, "Let's get back to Tom and see how he's doing locating the Energy Machine."

Nick and Rachael sat in Nick's suite at the Gritti Palace with a laptop open before them. Tom's face appeared on the other side of their video session.

"Do you remember that I worked on a GPS satellite program some time ago?" Tom asked.

Rachael and Nick both knew this and answered together.

"Yes."

"Well, I called in favors and gained some time on a satellite tonight."

"A spy satellite?" asked Nick.

"A satellite," repeated Tom. They were not getting more than that.

"The sensors on the satellite are superb. The guys I worked with said they could detect Ivan smoking a cigarette, let alone a rocket launch. I doubt it could really detect a cigarette, but, if the stakes emit a strong enough infrared beam, it should be able to locate them."

Nick, always impatient said, "Let's get on it!"

"Steady, Nick. I've set everything up, but I want to be sure that ground light interference is at a minimum. So, I need to have you turn the stake beacon on tonight after midnight."

Nick was puzzled. "And how am I going to turn it on?"

"There is a package waiting for you at the desk. I confirmed with the hotel that it's arrived. In it, there is a probe and tether you can lower from a boat. I know you have a man who can provide a boat."

"Sure, no problem. What type of probe are we talking about?"

"It's the type the Navy uses to communicate with whales. It's basically an underwater speaker system."

Nick smiled. "We're not going to attract whales, are we?"

"Not likely in the Venetian lagoon. In the package is a sounding device on which I encoded the message the Omni read from the stake that would turn it on. It's the same musical tones we used before.

"Go out near the stake, lower the probe, and play the code."

"How will we know it works?"

"I included two pairs of night vision goggles."

"Aren't you the supply master," quipped Nick.

Tom smiled at the recognition of his mastery in military manipulation.

"The goggles can see infrared light. I will keep my eye on what the satellite sees. We will be on phones, talking."

"OK. Let me talk to my friend Guido about the boat."

A cell phone rang near Tom.

"Guys, could you hold a minute? Birchmeier is calling."

As Tom took the call, Rachael commented, "Maybe he has an update on Lizzy."

Nick had not given Lizzy's whereabouts much thought, but could see that Rachael had.

Tom returned to the screen. "Nick, Rachael. Bad news. Birchmeier thinks Lizzy may have been kidnapped."

"What?" exclaimed both Nick and Rachael.

"Birchmeier is more than a little pissed his man failed to protect her. He told me they found that a private plane left Basel. A witness told them a woman matching Lizzy's description was taken on board. The witness said a man kept the woman on her feet and she appeared drunk."

"Drunk?" said Nick. "More likely drugged."

"That's what Birchmeier figures. I got to tell you, Birchmeier is determined to find her."

"Isn't that outside of TIGRIS jurisdiction?"

"That's what I asked Birchmeier."

"And?"

"He told me it was personal. I have no idea what he meant."

Rachael asked Tom, "Does Tanner know about all of this? About Lizzy missing?"

"I tried calling Tanner. No answer."

"He's probably out of range or can't respond. Who knows where he and Paul are now?"

Rachael pondered the situation beyond Nick's simple conclusion. "Whoever took Lizzy, they must know her relationship with Tanner. Could she be a hostage?"

Nick thought of something else. "She also knows more about the Energy Machine than Tanner does."

Tom quickly interjected. "But she doesn't know about our plan to locate it. I came up with that after I last saw her."

"Whoever took her doesn't know that," said Nick.

Nick considered the fix he was in. He wanted to move on separate fronts at the same time. He had to prioritize.

"Look," he said to Tom, "keep close to Birchmeier. Make sure he's on the kidnappers' trail. Tanner and Paul are tracking down Christy's killer. That's secondary to finding Lizzy."

"Unless they are one and the same," interjected Rachael.

Nick considered that prospect.

It was Tom who set the immediate priority. "Whoever kidnapped Lizzy is likely behind the break-in here. They want the Energy Machine. We need to get to it first."

Nick didn't add that Dowd may have killed Christine because she would expose his admission scam, but he might just as likely have killed her because of his hunt for the Energy Machine.

"I agree," Nick said. Turning to Rachael, "Ready?"

Rachael, who escaped a bomb in a cave, dodged an assassin's bullet at a castle, and had an attempt on her life in a grotto, realized a sensible person would not follow where Nicholas Foxe led. Maybe she wasn't sensible. In fact, she relished the idea.

"Ready," she answered.

Chapter 27

GUIDO STEERED the water taxi down the Grand Canal and into the lagoon. He normally piloted the craft at full speed in these waters, but stealth was the order of the evening and he was careful not to cause a wake. He had already loaded the package from the hotel before he picked up Nick and Rachael. Even at midnight, the city emitted life and light. Nick and Rachael boarded from a dock on the Grand Canal above the Pensione Accademia. Rachael noticed that Nick's expression changed as they floated by the pensione, apparently recalling unpleasant memories.

As they approached the lagoon, Guido was forced to stop as a huge cruise ship, the size of a condominium building, passed by.

"See," Guido said. "The big ships, they are returning."

Rachael said, "Look at all those admission tickets heading into Venice."

Guido scowled. "Not if I can help it."

Nick knew Guido would like to put a stop to Dowd's scheme, but he, even with his connections, was helpless against the likes of Nevin Dowd. That is, if the rumor was true. Rachael suggested Dowd was capable of killing Christine because she could expose his plot. Nick's gut told him that didn't seem likely. There was something more. He trusted Tanner to find Bosak and get to the truth. Now, he had to focus on the stake and the Energy Machine.

Was it the machine Dowd was after?

After the cruise ship passed, Guido moved forward and out to the location where Dowd had shown Nick the stake. Nick had Tom on his cell phone.

"We are nearing the spot," he alerted Tom, "but, we're taking our time."

"No problem," reassured Tom. "I have everything ready."

Nick rode beside Guido. Rachael positioned herself in the back of the boat to absorb the view of Venice at night. Nick noticed and walked back to join her.

"It's beautiful," she said.

"Yes, and unique in all the world. When Peter the Great built St. Petersburg, he created canals patterned after Venice."

"Often imitated. Never duplicated," she mused.

Nick smiled at Rachael's use of a phrase often used in commercials.

"But, all the money in the world can't save it from the rising seas," she said. "That's what Mose is all about."

Nick paused to consider. "I'm not a guy who believes the end justifies the means, but if Dowd can save this city, even if he gets even richer from it, at the end of the day, Venice survives."

"If he was the one who killed Christine, would you feel as generous?"

"If he had anything to do with that, I would kill him myself. But I don't think he did. Sounds too much like a conspiracy theory."

Rachael thought of all she had been through since she first met Nicholas Foxe and scoffed.

"Nick, everything we've been through together sounds like a conspiracy theory."

He realized the truth in what Rachael said and added, "Or the work of someone with an active imagination."

Nick had given Guido the precise coordinates of the stake's location. Guido's GPS blinked green.

"We're here," he whispered to the rear of the boat.

Guido cut the engine and walked to the back of the boat where he left the equipment.

Nick called Tom. "We've reached the location."

"OK," said Tom, "just put me on speaker and get the equipment in the water like we discussed earlier."

Nick and Guido worked together to open the canvas bag that contained the probe and the recording device. The probe was the size of a large can of beans, heavier so it would sink. It was attached to a thick black cable protecting the wiring.

"You need only drop it twelve feet," said Tom. "I put a white mark on the cable at that distance. That mark should be at water level. Then tie off the attached rope on the boat."

Tom was repeating everything they had covered earlier. So far, it was going as planned. Guido tied the rope off to one of the cleats on the edge of the boat. Nick pulled the recording device out of its bag. The device was the size of a brick, but much lighter. The electronics were contained within an aluminum body. This solid-state device was simple: a volume meter, a slide switch for play and reverse, and an on-off switch. Tom had recorded the code on the device. Nick plugged in the end of the cable.

"Ready," he told Tom.

"I'm ready. Turn it on."

The meter registered a high volume, but the reading was unnecessary. The occupants of the boat could hear the odd series of tones. Guido had heard nothing like it before, but Rachael and Nick had. This was the same type of music that unlocked the clues they followed to Italy, the ones they heard deep in a New Mexico cave. The same music that had released clues leading to the Omni. The markings on the stake were not like anything they had seen from the ancients of 10,000 years ago. The odd intervals of the melody assured them the source was the same.

Rachael put on the night vision goggles and Nick followed suit. A yellowish glow appeared beneath the water, invisible without the goggles.

Nick could not hide his excitement. "Tom, we see it! It's glowing."

"Great!" exclaimed Tom. "Now, let's see if it turned on the other two. This will take a few minutes."

Despite the goggles, Nick saw a large boat headed toward them. Rachael and Nick removed their goggles as a nimble speedboat now broke out of the darkness. Before they could react, it had pulled alongside them. At the wheel was Nevin Dowd with Commissario Russo and the policeman Matteo. Matteo was in uniform and wore a sidearm.

"Well, if it isn't my friend Nicholas Foxe!" Dowd said, smiling as though he was just passing by at this late hour.

Nick returned the salutation in an equal tone.

"Hello, Nevin. Fancy meeting you here."

Russo spoke up. "Mr. Foxe, we need to talk. Please join us."

"Who? Just me?"

Dowd added, "Please have Professor Friedman come along."

Nick turned to Guido. "Please return our equipment and the boat. We'll be in touch."

As Nick picked up his phone, he noticed that Tom had disconnected. Instead, he had left a text message. It was a simple one.

I found it.

Chapter 28

LIZZY'S WALK to her 'interview' chamber was helpful. She took in the hallway but could not spot any surveillance cameras. *Odd,* she thought, but she didn't question it. Her only impediment to getting out was Tweedledee at the end of the hall, whose chin now rested on his chubby chest as he snoozed. The item she grabbed from the interrogation room would be the key. Now to play damsel in distress.

She began to squeal like a ten-year-old whose little brother dumped a frog on her. Peeking around the edge of the cell, she saw Tweedledee awaken and stand. Lizzy climbed on the leather chair and continued her concert of distress. The guard, a man of few words, stood before the scene, and looked through the bars,

"What?"

"Mouse!"

"Where?"

"Over there under my cot. He's huge. Oh, please get him out of here. I hate mice. Can't stand them."

Begrudgingly, the guard pulled out his key card, held it up to the reader and slid the cell door open. He walked in as Lizzy pointed to her cot.

"Please, please, get him out of there!"

The guard turned his back on Lizzy. Big mistake. Lizzy jumped from the chair and grabbed on to his back as though daddy was giving her a horsey ride. The difference was Lizzy held a rag enclosing a vial of chloroform she had picked up from the floor in the 'interview' chamber.

Lizzy, crushing the vial in the rag and soaking it, held it over the man's nose and mouth. She remembered riding a mechanical bull in a bar. The limited training was now coming in handy as Lizzy rode this bull around the room. Tweedledee hit the chair and pushed it into the lamp. The Tiffany fell to the floor, shattering. He bounced off the bookcase, scattering a dozen tomes. All the while, Lizzy held the cloth in place. The man's arms floundered around his back trying to grab his nemesis, but Lizzy avoided them. For what seemed too long, the man remained conscious, but he soon began to stagger. The image of King Kong falling from the Empire State Building came to Lizzy and, as the man fell backwards, she jumped off. Tweedledee's mass made a splat on the floor.

Lizzy wasted no time taking the key card off the man. She was counting on the card opening more than just her cell door. She entered the hall and down to where Tweedledee normally sat. The door to the right had a window in it. She peeked through it. No one there. Just a hall that appeared more in keeping with a castle. Old stonework lined the walls and an ancient wooden door could be seen at the far end.

Lizzy took the key card and placed it on the keypad of the first door. It clicked.

Yes!

Lizzy pushed it open and crept down the hall, expecting someone to come through the other door at any moment. She reached it without that happening. She put her ear to the door and heard faint voices.

Here goes nothing.

She turned the large iron latch and slowly pushed the door open. The voices were near. One was familiar. Lizzy found herself on a ledge overlooking a huge room with a balustrade allowing her to peek at what was going on below. At the end of the ledge was a staircase going down into the room. At the bottom of the steps was a man who looked like a mafioso thug holding a machine gun.

Not going that way.

The room looked like something out of Game of Thrones, a room where one of the lesser kings held court. There was a huge fireplace at the far end and, just below and barely in sight, was a short man talking to two other men. Lizzy's face lit up. One of the two men was Tanner.

"Welcome to our humble abode," said Preston Smith to Tanner and Paul. Bosak was behind Preston, who paced around with a cigar as though he was king of the world.

"Where's Lizzy?" demanded Tanner.

"Patience, my good man, you'll see her soon."

Paul and Tanner noticed movement on the balcony above Smith's head. It was Lizzy looking through the rails. She returned a little wave. Paul glanced at Tanner. Tanner knew what he must be thinking.

Is that Lizzy?

Tanner returned a quick nod in affirmation. Both men suppressed a grin.

Smith was too immersed in his monologue to notice.

"Our boss asked me to bring you here, to convince you to work with us. Not against us."

"Who's your boss?" asked Paul.

"We use the codename Frost for the boss. You know all about codenames, don't you Mr. Allerton? Your business is known for them."

"What do you want?"

Smith pointed to two overstuffed chairs behind Paul and Tanner. "Oh, yes. I suppose you need to know what this is all about. Please have a seat."

Smith now had no height issue with the two taller men sitting. Bosak continued to pace and smoke.

"I believe Mr. Tanner is familiar with what this is all about," continued Smith as he walked toward Tanner to address him.

"Your Omni Scientia was a tremendous find. Imagine a device that contains a universe of advanced information. Potential cures for virus infections. Answers about space and time that stumped Einstein. Yet, there was one very important detail your team was keeping to themselves."

Paul was hearing this all for the first time, but he could see that Tanner knew what Smith was talking about.

"The Omni told all about how a new source of power could be derived. It could turn ordinary seawater into energy. Imagine!

"Oh, I can see why you would want to keep that one under your hat. No longer would the world dig into the earth to release an ever-dwindling supply of oil and gas. This new natural resource covers three-quarters of the planet. Think of how that would change geopolitics!

"Yet, the engineering is stumping the best minds. They think they can interpret what the Omni is telling them, but a working model would help, and guess what? The people who created the Omni left a working model. How convenient. But they didn't make it easy. They didn't just leave a simple map to find it. Instead, they invented a high-tech treasure hunt. But now your Mr. Littleton has found the location of the working model."

Tanner looked at the little man as though he was crazy.

"Quite a tale," he said. "What makes you think any of this is true?"

Smith sneered. "I know you are aware of the visit Mr. Bosak made to your lab in Basel. You probably thought he and his people were trying to take something. No, Mr. Tanner, they didn't take something. They left something."

Bosak smiled with pride at Tanner's confusion and took a long pull from his stogie exhausting it above the seated man's head. If Bosak could read Tanner's mind at that moment, he would not be so cocky. Tanner would have loved to wring his neck.

"They left a little package of code on your computer system that allowed us to monitor what you were doing. Mr. Littleton has just discovered the location of the Energy Machine. Isn't that delightful?"

"So, you have everything you need," said Tanner.

"Well, there is a missing piece. We need the code to turn the thing on. This was something that was not discussed with Mr. Littleton, at least not in a way his computer would have captured. Unfortunately, we were unable to bug the room in the limited time our people were there. We could not hear conversations your people may have had."

Smith turned to Paul. "It was this missing code that al-Muazzam's letter to his son talked about. Now you can see, Mr. Allerton, why this letter was so important."

Paul was a professional, but hearing this, he could barely control his anger. "And you had to kill Priscilla Westly for it?"

Smith expressed feigned dismay. "Such an awful waste. I'm sorry that happened."

Tanner, expecting Paul to leap upon the man, intervened. "So, you don't have the code to turn the thing on?"

"Not yet, Mr. Tanner, but we expect to have it soon."

"So, why do you need us?"

"Our boss is not at the top of the food chain, you might say. Frost has a benefactor who's taken a shine to Mr. Foxe and members of Foxe's team, although he's not met a single one of you. Frost is working on instructions from that man, an American I believe, to turn you to our side. There's a significant monetary reward for doing so.

"However, Frost has placed a limited time frame on the invitation. Mr. Bosak's brother attempted to deliver Mr. Foxe to Frost when he first arrived in Venice. Unfortunately, he underestimated the boatman's cunning and paid with his life."

Tanner and Paul noticed Bosak grimace at the mention of this death.

Did he hold Foxe accountable for his brother's death? Does the man have a vendetta against Foxe?

"And the pity of it all is that Foxe could have met Frost then and there and saved us all this trouble."

Tanner quipped, "Yeah, Nick never liked someone putting a gun in his face."

A guard posted outside entered the room with haste. He took Smith and Bosak aside, telling them something. Paul and Tanner could not hear the exchange, but it was clear Smith and Bosak were not happy. The guard left. Smith turned to Paul and Tanner.

"I'm afraid something has come up and we have to leave you."

Bosak reached for the sidearm he carried, but Smith put his hand on Bosak's arm. "No, that will be taken care of later. We have to leave."

With no other word, Smith and Bosak headed for the door. The guard at the foot of the steps walked up to Paul and Tanner where they stood.

The guard seemed prepared to use his weapon on them. Each man was calculating his next move when the unexpected happened. A redhead appeared on the balcony.

"Hey, bad guy!" yelled Lizzy.

The guard, caught by surprise, never saw the flowerpot Lizzy threw until it hit him between the eyes. The guard was dazed, but not down, until Tanner slammed his fist into the man's face.

Paul unwrapped the machine gun from the guard's shoulder as Tanner looked up, and with a smile called to Lizzy, "Nice pitch! Now get down here."

Lizzy ran down the steps and into Tanner's arms. As the big man's arms surrounded her, Paul slung the machine gun in place over his shoulder.

"So, this is the famous Lizzy Rodriguez," he said. "I thought you'd be locked away."

"Don't like jail. Never could spend much time there."

Tanner continued to hold Lizzy a foot off the floor when Paul said, "Don't want to ruin anything, but I think we need to be going."

They heard the rapid pings of automatic gunfire outside, joined by the unmistakable sound of a helicopter starting up. As Paul led the way out with his machine gun poised, they came upon two guards by the door firing at something outside the castle. The guard on the right noticed the escaping group first. He turned to fire, but left his back exposed to the gunfire outside and was saturated with bullets. A second later, the guard on the left turned, but Paul's machine gun quickly dispatched him.

Paul and Tanner hoped whoever was attacking the castle was friend, not foe. They cautiously approached the entrance. Tanner saw who the men were and said, "Not to worry. They're on our side."

Two guards high in a tower fired down on the newly merged force.

While the fight was underway, the helicopter rose from behind the castle and headed across the ocean.

"It's Smith and Bosak," yelled Tanner.

"Don't worry," said Paul. "We got Bosak once, we'll get him again."

The men assaulting the castle were pros. The guards in the tower were not. After a minute of exchange, they took out both guards.

As the dust settled, Tanner saw a familiar figure walking toward him.

"Lizzy," said Tanner, "I'd like you to meet Director Lukas Birchmeier."

Paul had to get his head around the fact that the director was far from home. "We're a little far from your territory, aren't we, Director?"

"When terrorists kidnap one of ours, we go where the trail leads us."

"One of yours?" asked Lizzy. "You mean me?"

"Indeed, Miss Rodriguez. You were under our protection. It was a great embarrassment to have you snatched away. It was the least we could do to find and free you."

Then Birchmeier smiled at the men. "But I see someone freed you first."

Tanner corrected the director. "You got it turned around, Director. Lizzy freed herself. Then she got us out of a jam."

Lizzy beamed at her man setting the record straight.

Birchmeier raised an eyebrow as he assessed the young woman. "Is that so?"

Lizzy's stoked pride showed.

"All in a day's work," she said.

Birchmeier briefly contemplated scenarios in which Lizzy could have possibly done this, but returned to the matter at hand.

"Was Bosak on that helicopter that just left?"

"He was," answered Paul, "and Preston Smith joined him."

"Preston Smith? Who's that?"

"He works for Nevin Dowd."

"You mean the man who's working on the Mose project?"

"The same."

Birchmeier pondered this new information. "Do you think Dowd had something to do with all of this?"

"Quite likely."

Lizzy interjected. "But Smith said he worked for someone with the codename of Frost. Seems odd that he would use a codename for someone we all know he works for."

"True," answered Paul. "But I'm betting that helicopter is headed directly to Frost. If we could find out where it's going, we could find Frost."

A TIGRIS soldier walked up to Birchmeier and told him something the others couldn't hear.

As the man left, Birchmeier said, "That's something that I can help you with. My man just told me they are tracking the helicopter on the ship's radar.

"The ship?" asked Paul.

Birchmeier smiled. "You don't think we swam here, do you? Please join me. There is someone you know on board."

Chapter 29

IN ANOTHER PART OF THE ADRIATIC SEA, an unusual yacht sped above the waves. Dowd's craft was a Russian-built thirty-seven-meter motor yacht with wing-like foils mounted under the hull. The structure allowed her to reach a top speed of sixty knots. Dowd, at the wheel, sped his guests, in the dark, into the Adriatic. Nick and Rachael felt nothing like guests. Being accompanied by Commissario Russo and an armed policeman negated any feeling of congeniality. Nick felt somewhat more at ease since, unlike Rachael, he had met Matteo before. He thought the young man was earnest but inexperienced.

Did Matteo even know how to use that gun?

Nick studied Russo.

What was his involvement with Dowd?

Although Russo had struck him as a Columbo type, a bungler but clever, he didn't expect him to conspire with the likes of Dowd. Nick and Rachael sat uncomfortably since boarding. Dowd was smiling as a host glad to have his guests on board, but Russo and Matteo remained inscrutable. Dowd just passed along a few words now and then.

"Wait a moment while I get her out to sea."

Dowd steered the vessel himself. No other crew was evident.

They passed through the Lido inlet and out to sea. Dowd opened the throttle and they headed into open water. The craft amazed Nick how smooth it ran at high speed. He reasoned they must be riding on hydrofoil wings.

Dowd chuckled at Nick's obvious appreciation. "Nice, isn't it? I'm putting it into autopilot so we can sit and talk."

Dowd threw a few switches and took his hand off the wheel.

"Autopilot?" asked Nick. "Really?"

"Don't you need to keep an eye out for other craft?" added Rachael.

"Another advancement from the labs of Vanessa Fabre. She took the self-driving car and made it a boat."

"Speaking of Vanessa," Nick said, "where is she?"

Russo spoke for the first time. "You will soon find out."

"Oh?"

"As you know, we wanted to interview Miss Fabre, but even her people were not able to contact her, not at first. However, we have talked to Miss Fabre. She asked us to come to her research ship to talk."

"And why are Rachael and me here?"

Dowd said, "She insisted you come."

"Why?"

"She said the whole picture would be complete with you there."

"What did she mean by that?"

"We shall see, won't we?"

Turning to Dowd, Nick said, "You know, you could have called. You didn't need to pick us up in the middle of the night."

"Yes, about that," Dowd said. "What were you crazy kids doing out there in the middle of the night? Seems you were conducting a little science experiment."

Rachael took the lead in lying. "It was my idea. I wanted to conduct some experiments in sound under water."

As soon as Rachael said it, she knew how lame that line of misdirection was. If there was any doubt, Dowd's expression confirmed it.

Nick assumed Dowd knew exactly why they were there. He was probably behind the break-in. He knew what the stake was for. However, he doubted Dowd knowingly took part in Christine's murder. He had such a large ensemble who worked for him, it could have been any of them. Perhaps it was someone trying to protect the boss without the boss knowing it.

Since Dowd probably knew everything about the Energy Machine, Nick spoke openly.

"We found that the stake is one of three. We took the markings from the one you found and successfully translated them into a code which we played through a speaker. It turned on an infrared signal on that stake and the two others."

Nick produced a scaled down narrative. He expected Dowd to fill in the blanks. As though hearing all this for the first time, Dowd added no additional knowledge.

"Nick, why didn't you tell me this earlier? I could have helped. I wondered why you were so mysterious in telling me what the markings on the stake meant. I'm hurt."

Nick thought Dowd played his part well.

Was he performing for the sake of Russo?

"So, what did the stakes designate?" Dowd asked.

"The location of a treasure."

I can play an actor's role, too.

"Ah, buried treasure! Now we're talking. After we visit Vanessa, let's talk further."

Nick considered where to take this little show when Rachael entered the act, taking it in a different direction.

"Perhaps not the treasure one can get from the price of admission to Venice," she said.

Dowd looked surprised at this woman's attempt to expose a secret, but his reply was smug and patronizing. "And what would that mean?"

"Are you working a deal where the government charges admission to Venice and you get a cut?"

Dowd glanced at Russo with a conspiratorial smile. "A cut? My dear, I get it all!"

"What?" Rachael was astounded.

"I have people who understand crowds. Some of Disney's best."

As Rachael began to object, Dowd raised his hand to stop her.

"My dear Doctor Friedman, I am not turning Venice into Disneyland. No theme characters. No rides other than gondolas, operated by gondoliers just as they are today. I will run the security, in cooperation with the police."

He nodded to Russo.

"I will do the ticketing, the timed entry from the cruise ships, and best of all, the preservation of the city. I've set up a trust fund which will drive the investment. The board of directors of the trust represent countries from all over who value this gem as I do."

In a few moments, Dowd had gone from evil to altruistic. Rachael was stunned. Nick was confused.

Is he Santa Claus or Jack the Ripper?

Dowd continued. "Venice has a special place in my heart. Did you know I spent much of my childhood here?"

"No," said Rachael. This was news to Nick. But Russo gave a knowing smile.

"My aunt had an art museum here. She envied Peggy Guggenheim's collection on the Grand Canal and tried to rival it. She seemed to want to duplicate Peggy's lifestyle. I was just a kid and my parents let me spend summers with her. I remember how elegant she was, wearing large hats, gliding along the canals with a cigarette holder up to her lips.

"When I wasn't with my aunt, I was with the local boys playing football in the piazza, getting into trouble anyway we could. There was a girl one boy was sweet on. We used to tease him about it. One evening, we passed by her house. Our buddy gave away her location by looking up at her window. We picked up little pebbles along the street. We each started throwing them at the window, trying to get her to open it. Our buddy was embarrassed and protested. But that just fueled our mischief. It may have been me, maybe another boy, but one of us hurled a stone too large and it shattered the window. All of us scattered.

"Unfortunately, I was the one caught by a young policeman. He asked me where I lived, and I told him. He knew my aunt and took me straight there. My aunt was beside herself and lit into me. But the policeman soothed the savage beast in her, defending my youthful indiscretion. I was just a boy, but I could see my aunt's attraction to this young policeman. They continued a relationship for several years.

Turning to Russo, Dowd said, "Didn't you, Bruno?"

"*Si*," replied Commissario Russo. "We were quite close."

This unimaginable history stunned Rachael and Nick. Nick had researched Dowd before agreeing to come, but these personal details were not public.

"What happened?" Rachael asked. "Where is she today?"

Russo's countenance saddened. "In San Michele."

Rachael looked to Nick for a clue.

"The island cemetery for Venice," he replied.

"Oh."

Russo continued. "She never liked doctors. She wasn't well and refused to go to one, until it was too late. They told her the cancer would kill her in two months. It took only two weeks, and she was gone."

"And you?"

"I found a remarkable woman, married her, and raised three fine children. But… I will always remember her."

Dowd put his hand on Russo's shoulder for a moment, then continued.

"As for me, after my aunt died, I stopped coming to Venice every summer, but tried to get here as much as I could. I think it's what got me into the water business, if you could call it that. Water is such an integral part of Venice, of Amsterdam, of many places around the world."

"And it is something climate change is forcing us to deal with," added Nick.

"And that is why I'm here."

Dowd paused, changing his demeanor to address the matter at hand. "Tonight, we are getting to the bottom of Christine's death."

"Paul Allerton and Tanner are after the killer," warned Nick.

"Yes, I know, but there is that missing element Bruno told you about, the drug someone slipped to Christine before she died. Bruno said that at that time, you were out of the country."

Dowd said this as though he doubted it to be true. "You must understand, I thought Christine was wonderful."

Nick saw in Dowd's expression more than a business appreciation.

Was Dowd having an affair with Christy? Could he have met her and drugged her?

But when and why?

"I want the killer, but I want to be sure we have everybody who may have something to do with her death," said Dowd.

Nick agreed. "As do I."

A beeping sounded from the pilot console. Dowd went to it, turned the automatic pilot off, and took the wheel.

"You'll have your chance soon. Vanessa's ship is up ahead."

Chapter 30

GUIDO WAS LEFT on his boat in the lagoon as Dowd's boat departed, clueless as to what to do next. He didn't have to wait long. His cell phone rang.

Who could this be?

He answered.

"Pronto."

"Is this Guido Bartoli?"

"Si"

"This is Tom Littleton. Nick may have mentioned me."

"Certainly. You provided this equipment I have now in my boat."

"Nick didn't answer his phone. Is he there?"

Guido filled Tom in on the events that had transpired.

"Look Mr. Bartoli," Tom said.

"Please, call me Guido."

"OK, Guido. I'm traveling. From what you told me, I will be seeing Nick soon. But that could be too late. There is something I've learned that's a matter of life and death."

"What could it be?"

"I understand that you have special relations with the authorities there," said Tom.

"Well…"

Tom didn't wait for Guido to respond.

"Guido, the Lido has to be evacuated."

A deckhand dressed in blue jeans and an aqua shirt helped board the group from Dowd's boat. The young deckhand's shirt bore the insignia of Vanessa's ocean research outfit, Fabre Robotique Equipe des Sciences de la Mer. Nick had noted that name before on the vessel Dowd used to take him underwater to the stake. Something about it gnawed at Nick.

He now realized why.

The deckhand led everyone to a living room, which would have been more at place in a luxury yacht rather than a no-nonsense research ship. A long white crescent of a couch was built into the center of the room against a console with built-in reading lamps. Across from the console were three heavy, blood-red leather chairs. A window curved around the front of the room overlooking the top deck and helipad.

"Miss Fabre will be with you shortly," the young man said before he retired from the room.

Nick and Rachael sat on the couch. Russo took a chair. Matteo, the only person armed in the room, stood guard. For what, he had no idea.

Dowd wandered around.

"I like her style," he said, appreciating the luxury of the room. "I wonder what the rest of the ship looks like."

"It's not like this," said Vanessa as she walked into the room. "We use this room to impress visitors."

Dowd shook Vanessa's hand. "Well, you've done it. How much am I paying you?"

Vanessa chuckled as though Dowd made a joke. She turned to Russo. "Commissario, I'm sorry I've been so hard to get in touch with. We experienced communications problems in our radio room."

She approached Nick. "Hello, Nick, I see you've brought a friend."

"Yes, I guess you've not met. May I introduce Doctor Rachael Friedman?"

Vanessa took Rachael's hand. "It's a pleasure to meet you. I've heard so much about you."

The young deckhand appeared at the door.

"Excuse me," said Vanessa as she walked over to him.

The young man whispered something. Vanessa replied, "Excellent," and walked back into the room.

Dowd remained standing while Vanessa addressed Russo. "So, Commissario Russo, I understand you have questions."

"Yes, we now understand Miss Blake took a benzodiazepine drug prior to her murder. We would like to know what you know about that."

"I would be glad to let you know," Vanessa said as she walked behind Matteo and opened a drawer, "but first I have to do something."

Nick heard the faint sounds of an approaching helicopter. He was about to end this charade with what he now knew, but he was too late.

Vanessa pulled a .32-calibre pistol from the drawer, stepped behind Matteo, and fired it into the right side of Matteo's head. The man careened to the floor. Everyone stood, unexpected shock all around, even Nick.

I didn't know she would go this far.

Now holding the gun toward the group, she said, "Please, everyone, sit down."

Everyone returned to their seats, except Dowd who had not been sitting.

"You too, Nevin."

Dowd took a seat in the chair beside Russo. As he did, the young deckhand returned with another man and took the body of the policeman away as though the murder was a part of a script.

Vanessa came around to the side of the seating area where she could see everyone, her demeanor icy, hand firm as she gripped the gun at her side.

"Now to answer your question, Commissario. I gave the drug to Christine. She had to die, but I didn't want her to suffer. So, we had some Champagne for old times. I placed the additive in her glass. She fell asleep."

Nick once disliked Vanessa. He now despised her. He knew the helicopter, now visible and headed to the ship, did not bode well.

"Why did she have to die, Vanessa?" he asked. "Or should I say, Frost?"

Vanessa had perfected the disparaging sneer. Nick had seen it before, and he saw it again at that moment. "Very good, Nick. How did you figure that out?"

"Your company, Fabre Robotique Equipe des Sciences de la Mer. In English, that's Fabre Robotics Ocean Science Team. FROST."

"One of the idiots I hired noted the acronym and tied it to me. I decided to use it as my identity. Usually, I take pains to avoid such obvious things. But then, I decided to embrace it. Nothing changed. Nothing! Even you, Mr. Nicholas Foxe, celebrated code solver, didn't break that simple code."

Nick let the comment slide off, although it gave him pause.

Would Christy be alive had I made the connection earlier?

"So, why did Christy have to die? Was she on to you?"

"On to me, Nick? You mean did she know I was about to find the greatest energy discovery ever? Yes, she did. Did she want to join me? No, she didn't. I pleaded with her. It would be like old times. But it was because of you, you bastard."

"Me?"

"Christine found out that I was the one who arranged the break-in of your lab in Basel. She didn't want to have anything to do with the deal since it would be disloyal to you. You still held sway over her. I told her I gave you a chance to join us the moment you arrived in Venice. My man on the water taxi was clumsy in his offer, but my intent was to have him bring you to me. I knew you wouldn't see me unless forced to do so. I told her I was behind that incident when you arrived, but I was only trying to give you a chance to join me. She knew you wouldn't do it.

"So, I arranged the meeting with her that night, had a no-hard-feelings drink with Christine, and put her to sleep. Bosch made sure it was forever."

"Bosch?" asked Nick. "Who's that?"

"You'll soon find out."

The helicopter landed. Two men got out and went below.

"So, why do you need us?"

"The break-in didn't go as planned. We wanted the Omni. But we got the next best thing. We planted some code that allowed us to monitor what was going on between Mr. Littleton and his computer."

"So, you have everything you need."

"Not everything happens on a computer. We know where the Energy Machine is. We don't know the code to turn it on. That, we need from you."

The door swung open and Preston and Bosak entered the room. Bosak held an assault rifle.

"Preston!" yelled Dowd as he stood. "What are you doing here? Who is this man?"

Preston grinned. "Settle down, Nevin. You're not the only one I'm working for."

Preston Smith had always felt belittled by Nevin Dowd, never getting the respect he deserved. Now he held power over his boss, and it felt good.

Dowd did as he was told, not out of respect for the little man, but rather out of common sense, considering a brutal man behind him held an assault rifle.

"Bosak!" exclaimed Russo. "It's you."

"Brilliant observation," sneered Vanessa. "I prefer to call him Bosch after Hieronymus Bosch, the painter who could envision hellish nightmares."

Vanessa took stock of Bosak's dull countenance. "But I believe such nuance is lost on this man."

Nick hesitated to mention the other members of the team on Bosak's trail, but he had to know where they were. "We sent two men after you, Bosak."

Vanessa turned to Preston and Bosak. "Yes. What has become of those men?"

Preston Smith had doled out information to Vanessa in limited packages. He told her about kidnapping Lizzy as bait. It was she who authorized it. She knew that Allerton and Tanner were on Bosak's trail. The plan was to bring them to a castle she owned. The latest news was they had taken care of the situation and were on their way to her ship. Preston had omitted the small detail of Birchmeier storming the island while he and Bosak ran for their lives. Preston assumed his men had finished off Allerton and Tanner and then went to the holding cell to kill Lizzy.

Bad assumptions all around.

Preston Smith lacked the villainous flare to be menacing, but he made a weak attempt anyway when responding.

"I'm afraid Mr. Allerton, Mr. Tanner, and Miss Rodriguez will not be joining us. Or anyone else for that matter."

The thought of losing Tanner and Lizzy stunned Nick and Rachael. Rachael could not help shedding a tear. Nick gritted his teeth. Whatever exceeded 'despise,' for Vanessa,

Nick felt it. Even though Vanessa already knew Nick's boiling hatred for her, she pushed it to another level.

"Now, as I was saying, seems the last thing missing is the code to turn the Energy Machine on. Preston had his man follow you to the Doge Palace where you found the sword with the code, but we understand that fool started a duel with you. The police took him away. We got to him, but he hadn't heard you repeat the code."

"You mean Robert Morrison?" asked Russo. "We found him hanging in his cell. Suicide."

Vanessa smiled. "Yes, wasn't that unfortunate?"

Turning to Nick, she added, "Looks like you must find another fencing partner."

Had Nick an *épée* in hand, he would have run it through Vanessa at that moment. Vanessa sensed it, but it only emboldened her more. She turned to Rachael.

"Doctor Friedman, may I call you Rachael?"

Rachael offered no response, nor did Vanessa expect one.

"You've been spending a lot of time with Nick. Seems you favor the man. I bet the feeling is mutual."

Now that Bosak had his assault rifle at the ready, Vanessa could freely use the pistol in other ways. She pointed the weapon point blank at Rachael's head and said, "Let's see if Nick thinks the code is worth your life."

Dowd bolted out of his seat. "Vanessa!"

Vanessa turned the gun on him.

"Shut up, Nevin. I'll kill everyone here one-by-one until I either get the code or a room full of corpses. You want me to take you first?"

"You don't scare me," said Dowd.

"Sit down," she said.

Dowd sat, gazing icily at Vanessa as she raised the gun to his head.

Vanessa laughed. "What was I thinking? Why would I kill Rachael first? She knows the code! Maybe I was too eager to see the hurt on Nick's face as his girlfriend's head exploded. Silly me.

"Oh, well. Let's see if you value Nevin's life. You know the drill. I count to three and pull the trigger, or I stop the count if you cooperate.

"Let's go… One…Two…"

"Stop!" yelled Nick. "Put the gun down."

"What's the code?"

"First, put the gun down."

Vanessa lowered her gun and asked, "Well?"

"It's pi."

"What?" asked Vanessa.

"It's the numerical value of pi."

"You mean 3.14?"

Rachael couldn't help but provide more accuracy. "Actually, it's 3.1415926. The first eight digits."

Vanessa considered this. She appeared dubious but both Nick and Rachael hoped she would take them at their word. Then she saw the logic. She laughed.

"Of course! No one had that accuracy until the twentieth century. The system was placed in the ocean, useless to anyone who had not advanced to the level required to solve pi to that degree. Everyone knew the relationship for centuries, but no one could solve it to even that simple level of eight digits. Even al-Muazzam couldn't do it. He just knew the key to power was there. Anyone trying to guess would go through over a million combinations."

Vanessa's joy turned sour.

"You're not joking with me, are you?" she asked Nick.

"No."

"We don't have everything from the Omni by a long shot, but we do have the basic coding for numbers. If we convert these digits to the sounds they represent, it will turn the machine on, won't it?"

Nick had no assurance it would work, especially since he had no idea if Vanessa had the right code translation for digits. So, he responded only as Nicholas Foxe would.

"Of course, it will."

Vanessa remained skeptical. "Well, I'm going on a little trip to the machine. I'm leaving you all under guard. If this doesn't work..." She looked around at everyone. "You'll not enjoy what happens next."

Vanessa exited through the door with Preston following. The two men who removed the policeman's body, now armed with assault rifles, entered the room to stand guard. Bosak followed the others and the door closed.

The guards were not as menacing as Bosak. Nick reasoned that they made that up in numbers.

There're two of them to take out, not just one.

Nick waved and smiled at the guards. They did not wave back.

Everyone could see Vanessa, Preston and Bosak climb into the waiting helicopter. The pilot started the blades. They were soon gone.

Nick would not wait for them to return.

Chapter 31

THE HELICOPTER LEFT the research ship with Fabre, Preston, and Bosak aboard. The room went quiet as each person considered their escape. None could read the others' thoughts, but each was thinking along similar lines.

Vanessa has no intention of letting us live.

Are there other armed men aboard?

First, we have to overcome these two guards.

Nick took stock of the two guards. Both seemed inexperienced by the way they held their weapons, more like terrorist rabble than trained soldiers. Even though there were two of them, he could sense their fear. They must be separated. Divide and conquer.

Nick turned to Rachael. "You look uncomfortable. Do you need to use the bathroom?"

Rachael spent just a second with a questioning look toward Nick before she understood the ploy.

"Yes," she said. Turning to the guards, "I really need to go."

The two guards looked at each other. The one on the right said, "I'll take her."

Rachael stood and walked to the door accompanied by the guard. He reached over her to open the door and she left the room.

"To the left," said the guard.

No crew, armed or otherwise, were in sight. Rachael noted the narrow width of the hallway. There was a fire extinguisher hanging on the wall.

Good.

"It's this door," said the guard.

"Thanks," she said. She opened the door to the bathroom and walked in. The guard closed the door behind her. Fortunately, the room was stocked with typical items for a lady's room. She saw what she needed.

Perfect!

The guard eyed Nick and the others with caution. Then the Commissario took the lead in this improv act.

Russo clutched his chest in pain. "Oh, my heart."

With the guard focused on Russo, Nick took action. He jumped the guard and took him down like a sacked quarterback. On top of the struggling man, Nick channeled his boxing days in college and slugged the man on the side of the head, rendering him sufficiently dazed. Nick yanked away the man's rifle, stood, and trained it on him.

"Not a word," Nick said.

"We need to bind him," said Russo.

"Do you have cuffs?"

"No, Matteo had them."

Dowd reached into the satchel he had brought on board and came out with a roll of duct tape.

"Here," he said handing the tape to Russo, who looked as amazed as Nick was that the man was carrying duct tape.

"You're a regular MacGyver, aren't you?" asked Nick.

"Who?"

Russo took the tape and put a piece over the guard's mouth and then wrapped his hands and ankles together.

As Russo bound the man, Nick asked Dowd, "What else do you have in there?"

To everyone's surprise, Dowd pulled out a small revolver. "This might be useful."

"You had a gun, all this time?" asked Russo.

"I didn't really have much chance to use it, did I?"

"Why did you have it?" asked Nick.

"Never leave home without it, but little good it did."

The guard heard the commotion from down the hall. Rachael did as well.

Time to act!

Rachael pushed the door open with all her weight behind it. As she hoped, the heavy metal door slapped the guard in the face. Knocked off balance, the guard struggled to get his rifle positioned in the narrow hallway. Rachael aimed a can of hairspray into the man's face and sprayed him in the eyes. As the man put his hands to his face, Rachael landed a vicious kick into his groin. The man bent over. Rachael grabbed the fire extinguisher and finished him off by slamming it into his head.

As Nick finished wrapping up the other guard, the door swung open and there stood Rachael looking like Rambo with the other guard's assault rifle slung over her shoulder.

"There's another one in the hall you need to gift wrap," she said.

"I will take care of that," said Russo as Rachael made room for the Commissario to exit.

Rachael examined the dazed guard and his bindings. "Who had the duct tape?"

"Dowd," Nick answered.

"You're a real MacGyver!"

Dowd asked no one in particular, "Who's this MacGyver?"

"We've got to get out of here," said Nick, who then eyed the assault rifle Rachael carried.

"You know how to use that thing?"

Rachael grinned. "Just point and shoot."

Nick's ego would not let him admit that he held an assault rifle for the first time in his life and probably knew as little as Rachael in its use.

Rachael, still in the doorway, took the lead. "Let's go," she said and began down the hallway.

Nick was followed by Dowd, who had his revolver in hand. Russo finished wrapping the guard Rachael had subdued and brought up the rear.

As they crept toward the door to the helipad, they heard a rapid exchange of gunfire and stopped. No one said anything. A moment later, the door swung open and Tanner stepped into the hallway.

Tanner couldn't suppress his surprise at seeing Nick and Rachael sporting assault rifles while Russo was gift-wrapping a bad guy.

"Uh." He paused, before asking, "Situation under control here?"

"Yes," said Nick. "But we're glad to see you."

The exchange of fire on deck stopped as quickly as it started.

Lizzy entered behind Tanner.

Tanner grimaced.

"I told you to stay behind."

Lizzy gave Tanner an elbow in his side. "Hey. I saved your ass, didn't I?"

If Tanner and Lizzy were welcome surprises, the person who entered behind Tanner was even more so.

"Tom!" exclaimed Rachael.

The lounge was now full. The TIGRIS forces who conducted the raid on the ship removed the two guards. Rachael and Nick relinquished their weapons to those now on board who could make better use of them. Birchmeier, standing at the edge of the room, received confirmation from one of his men that the ship was secure. Nick, Rachael, Dowd and Russo returned to their seats. Paul, Tanner, Lizzy and Tom now joined them.

Paul and Tanner informed the others about their pursuit of Bosak and about Lizzy's kidnapping. Birchmeier added, with some noticeable embarrassment, how Lizzy had been taken. TIGRIS had been determined to get her back, but Tom had insisted on coming with them.

Nick was puzzled. "Tom, you were just on the phone with me."

Tom understood Nick's confusion. Nick had assumed Tom was still in the lab near the Omni. He didn't know the Omni's search results for the Energy Machine were being sent to Tom's cell phone.

He smiled. "Phones move, Nick."

Tanner, with obvious pride, told how Lizzy had freed herself and saved them from being killed.

Nick explained how he concluded Vanessa was Frost. Birchmeier admitted that he should have figured that out, even though Nick said he was being too hard on himself. He hadn't seen the clues Nick had. There was enough guilt to go around. Tom looked upset when he learned about the code Vanessa's men had planted to monitor what he was doing. "Why didn't I suspect that?" he asked himself.

"You're not the only one who missed something," added Dowd. He shared how Preston Smith had betrayed him.

Nick knew they could no longer chit-chat. "Enough about all this guilt. Vanessa, Preston, and Bosak took a helicopter to the Energy Machine. They intend to turn it on."

The dismay on Tom's face was more than disappointment. He was troubled.

"That could be a disaster," he said.

"Why?" asked Nick.

"I did more research into what Omni could offer. She didn't have information on the location. We all know that came from her interpretation of the markings on the stake. However, she did have information on what the machine would do once operational.

"The energy it will produce will be in the form of electromagnetic waves. From what I can figure, they will be in the microwave range."

"Where will these waves be directed?" asked Rachael. The science behind the machine intrigued her.

"It's not clear. But that is not the most disturbing part. One thing everyone seems to have missed, a throttle."

"A what?" asked Nick.

Tom frowned at having to use a term he felt was half-baked. "It's not literally called that. I'm calling it that. From what I understand, there is a control for the amount of energy the machine will generate. If that control, the throttle, is not first set when the machine turns on, it will operate at full power."

"And what level would that be?" asked Rachael.

Tom paused. "Something above ten to the fifteenth joules."

Rachael sat back in her seat, appalled.

Nick was perplexed. "OK, in layman's language."

It was Dowd who answered. "Nick, you're familiar with an atomic bomb?"

"Yes," Nick said, fearing where this was going.

"Well, we're talking about a microwave beam with the energy of the first atom bomb you yanks dropped on Hiroshima."

"It'll cook any hamburger in its path, for sure," added Tom

"Are you sure of all that?" Nick asked Tom.

"No. Believe me, I hope I'm wrong. Just as I hope I'm wrong about the other thing."

"What other thing?"

Tom was reluctant to share additional theories of horrific possibilities, but he continued. "The amount of water it uses."

"Well, there's lots of that around here."

"It's not how much it uses. It's how fast it uses it. Omni didn't have specifics on the microwave beam direction, but she did have specifics on the water flow. The machine pulls water from the west. Why? I don't know. I didn't have time to figure it out. The machine generates the beam. Then, unless the control throttle is applied, within a minute, it releases the water, full force, back to the west."

"And therefore...?" prodded Nick, bracing himself to hear an answer he wouldn't like.

"Nick, I went over this again and again. It will generate a wave back to the west anywhere from twelve feet to over fifty feet high."

It was Nick's turn to be stunned. "A tsunami."

Dowd understood what the result would be. "It would crush Venice."

He turned to Birchmeier. “Do you have a satellite phone?”

“Yes.”

“Show me.”

“It’s outside. Come with me.”

Dowd left with Birchmeier.

Everyone remaining in the room was quiet, not knowing what more could be said. Russo, ever the investigator, broke the silence.

“Mr. Littleton. I have not met you before, but you seem to be a man who thinks things through. If your calculations are correct, what can we do to save our precious city?”

“When I couldn’t reach Nick, I called Guido Bartoli. I told him they need to evacuate the Lido. Do you think he made that happen?”

“I will make a call to be sure,” said Russo.

“Everyone need not leave the island, but they cannot be on the shore. But the wave will continue unabated through the inlet and on to the city, unless…”

“Unless what?” interrupted Nick.

“We need to block the wave. Can’t the Mose project do that?”

“Tom, the project may not be ready, and I’m not sure how effective it would be against a fifty-foot wave.”

"It may not be fifty-feet high. Remember, I said it would be anywhere from twelve to fifty feet. But it will be moving fast. Even a short wave will pack a punch."

"Or," said Russo, "It may not happen at all."

"True."

Nick added, "I'd rather get those gates up," just as Dowd entered the room with Birchmeier.

"So would I," said Dowd. "I called my men to lift the gates."

"*Magnifico*!" exclaimed Russo.

"Not so magnifico, I'm afraid," replied Dowd

"Why not?" asked Nick.

"We set the gates to rise one at a time and slowly. I need to get to the Lido inlet and switch the pumps to manual mode and raise them all at once, even the spares."

"Doesn't anyone else know how to do that?"

"Not with the new pumps we installed. It's a proprietary mechanism I was keeping under wraps. We have not yet trained the engineers on it."

"So, no one?"

Dowd scowled. "Preston knows, but he seems indisposed, doesn't he?"

"We're going after Frost," said Birchmeier, using Vanessa's codename.

"I'm coming with you," said both Paul and Tanner so simultaneously that they shot an amused look at each other.

"Me, too," said Lizzy.

Tanner took Lizzy by both shoulders and attempted to set her straight.

"No. I don't think so. I don't want you cooked by this thing if they turn it on."

"Hey, same here!"

Tanner grinned. "I got a lot more meat on my bones. They would have to turn it up high."

Dowd intervened. "We're going back to Venice. I could use someone like you."

Lizzy shot Dowd a sideways look.

"I mean, a woman who can take out a castle-full of bad guys could come in handy."

"See?" said Tanner.

"OK," responded Lizzy. "Just watch out for yourself."

"Hey," said Paul, "I got his back."

Tanner gave her a kiss on top of her head and left with Birchmeier and Paul.

"OK," said Dowd. "Let's get out of here."

As they walked out, Nick turned to Dowd. "I know you have a fast boat," Nick said, "but we may not have time to get there."

"Fast?" said Dowd. "You ain't seen nothing yet."

Chapter 32

VANESSA WAS PREPARED for the Energy Machine once they located it. The software her men planted in the Omni's computer system reported the location at the same time Tom received it. She had a platform towed to the site large enough to land a helicopter carrying a diving crew. When the machine came into view on the seafloor, it was clear it could not be easily moved. Vanessa had taken one of her submersibles down herself and was amazed at what she found.

10,000 years on the bottom of the sea settled the machine deep under layers of sand and marine life. Apparently, when the stakes were activated, the machine rose out of the sand and silt, awaiting the command for activation. Even after it rose out of the sea bottom, it could not have been detected if Vanessa's people didn't have the coordinates. The machine resembled a stealth bomber resting in the sand. Its angular body scattered sonar waves the way an aircraft diffused radar making it invisible to detection.

After probing and poking the surface of the machine, Vanessa's crew could find nothing that appeared to be a control. The thing was a huge lump of mystery metal. Vanessa had done her homework and knew Nick and his team had followed a trail left by the ancients which led to this machine.

The trail was filled with inanimate objects that responded to a code resembling music. Now she had the final code she needed to operate the machine.

While her divers worked to lower underwater speakers close to the machine, she pondered the simplicity of the code.

"Pi."

"Beg your pardon?" said Preston Smith, who stood with Bosak on the platform near Vanessa.

"Such simplicity, yet such a universal truth. The ratio existed before time, let alone 10,000 years ago. The ancients wanted us to become advanced enough to solve it."

"I suppose so," replied Preston on whom such philosophical theorizing was lost.

"And now it will soon be ours."

The maniacal expression washing over Vanessa's face gave pause to everyone, even Bosak.

Vanessa had two guards on watch, each armed with automatic weapons. With Bosak, that made three well-armed men. They would need them.

One guard turned to Vanessa and pointed to a boat speeding toward them. "We've got company."

As the hydrofoil settled into the water and slowed, she could see the armed men on the bow. She directed her men to stand down. Vanessa wasn't aching to be in the middle of a fire fight. She saw Paul and Tanner standing on deck and threw an icy stare at Preston who wilted before her gaze.

"So, the dead have rejoined the living, I see," she said.

Preston remained mute. Bosak gritted his teeth. Vanessa could see the Croatian wanted to correct his oversight. But she wanted cooler heads to prevail.

The boat came alongside the platform as Birchmeier walked to its edge to join Paul and Tanner. Vanessa, who had masterminded an operation in Switzerland, Birchmeier's realm, knew who he was.

What's he doing here?

"Permission to come aboard," requested Birchmeier.

"Permission denied," returned Vanessa. "We're in international waters and I don't see where a TIGRIS operative has jurisdiction."

The appearance of Paul and Tanner was an unpleasant surprise, but when Tom appeared beside them, Vanessa thought she had stepped through the looking glass.

"Tom Littleton! How unexpected."

Paul sniped, "Seems you have a problem, Fabre, in keeping people dead."

Vanessa said nothing, but her seething was palpable.

A diver emerged from the water on the other side of the platform. He raised his goggles, took in the situation before him, and considered returning to the depths. But Vanessa waved him over to the platform. He climbed the ladder and Vanessa consulted briefly with him. She marched over to the control platform.

"You've come at a good time. I know it's dramatic, but I've had my people wire speakers to this red button on the control box. I push it and, if everything goes the way we think, the machine will come alive."

"Vanessa," yelled Tom, "I need to talk to you before you do that."

Vanessa shrugged. "OK, if you must. But I can't continue talking to you up there above me. Come on down here."

Tanner turned to Tom. "Don't do it."

"It's too important. I've got to," Tom said as he walked away. He turned and told Tanner, "But watch my back, OK?"

"You got it."

Tom climbed down a ladder on the side of the boat and approached Vanessa. He exchanged a look of disdain with Bosak, the man on whose ear Tom left a permanent notch. As he walked past the man, Tom tilted his head and took a long look at Bosak's left ear. Bosak didn't miss that Tom was examining his handiwork. Bosak snarled. Tom smiled.

Vanessa noticed the cool Tom exuded.

I wish I had this man on my side rather than these buffoons.

"We haven't met, but I feel I know you," Tom said.

Vanessa began to respond, but Tom cut her off.

"And I know you respect what I know. You may have wanted the Omni for yourself, but I'm the next best thing."

Vanessa thought this man might have the good sense, unlike Foxe, to join her. Tom dispelled that notion.

"You don't have the whole story."

"What do you mean?"

"If you turn the machine on, it will operate at full tilt. And my calculations show that would not be a good thing."

Vanessa took another look at Tom.

Am I being conned?

Tom couldn't help but see Vanessa's suspicion, but forged on.

"You will generate a powerful microwave beam, but we don't know in what direction. We do know that the amount of water it takes in and releases will generate a large wave to the west. It may even be of tsunami proportions."

"Mr. Littleton…"

"Tom."

"Tom. You've given me a lot of maybe's. And 'maybe' I should believe you. But let me tell you the things I know to be true."

Up to now, Vanessa had shown a defiant attitude, bordering on irrational. Now, she was sober in her assessment. She had reached heights in her former business, only to see all she had worked for crumble. Vanessa was determined that her revival, her search for the machine, would be an unqualified success. She spared no expense and, unfortunately, no one's life to achieve her goal. Now, within sight of the pinnacle, she was determined to reach it, even if she knew she might never come down.

"I've been exposed. I'm responsible for some terrible acts, the assault on you being one of them. For that, I am sorry. I only wish I could apologize to other victims, especially Christine."

Vanessa paused, and Tom detected a tear.

"The men on that ship cannot arrest me, not here, not now. But undoubtedly, others will later. There is only one thing left."

Vanessa looked at the red button within her reach.

"Vanessa, don't," Tom whispered. "We don't know what havoc it may bring. It needs more study."

Tom could read Vanessa like a map. It showed a woman who regretted how she got here. He thought he could see some good in her. Although he was a victim of the attack she sponsored, Tom wanted her to survive this. He wasn't sure why, but he hoped she did, too.

Vanessa turned to Tom. "More study? And you would lead it?"

Tom could see Vanessa knew he was instrumental. He had to pursue that reasoning. "Yes. Of course."

"And I would monitor your success behind bars, wouldn't I?"

Tom couldn't pretend. It was the only fate Vanessa had before her.

"Tom," she said. "Perhaps, we could have reached here another way, a way where we were not surrounded by armed men."

She allowed herself a weak smile at her comment as she fought back tears. Tom could no longer see what she was thinking. It was as though he was dealing with two different women, one rational and feeling, the other malevolent.

Her eyes dried as the wicked Vanessa returned.

"But we are not dealing with alternative universes. This is the one in which we live. And I'll be damned if I let all I worked for, all I have struggled for, fail. Fail! No. No, not again. No!"

She looked at the red button as if one push solved everything.

Tom pleaded with her.

"Vanessa. Don't."

Vanessa slammed her open hand on the red button.

As dawn broke, Dowd's yacht raced toward Venice at sixty knots, the rising sun at their backs. Lizzy now joined Nick and Rachael in the main cabin with Dowd at the controls. Dowd threaded between small fishing boats out for the daily catch. The yacht rode high on its hydrofoil wings slicing the water and leaving little wake.

Lizzy brought the others up to date on what happened, from her kidnapping to her rescue at the castle. Rachael filled her in about their part of this escapade. Russo told her about Matteo, the policeman Vanessa shot and killed. It saddened him to think Matteo left a fiancée who would be devastated.

Lizzy had just met Russo, but the kind old gentleman was like the grandfather she never had. Lizzy put her hand on Russo's shoulder.

"I'll go with you to tell her, if you want."

"That is nice of you," was all Russo could offer.

Nick walked over to Dowd. "So, what is it you have to do to close those gates?"

"We installed the new pumps I talked about in my presentation at the Excelsior. They have not been activated. I know how."

"And no one else besides Preston?"

"No one at the site. Sure, I gave them plenty of instructions, but I left out a step or two."

"Why?" asked Nick.

Dowd hesitated. The answer embarrassed him.

"Because I wanted to be sure that I would be the one to activate them."

Nick couldn't tell which bothered Dowd more, being unprepared for an unforeseen emergency or his having to admit it.

"So, what are the missing steps?"

"Lido is the only inlet we have to worry about. There is an artificial island in the middle of the inlet. We have to get to it and enter the tunnels beside the gates. I have a code to turn on the pumps."

Nick smiled. "A code?"

Dowd understood. "You're not the only one with codes, my friend.

"We turn the system to manual, start all six compressors and use all lines to lift the gates at the same time. We would use four gates normally, but for this special occasion, we will lift the two spares as well."

"So, we are headed to that artificial island?"

"No," replied Dowd. "This boat's fast, but it's too big. We'll dock nearby and take one of the submersibles."

The Mose worksite came into view.

"There it is," said Dowd, backing off the speed and allowing the yacht to come to rest on its hull.

"I called ahead and told my men to have the submersible ready."

Dowd pulled alongside a pier where men were waiting to tie up the yacht.

"Nick and I are going to the submersible. It's best you all follow this man," Dowd said pointing to a man in gray overalls and a hardhat waiting for them. "He will take you to a shelter that should withstand any wave coming our way. The other workers here will join you."

Nick and Dowd ran down the dock to the building from which they first took the submersible to view the stake. A man stood by to assist. Once Nick took the back seat and Dowd the front, the man lowered the craft into the water. They closed the hatch as they were lowered into the murky waters.

If one could imagine a collective gasp, it was when Vanessa slapped the red button. The sun had come up and its rays were shining in Vanessa's eyes. She shielded them with her hand and looked at the button as though it was not functioning. Then she heard the faint sounds from the speakers in the water below. Everyone heard it.

What next?

The sounds stopped. Moments passed sufficient to elicit either disappointment or relief, depending on which side you stood in this drama. A few bubbles rose from the depths. Large bubbles.

Something was happening!

Bubbles turned into a roiling sea.

Tom turned to Vanessa. "You've got to get out of here."

"No!"

"This will end badly! Come on!" Tom pleaded as he headed to the ladder on Birchmeier's hydrofoil.

The men on the platform looked uncertain, especially Preston. One guard moved toward the waiting hydrofoil.

"No one leaves!" yelled Vanessa. As if that were his cue, Bosak raised his weapon and blocked the path to the waiting hydrofoil.

Tom reached the deck and yelled to Birchmeier, "Let's get out of here."

As the hydrofoil began to pull away, the machine broke to the surface. Its large mass tilted the platform. Two of the guards lost their footing and tumbled into the water. Vanessa steadied herself, grabbing the control panel while Preston held on for dear life beside her. Bosak had steady sea legs that kept him in place. The machine tapped the hydrofoil as the pilot pulled away.

The platform slid off the east side of the machine and floated level again. Water began flowing into the west side of the machine. The flow began slowly and increased into a torrent as though flood gates on a dam had been opened. The hydrofoil was the length of a football field away when the undertow created by the machine began to pull it back.

Birchmeier yelled to the pilot, "More power!"

The pilot pushed the throttle all the way forward. The craft moved away. As it did, Tom watched Vanessa in her triumph. She held her arms spread wide as a priestess would before a congregation, a broad smile on her face. It was her moment of glory.

Chapter 33

THE TRIP TO THE ISLAND was a short one. Dowd was at the controls of the submersible.

"Where are you docking this thing?" asked Nick.

"We'll pretend it's a motorboat and run it onto the sand."

Dowd accelerated. The submersible was soon three quarters aground. He pushed a control and the cowl raised.

"Follow me," he ordered Nick.

Rachael, Lizzy, and Russo waited with a dozen workers gathered in a concrete building. They were told that authorities had cleared the beaches and hotels had moved guests to upper levels.

"Ever been in a tornado?" Lizzy asked Rachael.

"Can't say that I have."

"I have. Mom took me shopping for back-to-school clothes, at a thrift shop, of course. It was in a shopping strip. The sky was as dark as night. Warning signals went off. I didn't know what they were. Sounded like some motor over-revving.

"The store manager ran up to us and told us we needed to get to someplace away from glass. The whole front of the store was glass. He led us outside. It was raining buckets. We all got drenched. He took us to a warehouse in back. No windows. A solid concrete bunker.

"This place reminds me of that one."

Rachael knew Lizzy. Ahe seldom saw concern on the face of this devil-may-care woman. She saw it now.

"Want to walk outside?" she asked.

"Yeah. Let's do it."

"Want to join us?" Rachael asked Russo.

"You go on. I'll stay here."

A man was stationed by the door, apparently tasked with ensuring everyone was accounted for.

"May we step outside for a few minutes?" Rachael asked the man.

"OK. But stay near and come back in when I tell you."

The deck just outside the door provided a fine view of Venice across the lagoon. It looked down on the pier where Dowd's yacht was docked. The inlet where the submerged gates would appear was to the right. Both women knew Dowd and Nick were somewhere there beneath the surface.

"I hope the guys are OK," said Lizzy.

"I'm sure they are," said Rachael, not too sure herself.

"Hey, what's happening to Dowd's boat?"

Rachael looked over in the direction of the boat to see a slight tug on the yacht, pulling it back toward the ocean. Then the large vessel began to drop.

"It's sinking!" exclaimed Lizzy.

"No," said Rachael. "The water level is dropping."

Venetians and tourists of the city were enjoying a perfect day. The morning sun lifted a cool fog from the squares and couples were enjoying gondola rides to no place in particular.

The Wagners, the couple who had shared a water taxi with Nick, were among them. They were first to get on a waiting gondola and now were being poled along a small canal where the gondolier pointed out Casanova's villa.

"You really think Casanova lived there?" The woman asked her husband.

"No, Casanova is alive and well and sitting beside you." A comment that elicited a playful jab in the ribs.

The gondolier began singing in a beautiful tenor voice.

Perfect.

The tenor stopped his concert abruptly. The Wagners did not understand why he looked confused, but it became clear. The gondola was reversing course, pulled along by a current, that was getting stronger. The gondolier now was using his pole to keep the craft from crashing into the sides of buildings. He ducked as they passed under bridges.

The Wagners hugged each other, not sure why they now were on what felt like a theme park water ride.

It only took a few minutes to return to the Grand Canal where they had started. They joined other gondolas and vaporettos pulling against the tug of this swiftly ebbing tide.

Dowd and Nick were in the tunnel under the inlet which was beside the gates. On the model Dowd used to show them the Mose operation, the shadows of people indicated the tunnel was large, but the enormity of the thing had to be seen in person. Nick felt as if he just walked into the Holland Tunnel under the Hudson.

"It's over here," Dowd said to Nick. "Let's go."

Birchmeier's hydrofoil was almost out of sight when the machine generated the microwave beam. Tom watched from the rail of the ship, hoping he was wrong about its intensity. He was not.

Birchmeier, Paul, and Tanner stood beside him when a storm of sparks the size of lightning bolts danced off the platform.

"What's that?" asked Birchmeier.

"You know what happens when you put metal in a microwave oven? That's what's happening on the platform."

Birchmeier considered the fate of those remaining there. "Poor bastards."

A white funnel cloud formed, swirling like a tornado, reaching progressively higher into the sky.

"What now?" asked Birchmeier.

Tom was lost in the science of what he was seeing and was losing track of the severity.

"Microwaves are invisible, but this one is so strong, it's vaporizing water in the air. The heat from that water is generating a narrow, tall tornado, but the microwaves themselves are headed out into space."

The artificial tornado generated its own lightning storm with bolts randomly flashing within the cloud. The phenomenon lasted little more than a total eclipse of the sun and was equally dramatic.

The beam quit as fast as it started.

"Now what?" asked Birchmeier.

"Now, the machine releases the water it drew in," Tom answered, but then snapped out of his science stupor.

"We've got to call Nick. A wave is on its way!"

Dowd reached the keypad for the code.

"Here's where I need you," he told Nick. "I enter the code and you pull that lever over there."

Nick reached the lever about ten feet away. Dowd pointed to him and said, "Ready."

Dowd punched in a code and yelled, "Now!"

The roar of pumps filled the tunnel.

Rachael and Lizzy saw it first. From the east, a gray mass appeared on the horizon and headed in their direction. In a few moments, the wave appeared, perfectly formed, a surfer's dream. A suicidal surfer. The beast was as high as a small ship. It moved rapidly, packing tons of force.

Rachael looked at the gates, now rising from the water. "They did it!"

"But where are they?" added Lizzy.

"Ladies, we must get back into the building!" yelled the guard at the door.

"Come on, Lizzy. They'll be OK," said Rachael, hoping she was right.

Dowd and Nick, their task complete, reached the surface in the submersible. The yellow gates were rising from the ocean like submarines coming to the surface, seawater rolling about them.

Nick had never seen Mose operate with such coordination and speed.

"It's working!"

Dowd, who was confident it would work was paying more attention to their submersible. The pull of the tide had left all of it in the sand on the shore, a few feet from the water.

"Look!" yelled Dowd.

Nick turned to the submersible.

"Looks like we're going to have some trouble with our ride."

"Not that," said Dowd. "That!" he said as he pointed to the horizon where a gray mass of water approached.

"Get back in the craft," ordered Nick.

Dowd didn't have to ask why. The safest place in a lightning storm is a car. The safest place in a tsunami is a submersible. Although, both men knew 'safe' was debatable.

Moments after Rachael and Lizzy reentered the building, the wave hit. Dowd's yacht slammed into the pier and was tossed like a toy. Water battered the concrete building, but it held.

The wave hit hard against the island, lifting the submersible like a surfboard, raising it to the wave crest. The gates became a ski jump as the submersible shot over them and into the air, coming down with a bone-jarring splash.

Nick had taken the driver's seat.

Dowd yelled, "Use the propulsion system to guide it."

"I am. I am," said Nick, focusing on staying with the flow of the wave, now significantly reduced by the impact against the gates. It was still a wild ride, maneuvering on a wave larger than ever experienced here.

Nick did his best to keep the submersible on the surface of the wave, pushing and pulling the throttle to keep it riding the crest. He steered the craft toward Saint Mark's Square.

"If we head to Saint Mark's we won't be slamming against a building."

Russo had alerted his men on shore. The police had worked quickly to clear the square should the wave hit at full force. Even the usual mass of pigeons sensed danger and quickly flew away.

The oncoming wave, still high enough for the submersible to clear the bank and deposit it in the center of the square, slammed into the docked gondolas, strewing them about the square and canal. The wave slammed into the surrounding walls around the square and rebounded back, shaking the submersible, but not dislodging it.

Neither Dowd nor Nick said anything. The square was accustomed to the flooding that it now experienced, but that flooding never brought an underwater vessel with it.

Nick broke the silence.

"Well, that was a quick way in, wasn't it?"

"We need to return to search for survivors," Birchmeier said.

Paul was cautious.

"Is it safe?" he asked Tom.

"It should be."

Although people acknowledged Tom as the expert, he knew he was lucky his educated guesses turned out to be right. But now, Tom was uncertain what they would find.

Paul could read the doubt on Tom's face and response, but Paul had to be sure Priscilla's murderer, Bosak, was dead. He had to see for himself.

The hydrofoil took little time to return in what was now a calm sea. It slowed as they approached the site. The machine was nowhere to be seen. Tom reasoned that it had returned to the sea floor. The platform remained with bodies strewn about. The ship pulled alongside the platform. Birchmeier, Tom, and Paul descended a ladder to the platform. Tanner stayed behind. Bosak may have been one of the bodies on the platform, but none seemed the right size. Despite armed men aboard the ship, Tanner wanted to keep guard over his friends himself.

The microwaves at platform level were apparently random. Two guards were charred beyond recognition. Tom figured the metal weapons they held attracted microwaves. There was Preston Smith, lying on his back, his face frozen in horror. Vanessa, the ice queen, was still beautiful in death. She lay on her back, one arm across her chest and one to her side. She looked like a woman who ate an enchanted apple, and was still sleeping. So much so, that Birchmeier was compelled to lay two fingers on her throat to search for a pulse.

"Dead," he said.

"There had been more men on this platform."

"They are likely in the water. We'll have divers search for them."

"There is one man missing I'd hope we'd find," said Paul.

Birchmeier knew who Paul meant.

"Bosak."

Chapter 34

TANNER STOOD WAITING outside a house in San Polo, a residential area of Venice. Lizzy had joined Russo in consoling Matteo's fiancée. They reported to her that the woman who killed him was dead. Tanner assured them of that.

The fiancée, a brave young woman, was heartbroken. Lizzy provided something Russo could not, an empathetic, loving hug and a shoulder to cry on.

When they returned to the street, Tanner asked, "How did she take it?"

Russo answered.

"Not well, but I am really grateful Miss Rodriguez joined me. She provided compassion in a way I could not."

"I was glad to help," said Lizzy.

"Well," Russo said, putting his rumpled hat on his head, "I must get back to the office. You can imagine all the paperwork the past few days has caused. *Ciao.*"

Before he left, he kissed Lizzy on the hand and gave it a loving pat.

Lizzy looked after him as he walked away. Tanner could see her affection for the Commissario.

"You like the old guy, don't you?"

"Do you have a grandfather?" asked Lizzy.

"Sure, but he died years ago," Tanner replied. Then he added with a sense of pride, "He was a marine."

"Your dad was in the service too, wasn't he?"

"Army. He died in Desert Storm. One of the few who did."

"I'm sorry."

"I was little. It was grandpop who was the dad figure for me."

"Must be nice."

"Nice?"

"You know I never knew my father. Let alone my grandfather. Guess I'm adopting Russo."

Tanner grinned. "I'm sure he would be honored."

Tanner noticed the time. "Hey, Paul and Tom are waiting for us. Let's get to the restaurant. I think it's near here."

Lizzy noticed a bonding. "Speaking of new relations, you and Paul are getting to be like brothers, aren't you?"

"Nah. Wouldn't go that far. But we looked out for each other."

Lizzy snickered at the male bravado at play.

They turned a couple of corners, making Lizzy doubt Tanner's sense of direction, until they happened upon the restaurant where Paul and Tom were waiting for them at an outside table. Guido was there as well.

"There they are!" said Paul as he stood to give Lizzy a kiss on the cheek and Tanner a handshake.

"How'd things go?" Tom asked Lizzy, knowing about her visit with Matteo's fiancée.

"She's tough. I can tell. She'll be all right."

While looking at Lizzy, Paul made an aside to Tom.

"Lizzy knows 'tough.' Were you aware of that, Tom? She saved our hides at the castle."

Tom beamed.

"Oh, yes. She covered for us more than once. You have no idea."

Lizzy asked Paul, "So what's next for you?"

"Well, I was on holiday on a sunny Greek island when all of this started. I head back there tomorrow to see if a certain young woman I left remembers me."

"Tom, how about you?"

"Going back to Basel. Rachael's joining me. We have a ton of data to go through. Rachael said she needed to have a working model to understand where the engineering was leading us. Now that we've seen the model at work, many questions are answered."

Lizzy looked skeptical. "You're not planning on turning that thing back on, are you?"

"Not anytime soon. Although we have the code that does it, we're not telling anybody."

"Speaking of Rachael, where is she?"

"She's with Nick," reported Guido. "I took them to Nick's hotel."

Lizzy couldn't resist suggesting a romantic nuance.

"So, they're having a little private time before she leaves for Basel?" She winked.

"I'm just glad that, whatever was going on between the two seems to have worked its way out," replied Tom. "I'll never forget how awkward it was when they met in my hospital room. I thought someone turned the thermostat down."

Nick and Rachael were at the door of Nick's suite once again.

"I'm starved," said Nick.

"Then let's head down to the restaurant," teased Rachael, knowing Nick wanted time alone with her.

"Let's order something sent up."

"Why?"

"We've been surrounded by people. Need some time alone, don't you think?"

Nick took his key card and opened the door. He led Rachael down the short hallway to the sitting room. Room service had placed a tray on the coffee table with a bucket of Champagne and a small bowl of fruit. There was a note card. Nick picked it up and read it out loud.

"'In gratitude for saving Venice from disaster – The Staff of the Gritti Palace.'"

Nick pulled the Champagne from the ice and peeled off the cork wrapping.

"Looks like our work's not going unrecognized, Rachael… Rachael?"

But Rachael had not yet made it past the closet door in the hallway. She thought she heard something.

The closet door burst open.

"Bosak!" she cried.

It was not Rachael the Croatian was after. He pushed her ahead of him like a rag doll. Rachael fell against the buffet table, hitting her head on the edge. She folded into an unconscious heap.

Nick had the Champagne bottle in hand working the cork loose when he heard Rachael scream and Bosak appeared. Fortunate timing. Nick popped the cork and, with steady aim, hit Bosak in the left eye. Bosak, stunned but not down, put his hand to his eye.

Nick grabbed the neck of the bottle, stepped up to the dazed man, and swung it like a foaming baseball bat, connecting with the side of his head. Bosak crashed backwards into the large screen television mounted on a short floor pedestal causing a shower of glass and sparks.

The hitman sat in a shattered screen struggling to get to his feet. Nick dropped the bottle to the floor spewing bubbly everywhere. He spotted what he needed in the opposite corner of the room and started to rush around a heavy chair to get to it, but Bosak grabbed Nick by an ankle before he could take three steps. The marble floor was slick with Champagne and Nick fell. Bosak got to his feet. Nick was surprised how nimble the big man was, but Nick was equally quick. He jumped to his feet and squared off with Bosak. Bosak made a grab for Nick's throat, but Nick put his arms up to deflect him. He followed by two left jabs and an uppercut to Bosak's chin. Nick felt like he was pounding a brick wall.

Bosak, dazed, landed a slap with the back of his hand against the side of Nick's head. The strike launched Nick toward the desk in the far corner of the room. He realized he was where he needed to be, but he couldn't move fast enough. He struggled to his feet as Bosak deployed his weapon of choice. Nick felt the leather garrote around his neck. He had been breathing heavily but now his lungs screamed for air. He was faint as he reached for the desk. Doing the counterintuitive, he leaned into the tight garrote.

Nick grabbed the letter opener from the desk, stabbed back and down, and sunk it into Bosak's leg. Bosak screamed in pain, loosened his grip but didn't release him. Nick pulled the letter opener from the man's leg, this time plunging it into his right side. Bosak reeled back, releasing the garrote.

Nick spun around, garrote hanging from his neck, faced Bosak and, with only a split-second hesitation, a visceral impulse prevailed. Nick held the letter opener given to him by Christine, the woman he loved, and before him was her murderer.

Nick plunged the letter opener into Bosak's heart.

He was on target. Bosak's expression turned from hate to shock as the large man fell backward to the floor. Nick collapsed onto the desk chair trying to catch his breath as he saw Rachael stirring. He went to her and sat on the floor beside her.

"Rachael?"

Rachael opened her eyes, trying to focus.

"Nick. Bosak!" she exclaimed as though only a second had passed.

"It's OK. He's over there."

Nick pointed to the heap of a man with a letter opener sticking from his chest like a small flagpole. A puddle of blood spread from around the man, but Nick had much of the bright red stuff on his hands.

"Nick, you're bleeding!"

"No, this is Bosak's."

Rachael touched the bruise marks on Nick's throat.

"Did he…?

"Yes. He tried."

Nick cradled Rachael protectively in his arms. They said nothing for a long time.

The top suite of the Excelsior Hotel on the Lido di Venezia had been a perfect vantage point for a man with a deep Texas accent to watch the effects of the machine.

Guido had succeeded in having the authorities clear the beaches. The police had not wasted time and had been dispatched all along the shores of the Lido, making sure everyone was off the beach before the wave hit. Excelsior staff evacuated guests to upper floors. The tsunami crushed the cabanas along the shore up against the hotel as water rushed into the ground level. It would take time to determine damage to the old structure, but it was sturdy and remained standing.

The Texan witnessed it all while sipping bourbon. He was the same man who last saw Nick Foxe at Dowd's presentation in this very hotel. He had told his assistant Nick would one day work for him. In a way, he had. This was the man at the top of the food chain. He had worked hard his entire life to be there and he liked it.

The Texan could see that the machine performed as Fabre had promised. Too well.

A young man approached the Texan with what he considered bad news.

"We can't reach Fabre. The phone she was using is dead."

The Texan was unfazed.

"Dead," The Texan repeated, "as Fabre herself may be."

"Authorities are all over the site. We can't get there to see what happened."

The Texan took another sip and drawled, "Well it looks like the thing works. Needs a little finesse. That's all."

"But sir, we no longer have anyone to work with."

"Patience. We know where the thing is now, don't we? I may not get it now, maybe not anytime soon, but I'll get it one day. One way or the other."

ACKNOWLEDGMENTS

I have been to Venice several times as a tourist, but this last visit was to do research for *The Ocean Raiders*. It was important to make sure the description of the water taxi struggle was realistic and the bridge at the Rialto market where Nick's attacker met his end was described correctly. We stayed at the Pensione Accademia in the fountain suite, Christine's room. My thanks to everyone at the Pensione and I apologize for the murder in your hotel.

My thanks to Romina Zago at the Gritti Palace who let us spend time in the suite which would become the place where Nick stayed and where Bosak met his end. Special thanks to Elena Zambardi and her team at Mose. We held face-to-face meetings and follow-up emails to get the details right for the book.

Thanks also to countless Venetians, from the police at the Questura di Venezia, to the staff at the Excelsior, and the men and women on the street. They all played a role in making this work of fiction realistic.

My wife and I cruised the Adriatic after leaving Venice taking notes on locations along the Dalmatian Coast since Tanner and Paul spend part of the adventure there. Thanks to Azamara Cruise Director Tony Markey for helping me introduce Nicholas Foxe and *The Code Hunters* to the guests on board.

Thanks go to my beta readers, Walt Curran, Frank Hopkins, Bill Kennedy, Barbara Guzak, Brenda Shaw, Pat Soriano, Susan Cleveland, Laura Maestro, Roger Schreiber, and John Walker.

The Ocean Raiders has a great look due to the cover design by Claudia Sperl at Label-Schmiede.

This book is dedicated to Ellen Coppley, my wife and partner in prose. We talk plot and place all the time. Her command of the Italian language, along with her charm, opened doors to us in Venice.

Read Where It All Began

The Code Hunters

A Nicholas Foxe Adventure

Chapter 1

The Code Hunters

Chapter 1

Afghanistan

They pitched themselves into the dark, cold night, 20,000 feet above the earth.

It was a high altitude, low opening descent, HALO for short. The acronym sounds ethereal, but at odds with a free fall dropping thousands of feet, the air rushing by at gale force. Their mother ship, the C-160 aircraft provided by the German allies, vanished into the night sky. The ground, devoid of the lights of modern civilization, floated below. When altimeters on their wrists read 3,000 feet, they pulled their ripcords. The sliders deployed, slowing and silencing the pop of the ram-air elliptical chutes that provided maximum guidance. The four men drifted about each other in the light of a quarter moon, aiming for the same few square meters of desert at the base of a mountain.

On the ground, they suppressed the air billowing their chutes, made their way to the team leader and huddled in silence. Intel indicated that no enemy would be near this spot, but caution prevailed in making their entry as silent and invisible as possible. Hand signals sufficed.

They were a team of experienced specialists, one that Central Command could direct to capture a key enemy mullah. With the chutes disposed of behind a clump of rocks, they made their way up the mountain. In the chill of morning air, the team waited in a secluded place. As dawn broke, they realized, too late, that the enemy knew they were coming.

In war, leaders make precise plans with well-thought-out contingencies. During the heat of battle, these plans go to hell. So it was with this team as the enemy surrounded them and they were hit by fire from all sides. A young Afghan boy who shouldn't have been there stumbled into the line of fire. No contingency plan for this moment.

A man makes a snap decision that sets in motion events beyond his imagination.

New Mexico – Two Years Later

Experienced cavers formed the team. The moniker 'spelunker' did not apply. Spelunkers once were scientists erudite in geology, but now the term is used for the general unwashed cave explorers. Cavers bring sophisticated equipment to navigate through challenges created by nature. "Cavers rescue spelunkers," say the experts. Tom Littleton, an experienced caver with chambers in the Pyrenees named after him, led the team. Carlsbad Cavern was well explored and tamed to facilitate the paying public. Winding trails bordered by chrome rails lead through limestone openings. Tourists usually were unaware of nearby cave systems much too dangerous for the novice. One, called Lechuguilla, resembled a child's ant farm enlarged a hundred times. It offered long drops where only rappelling experts could descend. Open chambers and lakes were connected by passages barely wide enough to crawl through. Littleton had already explored Lechuguilla's furthest known reaches but believed more remained to discover.

Tom had studied reports of a partially explored area. Cavers rumored the possibility of an undiscovered connection to Carlsbad. Littleton had heard of some half-hearted attempts. A suggestion by a stranger, and Tom's own ego, egged him on. He could do better.

The team winched into the shaft, one-by-one. Previous cavers had hammered and chiseled outcroppings, so that the trip down would be unobstructed. Yet it was laborious to lower equipment for a four-day exploration by means of rope and harness, piece by piece. Littleton and his two teammates worked for hours to get themselves and their gear down and set up a base camp.

The shaft's floor consisted of powdered limestone trampled by cavers before them. The sides of the shaft, jagged layers like rings of a tree, depicted years of sediment from prehistoric seas. It was a rough chimney through which a man could see the last vestiges of daylight. The air inside was cool and still.

Their bodies remained in tune with the sun. They took advantage of fading daylight seeping into the chamber to rest. After tonight, they would move into the depths of the cave where darkness became perpetual. Littleton shared a simple fare of beef jerky and tea with his teammates, Josh Peabody and Jeremy Miller.

Josh served as tactician for the group. He carried maps of previously explored areas and constantly referred to them. He was the man who assembled the gear for this trip and who checked each item to be sure nothing was omitted. In his early thirties and slight of build, Josh had blue eyes seldom seen. They were usually looking down, focused on a map or book, even as he walked along cave paths. It was no mystery why his helmet bore the most dings.

Jeremy was the contrast to Josh. Redheaded, sporting an inch-long matching beard, his fiery hair matching his lively personality. A mid-twenties man with a quick wit and a smart mouth, he was the teammate who constantly looked above and around.

Littleton was not a tall man. Growing up, the boys picked on him since his name fit his stature. But no boy ever picked on him twice. Quick to use his fists from an early age, he pelted his tormentors in an undisciplined series of punches, but they did the job. He had wanted to be an athlete. Baseball or track presented the only way forward for a small, but quick, boy. So, he became a pitcher from little league through high school. Then he discovered caving in his junior year.

Exploring caves was perfect for a man who could squeeze through tight spots. Yet something more made caving right for Littleton. Caves were another world, hidden from the one above. There, in that world, Littleton felt at home.

Littleton possessed a trait he took for granted, but one which his caving teammates assured him was rare. He had a well-developed 'proximity sense.' Many people experience that sense when they feel some unseen person is looking at them. Scientists suspect when we were prehistoric hunters, we had a well-developed proximity sense necessary for our survival. Even today, the blind demonstrate a sense for unseen objects in their path. For Littleton, that sense allowed him to know where the walls of caves were, even in the dark when he couldn't see anything. He sensed his teammates' positions without looking.

"You got everything?" Littleton asked Josh going through the checklist. Of course, Josh had everything. When did he not? Yet Josh, always the self-doubter, hedged with "I believe so." For Josh, 99% signaled failure.

"Well, that was easy," Jeremy quipped at the end of his descent. "This place looks like crowds have been here. Tell me again, why are we here?" He directed the question to Littleton who had convinced the team to come along. "Remind me."

Littleton took time to formulate an answer. How do you rationalize following a random rumor passed along by someone you don't know, mixed with a portion of gut feeling?

"It's all about the proximity to Carlsbad. No expert team's been here," Littleton explained, "Until now, that is." A modest boast.

Josh and Jeremy grinned. They were experts, and knew it, even the doubting Josh.

"I suspect there's a connection to Carlsbad," said Tom.

"And no one has found it because...?" Jeremy asked leaving Littleton to complete the statement.

"Because they looked in obvious places," Littleton responded. "Look, most cavers have tried to connect through the shortest distance between two points. That makes sense sometimes, but not always. I think we should try the path less traveled."

"Which means?" Jeremy asked.

"Which means, Carlsbad is to the east," said Littleton, pointing over Josh's shoulder. "So we go west." He smiled as he leaned back, pointing a thumb in the opposite direction.

Josh had done his homework. "Well, it's true the teams before us went east. Few went in the other direction. But in that direction, it peters out. I imagine most thought it was a dead end."

"How far has anyone gone?" Littleton asked Josh, already knowing the answer.

"About 3,000 feet."

"We can do that in a day, maybe two."

"Yeah," sneered Jeremy, "If we have to crawl all the way."

"Some deep knee bends may be necessary," laughed Littleton.

The exertion of lowering gear and setting up camp made sleep come easily; each man cocooned in his sleeping bag to ward off the coolness of the cave.

The next day, Littleton led the team into the "path less traveled." The first 3,000 feet were mapped as Josh pointed out the previous day. The team maneuvered over fallen rock and pits dropping hundreds of feet. It resembled a roadway crumbled by a major earthquake. As they continued, they descended 500 feet below the surface, still short of the 750 feet to the floor of Carlsbad. If successful in connecting to Carlsbad, they would have to find a passage that dropped further.

After hours of arduous climbing over rocks scattered along the way, the channel opened into a room the size of a small cottage. The team sat for a rest as they drank hot tea from their thermoses and considered their next move. Hot tea offered the antidote to both dehydration and the chill they would feel when the sweat evaporated after their climb. Above ground was the dry New Mexico air where perspiration disappeared as fast as it formed. But this was another world and another climate.

The walls of the room were made of limestone with its dusty white surfaces streaked with the browns and reds of iron oxide and occasional blues of carbon deposits. Although the path was cluttered with rock, the entrance to the room contained only a few that had rolled in eons ago. The rest of the room appeared clear. Josh and Jeremy sat on rocks the size of inverted kettledrums sipping tea. Littleton walked the perimeter of the room studying the walls. He examined each crack carefully.

Something is here.

"Well, so much for this idea. No way out," groused Jeremy.

Littleton stayed mute, focused on the cracks in the wall. Josh and Jeremy wondered if Littleton's rumored proximity sense was at work. Then, he announced "Here!"

Jeremy and Josh rushed over to Littleton. "What?" asked Jeremy.

"There's another channel behind this crack."

Littleton stood aside as Josh, then Jeremy, looked into the crack, shining their helmet lamps deep into the darkness. "There's nothing," Jeremy said.

"Look down," smiled Littleton.

Jeremy stood on his toes directing the light downward. Josh followed him, returning Littleton's smile at his discovery.

"I see it. There's something there," Josh confirmed.

"Yeah," said Jeremy. "We just need to shrink to ten inches wide to squeeze in."

"Not necessarily," said Littleton as he turned his back to the wall, took out his pick, and struck the wall at knee level near the crack. The soft limestone crumbled into the opening. He looked at his teammates and asked, "Shall we get busy?"

The men took turns hammering away. The first blows pushed through thin limestone at the edges of the crack, but later hammering worked against thicker layers and the progress slowed. Three hours of work provided a fissure just wide enough for each member to squeeze through. Though exhausted, adrenaline motivated each man to push on.

Littleton took a coil of rope and a large piton from his pack. He hammered the piton into the rock outside the fissure, snaked the rope through it and wrapped it under his arms, tying off with a bowline. Josh and Jeremy slipped on their rough cowhide gloves and grabbed the other end of the rope as Littleton lowered himself into the opening. He hammered another piton on the inside of the opening near the top and clicked his rope into it. His teammates would use that one to lower themselves down.

Littleton rappelled down the wall for seventy feet when he reached the floor. "Clear!" he yelled up to Josh and Jeremy as he unknotted the rope. The men each rappelled in turn.

Caves may be wet or dry. Under the surface of the arid New Mexico desert, Littleton had discovered a wet one. His helmet lamp illuminated stalactites and stalagmites surrounding him in a narrow passage, their sweating surfaces reflecting light brought into this chasm for the first time. A small stream flowed on the opposite side. The perfect clarity of the water allowed a view of the bottom only a few inches below. It was a narrow stream in a narrow cave. The water flowed deeper and swifter in another age. The floor of the cave offered a flat path carved by the much larger river parent. Small rocky rubble, falling every century or so, littered the path. Littleton felt like the first man on a secret moon. Josh and Jeremy were soon the second and third man to step foot in this hidden place.

"Wow," the simple exclamation from Josh.

"Yes, wow," responded Littleton. "And look which way it leads. West that way and east this way," pointing behind them and then forward.

"And east leads to Carlsbad," smiled Josh.

"So, we crawled 3,000 feet west to turn around and walk east?" questioned Jeremy.

Littleton grinned. "Well, at least it appears to be an easy walk."

"Yes, but for how long? And 3,000 feet just gets us back to where we started. Carlsbad is beyond that," stated tactician Josh.

"Guess we better rest," said Littleton. "And get our supplies closer."

"Which are up that way," Jeremy grimaced pointing back up the way they came.

"After you," Littleton responded with a wide wave of his hand.

Caving is hard work, but one never wants to be far from supplies. So, the team had no choice but make their way back to base camp. They returned over the same rocky path, exhausted by their efforts and immediately fell asleep. After eight hours of sleep and a dose of hot oatmeal washed down with tea, they returned to the same path, this time taking supplies to last the next extension of their exploration. They set up camp in the limestone room that once appeared to be the end of the line. Each man lowered himself through the crack and down to where they stood the previous day, now armed with food in their bellies and fresh batteries in their helmet lamps.

Once down to the stream bed, they made rapid progress over flat terrain. The team walked cautiously, but easily, along the path. The bright light from their helmet lamps enabled a view of their surroundings. As they walked upstream, seeking the source of the water, they calculated they had passed the 3,000-foot mark. That put them approximately where they started, only far lower.

Forward is Carlsbad!

Without speaking, each man's excitement grew at the prospect they might discover a new connection. They progressed well along the way for another 2,500 feet as the water flow increased. The stream generated a gurgling noise. But as they moved forward, it was joined gradually by the sound of a distant waterfall.

"Listen," said Littleton.

"I hear it," responded Josh, not hiding his exhilaration.

A hundred feet more revealed a shimmering waterfall cascading eighty feet from ceiling to floor. They stopped in silent wonder. Then reality took hold.

"Seems to be the end of the line," observed Jeremy.

No exit appeared. The waterfall covered the back of the chamber. Once again, Littleton refused to accept there was no way out, but back. He walked on a small ledge to the right of the waterfall. "It's not the end. Come on," he yelled over the roar of the water. Then he disappeared behind the fall. Josh and Jeremy rushed to follow.

Emerging from behind the waterfall, wet with a mixture of salty sweat and pristine water, they entered a small chamber. Just large enough to squeeze through, it led from behind the waterfall for a little more than sixty feet, and then opened into a larger area. It was much larger than the limestone room from which they started, and equally dry. As each man entered, their helmet lamps searched the wall surfaces. This time, no way out but back seemed evident. Even Littleton appeared less optimistic. Jeremy put his hand on Littleton's shoulder. "Not bad, my friend. I believe we've discovered a large arm of this cave. Looks like we have naming rights. What do you think? The Jeremy and Friends Cave?" He laughed.

"Wait!' Littleton said. "Look at the floor." Littleton walked across the room, pointing down as he neared a cascade of boulders on the opposite side.

"What about it?" asked Jeremy.

"The floor here is smooth, as if graded, and not by water. There is a place in Carlsbad with the same surface." Littleton's smile expanded as he patted one of the boulders. "I bet Carlsbad is on the other side of these rocks!"

Littleton had walked to the rocks around the left edge of the room. He returned walking directly across the middle. When he took a few steps toward his teammates, the earth gave way beneath him. He fell into an opening and disappeared from sight with only a cloud of dust remaining. Josh and Jeremy rushed over to the hole shouting Tom's name. Then light shown up from the opening. It beamed from Littleton's helmet lamp and bounced in all directions as though reflected from a large mirror.

At last, Littleton spoke. In a slow cadence he reported, "You are not going to believe what I found."

GET YOUR COPY TODAY OF ***THE CODE HUNTERS*** ON AMAZON OR AT YOUR LOCAL BOOKSTORE.

ABOUT THE AUTHOR

In addition to *The Nicholas Foxe Adventures*, Jackson Coppley is author of the novel *Leaving Lisa.* His short stories appear in *Beach Life, The Apollo Project, Bay to Ocean,* and other publications. He writes a daily blog on his web site www.JacksonCoppley.com where the entry, *Steve Jobs and Me,* won an award by the Delaware Press Association. A graduate in physics, Coppley's resume includes a career with world communications and technology companies and the launching of what the press called "a revolutionary software program." Now a full-time writer, his work focuses on adventure.

BOOKS BY JACKSON COPPLEY

Nicholas Foxe Adventures

- The Code Hunters
- The Ocean Raiders

Leaving Lisa

Tales From Our Near Future

SHORT STORIES BY JACKSON COPPLEY

- Apollo Summer
- Funland
- Sam Shade
- The Bomber Jacket
- Three Boys and the Moving Pictures
- Women in Cities

For more information, go to www.JacksonCoppley.com

Printed in Great Britain
by Amazon

30691765R00209